A Good Animal

A Good Animal

Sara Maurer

ST. MARTIN'S PRESS
NEW YORK

This is a work of fiction. All of the characters, organizations, and events portrayed in this novel are either products of the author's imagination or are used fictitiously.

First published in the United States by St. Martin's Press, an imprint of St. Martin's Publishing Group

EU Representative: Macmillan Publishers Ireland Ltd, 1st Floor, The Liffey Trust Centre, 117–126 Sheriff Street Upper, Dublin 1, D01 YC43

A GOOD ANIMAL. Copyright © 2026 by Sara Maurer. All rights reserved. Printed in the United States of America. For information, address St. Martin's Publishing Group, 120 Broadway, New York, NY 10271.

www.stmartins.com

Designed by Jen Edwards

The Library of Congress Cataloging-in-Publication Data is available upon request.

ISBN 978-1-250-38356-3 (hardcover)
ISBN 978-1-250-38357-0 (ebook)

The publisher of this book does not authorize the use or reproduction of any part of this book in any manner for the purpose of training artificial intelligence technologies or systems. The publisher of this book expressly reserves this book from the Text and Data Mining exception in accordance with Article 4(3) of the European Union Digital Single Market Directive 2019/790.

Our books may be purchased in bulk for specialty retail/wholesale, literacy, corporate/premium, educational, and subscription box use. Please contact MacmillanSpecialMarkets@macmillan.com.

First Edition: 2026

10 9 8 7 6 5 4 3 2 1

Because of Ryan

Some time when the river is ice ask me
mistakes I have made. Ask me whether
what I have done is my life.
—William Stafford, "Ask Me"

A Good Animal

Prologue

SAULT STE. MARIE

When I walk these fields, I feel generations beside me. All those Lindts, bending over this wet clay soil, putting their hands in it, their shovels and seeds, their sweat. They pulled stones from the land to set the foundations for the house I live in now. They saw these same rose-colored skies glowing over the St. Marys River in the morning; the same June grass poking up bleached and dry through the crusted snow.

They walk beside me, and I tell them what's on my mind. I tell them my plans for the farm, the price of hay and show lambs. I tell them about my wife and daughter. But mostly, I talk to them about Mary. I tell them about those nine months we had, screwing to beat hell, driving my piece-of-shit Ford with roads and roads before us, gravel jumping up and biting the undercarriage, dust flying up behind.

I tell them about that cold May night, when Mary stared out my truck window, far away and unreachable, with the St. Marys churning behind her like it's done for ten thousand years. They were there that night. They saw everything. And they're the only ones I can tell it to.

Summer 1995

Chapter 1

The phone rang so early, the coffeepot was still brewing. There were no clouds, and already the sun was a sharp white coin suspended above the trees in the east. The fields around the house were rich and green and the ewes rested in a loose group like scattered stones. It would be a beautiful day, and hot. Dad had already left for his job at the road commission, and Mom was in the bathroom blow-drying her hair. Katie was in the living room watching TV, and Jay, of course, was still in bed.

"Moisture's about right," Roy Mason said. "You boys can plan on baling today."

"I'll let Charlie know," I said.

You wanted your hay's moisture level around 15 percent. Any higher and it would mold or heat up, even combust. You could buy moisture testers that looked like enormous meat thermometers, but Mason knew by feel. He would walk out in the field and pick up a fistful of hay, twist it, and if it sprang back with just the right amount of brittle, he knew it was ready to bale.

I knocked on the bathroom door, loud enough so Mom could hear over the dryer, and when she opened the door, the damp warmth of it hit me, the oven smell of hair spray and heat.

"What do you need, Ev?" she said.

Her hair was soft and loose around her chin, the color of the foxtail barley that grew up behind the barn. She had her eye makeup on, something shimmery just under her brows, and it struck me, like it often did, that she was beautiful. And not in the way you'd think with her blond hair and blue eyes, but because her face was the beginning and end of each day.

She was wearing one of her credit union outfits, a white and satiny blouse, cuffed at the wrists with pearly buttons, shoulder pads. Shoes she had no business wearing on a farm. Open-toed, flimsy things with heels. Just begging to get scuffed or shit on. When she wasn't working, she wore a housecoat most of the day and her face was shiny and bare. But her hands, no matter what she wore, were thickened and rough, the knuckles red from scouring pails, or nicked from closing a gate too fast, or any one of the hundred tiny accidents that happen each day on a farm.

How she could shift like that—two women in one—made me wonder if she liked one more than the other. Once, I'd waited in line at the credit union to deposit money and watched while she chatted with the customer ahead of me. She cupped one hand behind the other, or held them at her side below the counter, keeping them out of sight. And I thought I knew which version of herself she liked better.

"Can you get a sitter for Katie? Mason called and I need Jay."

"Jay? For what?"

"Raking."

"No."

"Mom—"

"He's too young. Find someone else."

"I was haying at his age."

She turned away from me and unplugged the hair dryer. Then picked up a section of her hair and wrapped it around a curling iron.

"Mom," I said. "We need him."

She tapped her fingers against the tightly wound hair and sighed. I knew that meant she was going to say yes, and I turned to run up the stairs and get Jay.

"Everett!" She released her hair and it fell in a single spiral on the side of her face. "Make sure he brings something to drink."

"I'll keep a good eye on him."

Jay was such a runt and burrowed in so good, I could hardly tell he was in the bed. I shook a lump, which felt narrow and sharp under the blanket. It turned out to be a shoulder.

"Me and Charlie need a raker today."

"I don't know how."

"I'll teach you. You're good and old enough now."

I pulled the covers back and there he was with his bare little chest, his arms like maple twigs. He was twelve and built like me at that age. He looked like me, too, with brown hair that curled up behind the ears and Dad's mud-puddle eyes. We walked the same, slowly, feeling the soil with each step and bending our faces to it. Our shoulders slouched, as though our bodies were tired, which they often were. There was no denying we were brothers. Or Dad's sons. "Robert," people would tell him, "you cannot deny those boys."

We had Dad's face. We walked around in his skin. A cast from his mold, which was cast from an even older one: the grandpa I was named for, Everett Lindt. The Lindt farmhouse was long gone, and so were Grandpa and Grandma Lindt, but the foundation stones remained, and so did we.

"We'll split the money," I said. "Three ways."

He sat up. "You, me, and Charlie? Equal?"

Now I had his attention. "Three ways."

Charlie would get his full half. Jay's cut would come out of mine, but I didn't mind. It wouldn't be that much. Let him feel big.

"Better get up and eat if you're coming," I said.

Katie, who was seven, was still sprawled out on the floor, wrapped in a brown-and-orange zigzag afghan that she'd pulled off Dad's recliner. Grandma Lindt had made it for him. It was the ugliest thing in the house, but Dad said he could feel her in it, and sometimes even Mom snuggled up in it, saying, "She was my mother too."

Out of us three kids, Katie was the one who looked like Mom, straight and pale as a paper birch, with big, owly eyes that took in everything. She lay with her head on her old baggy stuffed rabbit. The news was on, reporting on a heat wave downstate, warning people to close their shades and drink water, showing images of emergency workers loading people on stretchers into ambulances. The broadcast reflected on her eyes. The stretchers looked like they were sliding right into her brain.

"You don't need to be watching this."

I picked up the remote and found a kids' show.

"Hey!" she said, but quickly sank back down into the afghan, the bright colors of the cartoon lighting her eyes.

"Jay!" I yelled up the stairs. "Let's go!"

We got to the fields as soon as the dew lifted from the ground, and Charlie was waiting for us, leaning easily on his truck, ankles and arms crossed. Haying this summer had bulked him up, streaked his hair with brass, and turned his shoulders copper. He had an athlete's body that was most comfortable in motion and if he would've given two shits about school, he could've been on the baseball team or football even, but neither one of us had much use for school. He'd inherited a big, fleshy smile from his dad, but that's where the resemblance ended. His parents were built like blocks. His dad's stomach poured over his buckle and his mom's limbs were as thick as fenceposts. Mr. King called her his best farmhand. And somehow, like a pair of Belgians siring a Thoroughbred, the two of them had created Charlie. We'd been best friends since kindergarten, riding the same bus to Soo Township School, drawn to each other because we both lived on farms: My family had sheep and his had hogs.

We'd been haying partners forever. Our corner of the Upper Peninsula flooded each summer with oceans of clover and trefoil, orchard and timothy grass. The soil was always cold. Winter came fast and stayed long, so the hay rose up year after year, flourishing because it was the only thing that could. Each summer, we rolled over Chippewa County three times—once to cut, once to rake, and once to bale.

Charlie pointed his chin at Jay. "What's Little Lindt up to?" One of his nicknames for Jay. That or Dryer Lint or Sweater Lint and their spin-off, Fuzzball, which eventually became Fuzzy or Fuzz. Jay answered to them all. "You catching bales?"

"Raking," Jay said, stretching himself up straight. "First time."

The way it would work was like this: Jay would drive the tractor that pulled the rake, combing the cut hay into long fluffy windrows. I would come behind him on a tractor pulling the baler and wagon. The baler would lick up the hay, like an enormous vacuum cleaner, and pack it into bales. Charlie would ride the wagon, catching and stacking the bales as they came down the chute. When he got tired, we'd switch.

That day, we were baling Mason's fields on Ridge Road. His three-story redbrick farmhouse sat on top of the ridge the road was named for. He'd notched out two acres in front of the house and put up a tiny tan modular home for his oldest daughter. His grand scheme was to have all four of his girls settle down in a row in front of his house like a clutch of goslings. But so far, none had bit. They'd all migrated downstate for college and stayed there. His last hope was Kylie, the youngest, who'd brought us lunch in the field every day that summer. We watched for her, our stomachs tight, our mouths dry. And then she emerged from the road dust in Mason's truck, her hair moving like loose autumn leaves around her shoulders, bringing sandwiches and ice-cold pop, a twenty-minute break from the field, thirty if we actually chewed between bites. Charlie ate as slow as he could, watching her, hungry, I knew, for more than just lunch.

"I'm going to take Jay on a few laps," I said. "Won't take long."

I perched on the tractor fender beside Jay while he made his first passes back and forth across the field. His Kermit the Frog arms moved over the controls and I barked at him when he reached for the wrong one. Mason's tractor was an old open-station Massey Ferguson that dipped and bucked, trying to throw me. My ass ached, but I held on, and pretty soon, Jay's movements got smooth and easy.

Dad had taught me the same way, at the same age. The tractor had rumbled under my hands, and I'd been afraid, but Dad had crouched beside me, giving instructions as we circled the field, sometimes placing his hands over mine and moving the wheel or the throttle and my hand all at once. And then, just like that, he climbed off the tractor, and I was on my own, alone with the field stretching out before me, sunlit and hazy with pollen and fragrance; the heads of hay sparkling as they bent in the breeze. Dad loped back to the house and didn't look back once. But that was where I'd be different: I'd be coming up behind, and Charlie would be with me. Jay wouldn't be alone.

I nudged his shoulder. "You good?" We were coming back around where Charlie was waiting with the baler and wagon.

"I'm good."

He paused the tractor long enough for me to jump off and I watched, hands on my hips, as he pulled away.

"Yo, Rett! We baling or not?" Charlie slapped his Detroit Lions cap against his thigh. The hat was a thing of beauty: perfectly curved and broken in; old, with tiny frays along the bill, a yellow strip of dried sweat below the logo. He was standing on the empty hay wagon, looking up at the thin, high sun.

I jogged over to the tractor and climbed in. I eased out into the field, the conductor of a rickety train of Mason's aging equipment. The baler thudded and clanked as it pulled in the hay, rammed and bound it, and shoved it down the chute, one fifty-pound bale at a time. Charlie stacked the wagon for a good hour, then the back of his neck got slick and he yelled over the engine noise for us to switch.

"Your turn, man." He stripped off his T-shirt and wiped his face, then stuffed it into the back pocket of his jeans, where it hung the rest of the day like a damp tail. He examined the two-week-old tattoo on his left biceps: Vulcan, god of the forge and unofficial mascot of the high school welding shop. Vulcan was ripped and bearded, the way I imagined Moses, only with a blacksmith's hammer raised high above his head and standing before an open flame. It was Charlie's first tattoo and he rubbed Vaseline into it every morning.

I took the hay hooks from him and got on the wagon, bracing my knees for the tractor to lurch forward. I swung the hooks into the bales and stacked them in snug north–south, east–west rows. My breathing increased and the bales peppered my face and arms with papery chaff that worked its way under my eyelids like glass. My forearms screamed from the sun. God, was I ripe.

After a while, a cloud of dust rose over Ridge Road. Charlie saw it too.

"Lunch!" He steered the tractor toward the gate. Jay did the same.

I climbed to the top of the stacked hay and rode across the field like a hen on a nest. Seagull shadows spiraled over the ground as they watched for grasshoppers and voles fleeing the tractor treads. They picked through the windrows for skipper worms, twisting their heads and gurgling warnings to each other, stuffing themselves so full they strained to fly.

I peeled off my work gloves and lay back, folding my hands behind my head, letting the brilliant summer sky cover me like a blanket the color of a blue jay's back. The brittle stalks dug into my back as the wagon plodded along; my arms were crisscrossed with fine white scratches, but I could have dozed off right then and there, lulled by the lurching wagon, my tired body, the warm sun.

Kylie drove Mason's dust-covered dually through the entrance to the field. From my nest, I watched her and that cloud of unruly hair get out of the truck and start setting lunch on the tailgate. Another girl was in the truck with her. And when she got out of the truck, what hit me was how out of place she looked. She was small and skinny, not like most of the girls around here, who were wide-hipped and hearty; corn-fed, like Kylie, who filled out a pair of jeans real nice. Her hair was black and smooth down to her waist, and the pale skin of her face looked too clean next to the truck, too cool against the summer sky. She wore brand-new gleaming white Keds and placed each foot deliberately on the gravel drive. She handed a plastic bowl to Kylie, then looked around, a hand over her eyes, shading her view of the field. I swear she looked right at me.

I slid off the hay before Charlie even stopped the tractor.

Kylie paused from arranging paper plates, napkins, and plastic utensils and said, "This is Mary."

I felt for the first time the weight of Mary's steady, unflinching gaze, the same stare the ewes gave me when I walked through the field, how they weighed my every movement and sound. Her eyes were big and brown, just like those pretty Jersey cows at the fair. Jersey eyes, I thought. So deep you could drown in them. But so pretty you couldn't look away.

"I'm Everett."

"Hey, Everett," she said.

Her voice was feathery and low. Everyone always pronounced my name with two syllables, like Ev-ritt, but Mary pronounced it with three: Ev-er-ett. I liked it. The more syllables, I decided—the longer my name was in her mouth—the better. She wore a black choker and a tour shirt from a band I didn't know, the back a list of cities I'd never been to.

"Mary just moved into Dad's modular," Kylie said. "She'll be in our grade."

I rubbed my hands on my thighs, not sure what to do with them, aware of the oil and dust under my nails, my pitted-out shirt, the chaff in my hair.

"Hell of a time to move, senior year," I said.

"My dad didn't exactly ask my opinion about it. But it's fine. One more year and I'm on my own."

"Then what?"

"Far away from here." She looked up at me. "No offense."

I shrugged. "People say you got to be born here to love it."

"You love it?"

I looked over at the ridge beyond, where the land welled up to meet the sky, scrubby near the fence line, but sweet and lush as it rolled back.

"It's all I know," I said.

Charlie parked the tractor and came over, swinging his golden arms. His blue eyes popped against his skin and both girls turned from me to him, like their heads were attached to strings and he held the ends. It was always the same. When Charlie was around, it was like I wasn't. Then Jay walked up, and Kylie introduced them all. Charlie peppered Mary with questions. She gave him one- or two-syllable responses parceled out in small wispy bites.

"Any siblings?"

"No."

"What brought you here?"

"Coast Guard."

The St. Marys River was a revolving door of Coast Guard families. They dropped down like geese on the water, stayed a few years, then took off again, barely leaving a ripple behind. It was a life I wouldn't wish on anybody.

"Where'd you come from?" he asked.

She counted the places off her fingers: Puerto Rico (pinky), Massachusetts (ring finger), Florida (middle finger), New York (pointer finger). Then she hooked her thumb. "Here."

"New York City?"

"No, Buffalo."

"Buffalo! Holy Christ, you tired of losing Super Bowls yet?"

She glanced up at his yellowed Lions cap and smiled. "At least they went."

"Ouch," I said, and laughed. I couldn't help it. A good burn was a good burn, and Charlie didn't get burned often. A cloud passed over his face. Mary had found his button and pressed hard, and she stood there calmly with her hand tucked up on her hip. Who was this girl? A whip of desire cracked through me, and I leaned into the bed of the truck, pretending to check out the food, while my dick pulsed.

Mrs. Mason had put together a good spread: goulash in the Crock-Pot, bread and butter, green salad with sliced-up cucumbers and radishes. She'd even thrown in cottage cheese and melon balls. You'd think a steaming pot of goulash would be the last thing you'd want to eat when your muscles were screaming and the sun was sneering down on you but haying made us crazy with hunger. The bright summer air, the hours spent lifting and stacking. Every cell felt worn-out. The hotter, the thicker, the heavier the food, the better.

Kylie peeled the Saran Wrap off the food and we crowded against the tailgate, reaching around her to get at it. The sheep swarmed me the same way every time I climbed into their pen with a feed pail or an armful of hay. Their bodies were a current that wanted to sweep my feet out from under me.

"Stand back, Mary," Kylie said. "You might get bit."

We ate in silence, singularly focused on filling our bellies, swallowing forkful after forkful. Then we scoured the dishes for crumbs and bits of fallen lettuce and pushed those into our mouths as well. When everything was gone, we stood around, gorged as gulls. We looked over the fields, at the work we still needed to do, and leaned back against Mason's truck, unmoving. There was sweetgrass in the air and the sound of chickadees. The velvet-brown heads of cattails drummed against each other in the ditches.

"Oh," Kylie said. "We brought cookies too."

She held out the plastic container to Charlie alone. He plucked one out and took a bite, grinning at her as he did. Her eyes lingered on his bare arms and chest, and he made sure she noticed the tattoo. He rotated his arm so that she could admire the shadowed dimple of his triceps. She trailed her index finger across Vulcan's face, the fire between his hands.

"When did you get that?"

"Two weeks ago." He curled his arm to make the muscle bulge. "I designed it myself."

"Must've hurt." She bit her lip.

"Wasn't too bad."

She sat beside him on the tailgate, and he gave her knee a nice little squeeze. She smiled down into her lap, flames on her cheeks, and he moved his palm a few inches up her thigh. He lifted the pull tab on his pop, releasing a long, slow hiss of carbonation that blended with the droning undertow of meadow locusts and birdsong. She dropped her head onto his shoulder. Her glossy curls brushed against his bare skin, and I shivered.

Jay's mouth hung open, bits of lettuce on display. The little shit learned a lot that day.

Eventually, Jay wandered off to a scrub of trees to take a piss, leaving me to talk with Mary. Her hair looked liquid in the sun. I imagined it gliding between my fingers or skimming my chest the way Kylie's hair had touched Charlie's. I pulled my work gloves out of my back pocket, folded them up, and stuffed them back in. I cleared my throat.

"That's a big town, Buffalo, isn't it?"

"Not huge, but way bigger than this place."

"It would be huge to these guys," Kylie piped up. "They've crossed the Mackinac Bridge, like, twice in their whole life."

"Like you've ever been anywhere." Charlie stood in front of her, making sure his abs were nice and tight.

"I visit my sisters in Traverse City all the time," she said, like it was China. "Which is more than you can say. You guys are all going to live and die, like, ten miles from here." She cocked her head at Charlie, leaning in so close that her hair almost stroked his face.

"News flash, Ky," Charlie said. "You'll be right here with us." He leaned forward too. Their faces were an inch apart.

"I'll be downstate." She play-pushed him. An excuse to touch him. "Tired of hanging out with rednecks."

"Rednecks! What rednecks?"

"You! Both of you." She swept her arm to include me.

Charlie opened his mouth to say something, but then he turned to me.

"Everett's the redneck," he said. "Look at him."

I slid my hand over my neck. "I'm not a redneck."

Charlie came up to me and plucked at my shirt. "Sure you are. I bet Mary's never seen a real redneck before. Come on, give her a peek. Show her that farmer's tan."

"Cut it out."

"Show her. You want to see a redneck, don't you, Mary?"

"I said cut it out!"

I shoved him. Not too hard, a warning. But then he pulled me into a headlock, pinning my face against his side, stale and rank after the morning in the field, and underneath that the peculiar odor of hog shit that pig farmers can't ever wash away, sweet like oranges, thick like chalk. I tucked my head and tried to roll out of it, but he was stronger. He yanked my shirt up over my head.

"Lookit! Lookit!" he crowed. "White as a baby's ass!"

I slammed Charlie into the side of Mason's truck. My shoulder caught him right in the gut. He grunted and I knew he felt it, but he didn't let go.

Sheep pulled this shit all the time. Rams, lambs, even ewes fresh from lambing with their udders swinging all over; they would knock each other around, trying to put each other in their place. Ewes and lambs settled things pretty quick, but rams wouldn't stop till one of their necks was broke.

"Knock it off!" Kylie shouted. She climbed into the bed of the truck and stood there with her hands on the edge, staring down at us. "You do something to my dad's truck and you're dead."

Charlie loosened his grip, and I threw him off. He rolled on the ground laughing. "Oh, shit, man—your arms. That's prime redneck right there, Mary. Take a good, long look. You can tell your fancy friends in Buffalo about it."

They all looked at me, my pale chest, the sharp lines dividing my biceps into red and white, but it was Mary's unhurried eyes that felt hot and bright as a spotlight. I snatched my shirt off the ground.

"Fuck you, Charlie."

"I'm just messing with you. Jesus."

I pulled my shirt back over my head and walked back to the tractor.

"Oh, come on!" Charlie called from the ground. He draped his arms over his knees. "Retty baby, it was a joke, OK? I was joking."

I turned on the tractor just to drown him out and leaned back in the seat, taking deep, slow breaths of the thick summer air. A horsefly landed on my arm. I watched it knead my skin and slide its long black mouthparts over my arm before fanning it away.

Truth be told, I didn't mind how I looked. A few summers ago, I was as scrawny as Jay but now I was tall and tight, not chiseled like Charlie, but filling out. Those were Mom's words: "You're just filling out so nicely." The top of her head came to my chin now.

I wasn't ashamed of the farmer's tan either. The sun left its mark in reds and creams, what it had touched and not touched, darkening my hands and arms and neck. My shoulders were hard. I was a worker and it showed. My skin told me who I was. If those Lindts who came here to farm so long ago saw me, they would recognize themselves in me and be proud.

Mary was helping Kylie pack up, bending into the truck bed to gather the napkins we'd been too hungry to use. I took in the curve of her body, the smallness of her waist before it flared into her hips. She reached for something, and her shirt rose an inch, revealing a ribbon of creamy, soft skin. I imagined walking up to her and sliding my hand around her waist, just under her rib cage, pulling her body up close against me, and bending into that silky hair, how it'd smell like nighttime and white clover. She lifted her head before I could look away and I spun around, gripping the steering wheel, feeling the heat rise up my neck. Red now for sure.

Then, oh shit, she was walking toward me, moving through the honey-colored air, her Keds blinding. The whole landscape blurred around her. The fresh-opened buttercups, Mason's truck, the wagons. Charlie, Jay, and Kylie. They all merged and faded, like tunnel vision narrowed to focus on her. I killed the tractor.

"You OK?" she asked, squinting up at me.

"Me? Fine. Why?"

"You guys were really going at it."

"We were just horsing around."

"Is he always such a douche?"

"What do you mean?"

"Trying to make people look bad so he looks good."

"Charlie? Nah. He's not like that. He's—we were just being stupid."

I looked back at him. He had his arm around Kylie, the way just moments before I'd imagined holding Mary.

Kylie yelled over. "Mary, you ready?"

"Yeah." She turned back to me. "Guess I'll see you."

"Yeah," I said. "See you."

I watched her walk away, the way her jeans hugged her thighs and ass just right. Jesus. She climbed into Mason's truck without a word to Charlie and closed the door behind her.

It bothered me what she said though. Charlie was my best friend. Had been since forever. Yeah, rams jostled for dominance, but there was never anything like that between us. He was Charlie. He was golden. I knew that. It was roughhousing, a joke, just like Charlie said, the way young rams will play-fight, practicing for battles ahead. What did she know? This strange new girl. I sat in the tractor, looking out over Ridge Road, unchanged as long as I'd been alive. But her words wouldn't leave me alone. And something else came to mind, a lesson I'd learned from Dad long ago: Don't ever turn your back to a ram.

When Kylie had finished packing up, Charlie walked over to me, loose and easy, like nothing had happened.

"I don't have a thing to say to you," I said.

"You still got your little redneck panties twisted up?"

"Just get on the wagon."

He pulled out his cooler from where he'd stashed it between bales.

"Thought we could have a cold one before we got back at it. Got something other than Old Milwaukee for once. But I guess I'll drink them myself." He hoisted himself on the wagon and plopped down on top of the stack of bales. He took two amber bottles out of the cooler and waved them at me. "You sure? Nice and cold." They shone with condensation. He twisted off the tops.

Fuck it, I could use a beer. I got off the tractor, pulling up a fat stalk of grass on my way to the wagon. I bit its tender white base. A hick habit, I knew, but I loved the starchy, muddy taste. Sometimes I craved it. I probably wouldn't be an unhappy sheep, wrapping my tongue around one blade of grass after another, breathing in the bright scents of each season, following the sheep ahead of me all day long. I sat beside Charlie.

"Atta boy," he said.

He clapped my back and handed me a bottle.

"Coors Light," I said. "Fancy." I pressed it to the side of my face, cool and wet.

"Mom bought it. Dad won't touch it."

His parents had a beer fridge in the garage, a fact we had used to our advantage quite a bit over the years. We'd be tinkering beside his dad in the hog barn, and he'd turn to us with a sweaty upper lip and say, "Run on up to the house, now, and grab me a beer." So we would. And some for ourselves too.

Charlie raised a hand in farewell as the girls pulled away.

"Fucking city people," he said. "Did you hear that chick? The first words out of her mouth are how shitty she thinks this place is. How she just can't wait to get out of here. Watch, Kylie'll bring her around all the time now."

"I didn't think she was too hard to look at, myself," I said.

He looked at me. "You like her? Christ Almighty."

"It was pretty funny the way she shut you up over the Bills."

"Last time I checked you were a Lions fan too."

"Never said I wasn't."

"OK, then she burned you too."

"Nah, pretty sure it was just you."

Jay trotted back from his piss break, pulling the seed tops off the bromegrass as he came, dropping them like breadcrumbs behind him. The wind billowed his T-shirt around his reedy chest, making him look like a big-headed paper doll. One of the big boys, my ass.

Charlie smiled down at him, dazzling. "Little Lindt! My man, the big hay raker. How do you feel?"

"Good," Jay said. "Real good." He was breathless, beaming. I could tell he wanted to climb up and sit beside us. The girls, learning to rake, the prospect of a cut of our pay—he looked so pleased with himself he could hardly stand it. If Charlie had offered him a Coors, he probably would have self-combusted right then and there.

"That's what I like to hear," Charlie said. "So, why don't you hop up on that tractor over there and get a head start on us?"

Jay's face fell. Without a word, he climbed onto the other tractor and pulled away, the rake bouncing behind, folded up like grasshopper legs.

Charlie took a long pull from his beer. He picked daisy heads out of the hay and pitched them to the ground.

"Listen, man, no hard feelings, right?" He looked at me quick. "It was a dick thing to do. I don't know why I did it."

That was the thing that always amazed me about Charlie, how he could lay himself bare like that, belly-up, and make himself vulnerable. When it was just the two of us, he could set the swagger aside. It was the reason we were still friends—he always asked for forgiveness, and I always gave it.

I clinked the neck of my bottle to his. "All good."

We watched Jay for a while, mesmerized as he moved back and forth. I took off my hat and the air cooled my temples where my hairline was still damp. By now my beer was empty. I tucked the bottle back inside the cooler.

"But did you see me and Kylie though?" Charlie asked.

"I saw. Thought I'd have to give Jay the Heimlich. What did that tattoo cost you?"

"Two hundred Canadian."

"Worth it, I'd say. Looked like she wanted to lick it right off you."

"Hell, yes. We're hanging out tonight. Soon as I shower up."

"Good luck with Mason."

"Mason can kiss my ass."

He held out another Coors, but I shook my head. I was thinking of Mason now, imagining him looking out the third-floor window of his farmhouse wondering why only one of his tractors was moving.

"Let's get going."

Charlie groaned and flopped backward on the hay, but I ignored him. He'd move when the bales started coming.

"Hey, Lindt!" he said, sitting up. "You want me to get Miss Fancy Pants's number? Kylie'll have it."

I pulled up a new blade of grass, a deep-blue one, stringy and sweet, and clamped it between my teeth. It was cool and fresh on my tongue after the bitter beer.

"You heard her. 'Far away from here,'" I said.

"Huh?"

"That's what she said. 'Far away from here.'"

"That don't mean shit. She's just talking big."

He was at the edge of the wagon now, leaning over me, thumbs in his belt loops. Behind him, the ridge rolled west in a singular sodden ripple and the sky flattened everything around us. Spring-born lambs are scared when they're first turned out. They spend the first few days wrapped around their mothers' legs, cowering in the shadows of their bellies, bleating. But it's not coyotes they're scared of, or hawks. It's the sky. Enormous, yawning, and blue.

I smiled up at Charlie, extra wide, showing him the green grass flecks in my teeth.

"Something tells me I'm not her type."

"You're a pussy, you know that? A big, wet, floppy one." His eyes matched the sky behind him. "It's a phone call. It's not like you're spending the rest of your life with her. You think I'm spending the rest of my life with Kylie? With Mason? Christ, no." He looked to the road where the last grains of gravel dust from Mason's truck were still falling. "But I bet she'll make senior year a little more fun."

I thought about Mary's Jersey eyes, the way she'd tossed Charlie's words right back in his face. How she'd stood looking around the field, like something sleek and beautiful dropped from the sky.

"Seriously, man," Charlie said. "What's the worst that could happen?"

It was just a number. Just a phone call. There was nothing to lose.

"All right," I said. "Get it."

Chapter 2

The forever July light still lit the yard when Jay and I pulled into the house. There were hours yet before stars would break onto the sky. Mom was at the kitchen window, framed in a yellow square of light, probably washing dishes. Dad and Katie were in the yard leading the 4-H lambs in single file like hoofed dogs. Dad led mine and Jay's by halter; Katie led hers with her tiny hand cupped under its chin. It was her first year showing sheep. Her market lamb, a pretty ewe she'd named Fluffernutter, was a bottle lamb that she'd raised herself. Milk was a powerful pull, and now Fluff followed Katie like a sloppy pup, thinking she was her mom. They even looked like mother and daughter, or at least the same species, the way they almost glowed like angels, Katie's hair and Fluff's fleece, shining in the vanishing daylight.

"I'm starved," Jay said.

"Lambs first, then eat," I said.

He rolled his eyes and pushed open the truck door.

"Hold on," I said, taking out my wallet. I gave Jay his cut.

"Mom was worried, but you did good. You saved the day. You really did. I don't know who I would've called."

He pushed the bills into his pocket. "Thanks."

Walking the lambs was our nightly summer ritual. There was no shortcut to training a lamb for the show ring. There was no telling it what you wanted it to do, no magic wand, no treat. There was only ritual. Repetition. We halter-broke them first, then weaned them off the halter altogether. We increased a single lap around the yard at the beginning of June to a full mile by August. We pressed down the rises in their spines, we held their heads high, we stretched their stance into an elongated rectangle until the position was second nature to them. We fed them high-protein feed, lots of it, and not too much hay, so that they doubled in size over the summer. We washed and sheared them, using Orvus soap to make their fleeces bright, and baby oil to make their faces shine. At the end of August, we loaded them, grown and slick-muscled and completely transformed, onto the stock trailer and brought them to the Chippewa County Fair with the hope that one of them would bring home grand champion.

Every 4-H kid wanted market lambs from breeders who produced grand champions, so every animal on our farm existed to create them. You weren't getting a grand champion without a good sire and dam. That was where it all began: putting two special creatures together and hoping they'd make something extraordinary. There was Curly, Dad's freight train of a ram, a big Suffolk with a domed head and drooping, low-set ears, a short body, and heavy shoulders. Dad also had thirty ewes, sturdy females with deep bodies who had easy births and gave good milk. He culled any that rejected their lambs. That was the worst, in his book. If a ewe wouldn't mother, he wrote her ear tag number down and said, "That one's going to sausage camp." Then he'd drop her wailing lambs in a cardboard box for me to take up to the house for Mom and Katie to bottle-feed.

Each spring, Dad sold about sixty market lambs. 4-H kids started calling him in February to get on his sale list. He'd wallpapered the barn manger with newspaper clippings and pictures of kids wearing bright-blue Lindt Lambs hats and draping rosettes over the backs of lambs they'd bought from him. Dad pinned the pictures right by the light switch, so that they were the first thing he saw when he entered the barn and the last thing when he left.

Jay and I took our lambs from Dad, and he started playing judge, standing in the middle of the yard while we led the lambs in a wide circle around him. He was wearing a gray plaid work shirt, the first few buttons undone, revealing the bright collar of his undershirt. On the back pocket of his jeans was a faded Skoal ring. On his head, the foam-and-mesh Lindt Lambs cap. He motioned for us to line up the lambs facing him and set them up. He walked around us, touched the lambs. It was all practice for the fair, to get the lambs used to the show ring, starting and stopping, being handled. He motioned Jay to walk his lamb toward him. The lamb planted his front feet in the earth and refused to move.

"Stupid thing!" Jay cursed. He pulled on it, hands around its neck, like he wanted to twist its head right off. The more he pulled, the deeper the lamb dug into the ground. Tufts of grass threaded up between the clefts of its hooves.

Here's the thing about sheep: They won't do things alone. They only want to do what the other sheep are doing. So Jay's lamb was thinking, My buddies are standing back there. No way in hell I'm going anywhere with this kid. That's what training is for. You have to train that herd instinct out of them. You got to work with them so much that you become the herd. Anywhere you go, that lamb's got to want to go. Yanking on its head is not the way to do it. No matter how tired or hungry you are.

"Hey!" Dad shouted. "What happens when you squeeze bread?"

"Gets squished," Katie and I said. He'd told us this before. Many times. That we had to think of the lamb's head like a loaf of bread, keep our hands light and open, stay calm, never get rough.

"I'm asking Jay."

"I hate sheep!" Jay said. He pulled on the lamb with all his body weight. The lamb reared back and shook its head, wresting away from his hands, and trotted off. He chased after it like a fool, looking like he was going to cry.

"Get in the house," Dad said, and Jay stomped off, acting mad, when he was getting exactly what he wanted—going inside, showering, eating—while I was still out with the sheep. All he had to do was throw a little temper tantrum and get exactly what he wanted.

"Must be nice," I said.

His lamb came up beside Fluff and Katie crooked her arm around its neck. Dad took it from her and the three of us continued the session. All the while, Katie stroked Fluff's back and rubbed her face against the nap of her head.

I worried it was too much love. Mom and Dad had let it go too far. Dad should have never let her pick Fluff for the fair. No matter that she was a beautiful lamb. One of the best Dad had ever produced. He should have said, *Sorry, Kate, not you, not this lamb*. He should have kept Fluff for breeding or sold her to some other 4-H kid. Ripped that Band-Aid off early. Now it was too late. I dreaded the end of August when we'd load Fluff with the other show lambs onto the trailer and bring her to the fair.

The three of us walked on. I cupped my lamb's head in my hand, keeping him close. I felt his delicate under-chin skin glide along his jaw. The slightest nick would reveal bone. My other hand was at the base of his ears, the very spot where the ewes sniffed their lambs moments after birth to memorize their smell.

A week later, I was on my back under Mason's baler, watching Charlie's boots pace. We'd run out of sisal twine, the blond cord that binds bales together, and the baler had spit loose sheaves all over the wagon. Charlie gathered them up and scattered them over the windrow, where the baler would lick them up again.

The weather had been so good lately—dry, with days of cloudless, open sky—that the county rippled with hay. Bright swaths of trefoil looked like gallons of mustard smeared on the fields. When the engine was off, I could hear the hay growing, a buzz one level below the sound of the flies and grasshoppers; the electricity of expansion, of something lifting its head and stretching its arms, taking up space it had every right to take.

We couldn't put it up fast enough. We nudged the throttle until the equipment wanted to shudder apart right out from under us. We finished Mason's fields, then cut for other landowners who hired us through him.

It was a sorry-ass job, crawling under the baler. There were just a few inches between my chest and the baler's rusted underbelly and, once I was there, I tried not to think about how old it was, how much it weighed, how I was in the middle of a field in the middle of nowhere. The best thing to do was talk. And Charlie was good at that.

"How much do you think these people are making on this hay?" he asked.

"More than us."

"Fifty bucks a ton, you think?"

"A hundred."

All the hay I cut for Dad went to the sheep, but other landowners, like Mason, made more hay than their livestock could eat and sold the extra to hay markets in the South. When I watched the Kentucky Derby on TV, I liked thinking about those pretty, fine-boned Thoroughbreds prancing up to the starting gate, their hides glowing in the Southern sun, having eaten Chippewa County hay for lunch.

"And how many tons per acre?"

"Two or three. Depending on how good the hay is."

"This field's forty acres."

It came out to anywhere between eight and twelve thousand dollars. I tied off the twine in silence while the math sank into Charlie's skull.

His boots stopped at my head and he whistled. "We're at the wrong end of this process," he said.

"Yep." I pulled myself out from under the baler. "But someday we'll be on the other side."

As much as we liked to rag on Mason, the truth was we admired him. He had what we wanted. When we imagined ourselves as grown men with our wives and kids and jobs, we saw ourselves like Mason, sitting in our tall houses, driving our Super Dutys, surrounded by acres of flat, bare land filled with our animals. We'd have a handful of tractors and wagons, and every summer, we'd hire a crew of kids to hay.

"Almost forgot." Charlie dug into his front pocket and pulled out a piece of paper, folded cleanly and evenly, which told me that he hadn't been the one to fold it. The sun struck it, a blinding whiteness, and I shielded my eyes.

"What's this?"

"It's her number, dipshit. I told you I'd get it, so here it is."

My heart jumped, something like a spooked rabbit thumping its hocks against the inside of my chest. Fine lines of graphite looped across the sheet in a light, rounded hand, definitely not Charlie's dull-pencil scrawl. Three digits, a dash, four more digits, and then that single, simple name: Mary.

Part of me was glad he'd remembered. I looked down at the paper fluttering in my grease-stained hands. I could see her long hair and faraway eyes. That ribbon of waist. How she hadn't given Charlie the time of day. But the other part of me had hoped he'd forget. I could think of a hundred other things I'd rather do than call her. Crawling back under that baler was one of them. I'd never been like Charlie, making a fool of myself flexing and posing. Sweet-talking. It was easy for him. Impossible for me.

"Did Kylie say anything?"

"About what?"

"When you asked for Mary's number."

"I got it right from Fancy Pants."

"You did not."

"She was at Mason's the other night, and I told her you wanted it."

"Why would you do that?"

"You wanted her number. I got it."

"You said you were getting it from Kylie. Now Mary knows."

"Exactly. No more being a pussy, man. If you don't call her, she'll know you're a pussy. And so will me and Kylie." He smiled as he said this, pleased with his little setup.

"She's going to say no anyway. What's the point?"

He held out his hand. "You want me to take it back?"

The paper waved in the space between us. She had come back to me though. Asked if I was OK. Squinted up at me with those bottomless eyes. I folded the paper back up and slid it into my pocket.

"That's what I thought," Charlie said, his smile even bigger. "When are you going to do it?"

"I don't know." I stepped toward the tractor, eager to get back to work. There was so much hay to put up, so little sun left. We'd already wasted too much time on the twine.

But he didn't move. "When, Lindt?"

"Tonight. OK? Happy?"

He smiled. "Happy."

He got on the wagon, and as we looped around the field, the sharp point of the folded paper bore into my groin, no matter how I shifted in the seat.

A turkey vulture landed on a nearby windrow. Crashed was more like it, her big body looking like a used black Hefty bag. She picked through the stalks, scaring off the seagulls, eyeing me with her horrible, hooded eyes. As I got closer, even with the baler grinding behind me, she didn't budge. I'd baled up voles before, a dead skunk, and a pile of seagull feathers. When I was twelve, I baled up a nest of fresh sparrows. I'd stopped the tractor and run all the way to the house to tell Dad.

"Extra protein for the sheep" was all he'd said, and he told me about a three-foot-long garter snake he'd once baled that was still hissing when he unloaded the wagon.

The turkey vulture watched me get closer and closer, daring me to hit her. I could see the red, brainlike ripples on her hood.

"You ugly son of a bitch," I said, aching to run her over now, just to make her move. And then, when I was three yards away, she hopped to the next windrow over. She carried on like that the rest of the day, glaring, filling her gullet, waiting for me to get just a few feet away before she moved, until every windrow was baled and she had nowhere else to go but back into the sky.

That night, I held my hand under the showerhead waiting for the water to warm. I looked sideways in the mirror and traced the line on my arm where the sun had divided my biceps neatly in half, one side the mottled browns of heat and sweat; the other side the pale coolness of cotton sheets. There was no extra flesh on my body, no softness anywhere, but there was no weakness either.

All summer long, I'd watched my neck widen. It sloped down to the divots where my collarbones and shoulders met. Each bale lifted, tossed, and stacked had marked my body, the same way the sun had.

What had Mary seen in the field? A neck thickened and reddened by work? Or a body growing into itself, taking the shape of what it would be? Steam rose behind me and licked the backs of my legs. The water was plenty hot but still I waited. I squared up in front of the mirror and rolled my shoulders. I had balance, a skeletal correctness that I looked for in my lambs: straight in the lines from my shoulders to the ends of my fingers, from my hips to the heels of my feet. There was fleshing ability, growth potential.

I leaned into the boy in the mirror, his nose an inch from mine.

"I'd buy you," I told him. "If you were a lamb. I'd buy you in a heartbeat."

The spot where Mary's number had rubbed all day, just inside that soft hollow between bone and hair, radiated red and warm like an early tick bite. It was tender to the touch. I picked up my jeans from the floor and fished the paper out of the pocket. There it was, not quite so crisp anymore, but seeing it again—those numbers and letters plain as day—loosed the rabbit in my chest. The powerful strokes were visible in the mirror. My chest pulsed as though my heart lay directly beneath the skin, unprotected by rib, open and vulnerable.

"It's a phone call," I said, repeating Charlie. "It's not the rest of your life."

I ducked into the shower and almost purred when the water hit my shoulders. My muscles softened. The water ran off me light gray and then clear. Bits of grass swirled at my feet.

Mom looked up from the couch when I lifted the telephone on the wall in the kitchen. Her rule was no calling after eight PM. It was rude.

"Just calling Charlie real quick."

I stretched the cord all the way to the back door, sheltering the receiver between my shoulders and the wall. That phone was the only difference between me and Dad's ram Curly. When Curly wanted a ewe, he let her know. He batted her leg, dipped his head, and growled. Sometimes he licked her shoulder, dying for her, even if it was just the taste of her lanolin on his tongue. There was no mistaking what he wanted, what he needed. In response, she let him mount her or turned away. It was as simple as that. Yes or no. Me calling Mary was essentially the same thing. I could call, but everything else was up to her.

Her dad answered on the very first ring. A voice that was deep, stripped of warmth, hard as ice. The rabbit wanted to kick its way out of my chest.

I cleared my throat. "Is Mary there?"

He snorted. "You boys are quick around here. What's it been—a week? Sniffing around already."

I held the receiver over the cradle and let it hover there. It would be easy to let it go. One smooth, clean click and I'd never hear this voice again. But I could already hear Charlie laughing at me, calling me pussy. There was no way I was hanging up. I unlocked my tongue from the top of my mouth.

"Can I talk to Mary, sir? Please."

He covered the receiver and there was an exchange of words. The receiver creaked and at last I got what I wanted.

"Hello?"

"Mary? It's Everett. Not sure if you remember."

"Charlie's friend."

It was always the same. Charlie's friend. Dad's face. Grandpa's name. When would I ever be known for myself alone? Just Everett. Period.

"I was wondering if we could hang out sometime," I said. "Maybe I could show you around or something. I have a truck."

There. I'd batted her leg. Whatever happened next was up to her. I pushed my thumbnail into the doorframe, leaving a cascade of crescents in the soft pine, and waited. I pictured her bunched up like me against the wall, trying to carve out a little privacy at the end of a stretched-out telephone cord. Her lips would be less than an inch from the receiver, speaking words into the line, straight to me. A kiss couldn't bring them closer. I laid a palm to my chest, feeling the strong, rhythmic strokes.

"You seem really nice and everything, Everett."

My name. All by itself. The stretched-out way she said it. Her throaty voice. I wanted her to say it again. But she was silent for a long time. And in that silence, I knew I was doomed.

"I'm just gonna focus on school while I'm here, you know? Getting ready to apply to college. But it's nice of you to ask."

"Yeah," I said. "No, yeah. I get it. I mean, I figured. 'Anywhere but here,' and all that, right? I just thought—"

She said other things. Nice things. I thought I said goodbye. And then I placed the receiver on the cradle, slowly, softly, as though my whole family were asleep and one little click would wake them all up. As though I could make it so the whole conversation had never happened. I walked back through the kitchen to the stairs, feeling whipped.

Mom set down her magazine, following me with her eyes. "You look upset."

"Just tired."

"How's Charlie?"

"Charlie? Oh, right. He's fine."

He'd be more than fine. I'd gone through with it and called Mary and he would be laughing at me anyway. I couldn't think of one girl who'd ever said no to him. At least he couldn't call me pussy. He'd have to come up with something else.

I climbed the stairs to my bedroom. Jay was in his bed with his eyes closed and earphones on. He tapped his thighs with his fingers. Good. I didn't want to talk to him. My body was tired and so was my brain. My heart was tired too. I tossed Mary's number into the garbage can and dropped onto my bed, rolling onto my side, looking out the window.

Our house was shaped like it had been drawn by a little kid: a yellow square with a triangle on top. My and Jay's bedroom was in the triangle and from the window, I could look out onto the pitted gravel driveway and see everything that came and went. I could see the aged barn with its paint peeling in large, faded red flakes, revealing sun-worn, spongy gray wood beneath. If I pushed up the window and leaned out a little, I could see the St. Marys sparkling in the east with Sugar Island rising up forested and dark on the other side.

Why did she give Charlie her number if she didn't like me? That was what was bothering me. I fished the paper out of the garbage and read her number for the hundredth time. I ran my finger across her name. The pencil smudged easily. Maybe something I said made her change her mind.

I have a truck.

Jesus. I couldn't blame her.

Jay shifted in his bed, and I snapped the paper closed. When I was sure he was minding his own business, I tucked her number inside my wallet. She'd changed her mind, is all. And if she'd changed her mind once, maybe she'd change it again.

The next day, a gray shelf of clouds covered the county, threatening rain, making the air thick to breathe. Charlie and I had a field to bale before it came. After that, maybe a few days off.

"So?" he asked. "How'd it go?"

"It didn't." I reached into my pocket and touched the tender tick bite. "I'm really nice though."

Now was the time for him to ridicule me, and I waited for it, eager to get it over with, but instead he was thoughtful. He pulled up a blade of orchard grass and handed it to me. "The fair's coming. You'll hook up with someone there."

"I'm not trying to just hook up with somebody. Jesus! I just thought she was"—I put the stalk in my mouth—"interesting, you know?"

He put a hand on my shoulder and looked me in the eye. "Dude, if you hook up with someone, I guarantee you're going to think she's pretty interesting too."

I looked off to the sky. The heat with no sun, the heaviness, was strange.

"If the weather holds off, me and Kylie are going to Dunbar tonight. You should meet us. I'll tell her no Fancy Pants."

"Are you fishing?"

He winked at me. "Swimming."

Dunbar was a forested wedge of land carved out from where the Charlotte River emptied its tea-colored water into the St. Marys. When I got there, a half dozen classmates were leaning over the edge of the bridge, ready to drop into the river fifteen feet below. The guys wore boxers or gym shorts. They were already wet. I hadn't seen most of them in months, and they were taller now, their jaws wider. A handful of girls stood around shivering in their bras and tank tops. Charlie, of course, was in the center of them, shirtless. Kylie wore jean shorts and a blue bra with little flowers all over it. Her hair was slicked back and her skin glistened. Everything about her was full and broad, and while the other girls were huddling in a tight pack, with their arms crossed over their chests, she climbed onto the metal guardrails, shoulders above everyone, and shouted for Charlie to get up there with her. She'd taken to calling him Charles.

"Charles, let's go!"

He climbed up next to her, all smiles, like there was no other girl on that bridge, no other girl in the whole Upper Peninsula. And Kylie looked back at him the same way. She took his hand and they jumped, shrieking like little kids. He jumped farther and wider, but she anchored him, and they hit the water together.

The bridge was a long concrete slab supported by more concrete. Kids had scratched their names and initials into its underbelly with rocks. Someone had spray-painted a single droopy penis. A trio of wooden pylons, left over from the original bridge, listed in the water, wanting to topple and rot, but the riverbed held them firm. There was a smashed beer can wedged into a split in the tallest one. I leaned over the guardrail and looked for Charlie and Kylie. They'd swum out of sight under the bridge, but I could hear her laughter ricochet between the concrete and water.

On the count of three, everyone else jumped in, feet and arms kicking, and they churned the Charlotte like a school of fish fighting for food. Charlie and Kylie swam to the bank and scrambled out, stepping barefoot on twigs and leaves.

Kylie waved when she saw me. "You going in? It feels great!" She held out her arms to the muggy air, warm even though the sun was hiding. One of her bra straps had slipped off her shoulder. I took off my boots and socks and peeled off my shirt.

"He won't jump," Charlie said. "He's a—"

Before the word was out of his mouth, I swung my legs over the railing and leaped. The water surged over my head and bubbled against my skin, sloughing away the heat and stink of the day. I took my time coming up. I could make out swirling black bits of leaves in the clouded water, the sweep and surge of kicking legs. The kids called mutely to each other, and my jeans felt heavy and stiff. I touched the mush of the river bottom with my toes before pushing to the surface. When I broke through, the voices around me became crisp again and I rolled onto my back and floated, looking up through the spruces leaning over the water. Someone had cast a line and snagged a red-and-white bobber in the branches. It could have happened twenty years ago or last week. I filled my lungs as deep as I could with the dirt smell of the river. I lifted my head as the water erupted in goose bumps and the rain fell on us all.

Chapter 3

Our show lambs grew. The timothy feathered lavender and pale and the summer tilted to an end. Mary never came back to the fields, but I'd be a liar if I said I didn't look for her smooth black head every time Kylie pulled up in Mason's truck. The last Monday of August, we loaded the show lambs into the stock trailer and hauled them to the fair. Weigh-in was from ten AM to nine PM. If you didn't get in line before nine PM, you didn't show. If your lamb didn't weigh at least eighty pounds, you didn't show. If your lamb had the shits, a snotty nose, ringworm, or a cough, you didn't show. All day long, the weigh-in line wrapped around the fairgrounds, a train of screaming hogs, moaning steers, sheep pushing their noses out the trailer slats. Jay hopped out of the cab and hoboed up and down the line looking for his buddy Chase. Katie got out, too, and balanced on the trailer runner as we inched forward. She stretched up on her tiptoes and reached inside the trailer, seeking Fluff's nose.

I sat in the cab with Dad, watching her in the side mirror.

"Did you talk to her about the sale?" I asked.

"It's no secret," he said.

"That's not the same as telling her."

Because the fact of the matter was the fair was terminal. Once we led the lambs off the trailer and through the scales, they'd head to the sheep barn, where they'd spend the last week of their lives. On Saturday, they'd take a final spin around the show ring while the auctioneer sang over their heads. On Labor Day, a new line of trucks and trailers would wrap around the fairgrounds, this one made of packer trucks from the area meat processors, some coming from three hours away or more.

That's when it dawns on first-time show kids that there is a day after the fair. Up until then, they've kept their feelings in little compartments, only letting themselves think about how their lambs would do on show day, who would win grand champion, how much money they'd make. Then fair week is over, and the packer trucks come. All the compartments smash together and reality hits. Hard. I can't tell you how many kids I've seen chasing after those packer trucks, bawling, shaking a feed pail, wanting to give their animals one last comfort before they went.

My first year showing, I watched the barn superintendents spray bright stripes down each animal's back. My lambs had red stripes and I asked Dad what it meant.

"The animals with red stripes go on that truck," he said. "The animals with blue stripes go on that one. And the animals with green stripes go on that one."

"Where are they going?"

He looked off to the side for a moment and pulled on his chin. "Oh, different farms downstate," he said finally. "Yours are going to a family that has a giant field of red-top clover. They keep sheep as pets."

That satisfied me, pleased me even. I couldn't think of a better life for my lambs.

But Charlie had laughed when I told him what Dad had said. "They're headed to someone's plate, you dummy."

We were standing by the idling trucks, drawn to them because they vibrated with a power that felt dangerous and thrilling. We touched their mud-splattered fenders, watched them heave as the animals moved inside.

He climbed up the side of the trailer and I followed. We looked down at the jammed-in animals, each species partitioned by a metal gate, each back marked with a bold red stripe. I picked my lambs out of the press of bodies. They saw me and called out. Their cries spread through the trailer, like the first drop of Hershey's syrup darkening a glass of milk, until every animal was bellowing, and the entire trailer rocked with noise.

I'd decided I would never do that to my own kid when I had one. None of that fairy-tale shit. No compartments. I would tell them the truth, right from the beginning. No matter what, they would hear it from me.

We sat in the weigh-in line two hours. Katie hopped on and off the trailer the whole time, picking dandelions and threading them through the slats to Fluff. Jay must've found Chase because he hadn't come back. Dad and I watched truck after truck unload its cargo into the scale house and bounce away, lighter.

The MacGowans' trailer was ahead of us, a brand-new gooseneck with their farm crest painted on the side. The MacGowan girls were airy and plain-faced. They wore their hair in painfully tight French braids. One was my age, the other was a year or two younger, but neither one was any bigger than Jay, and beside them their lambs would only look larger and all the more beautiful. A few exhibitors stood around the scale house, waiting for the MacGowans to open the trailer door and unveil its contents. Lindt Lambs weren't good enough for Mr. MacGowan anymore.

He informed anyone who would ask that he had purchased his girls' lambs in Indiana that year, as if that alone made them superior.

But when the tight, leggy lambs leapt from the trailer, more deer than sheep, my breath caught in my throat. They were long, sleek-bodied, and square off their tailheads; the gleaming products of intensive breeding. They moved like royalty, stepping tall and quick, holding their noses high. They led the two MacGowan girls into the scale house instead of the other way around. I could have watched those lambs all day. You can't train attitude like that; it comes from something an animal understands about itself.

Dad leaned forward and snorted. "That's what seven hundred fifty dollars' worth of lamb looks like?"

"Each," I said. Because Mr. MacGowan also informed anyone who would ask how much the lambs had cost. "And that's before he put feed in them."

Dad shook his head. He pressed an old Coke bottle to his lips and spit out a tobacco-stained stream of spit into it. The dank liquid sloshed as he screwed the cap back on. Charlie had dared me to drink it once, just one swig; offered me money even. But I'd refused.

"Where the hell is your brother?" Dad asked.

The scale house was a tiny sugar cube of a building, limewashed like every other building on the fairgrounds, with large swinging doors at each end. Inside, the unlit, unfinished walls and the caged scale gave it the feeling of a Wild West jail. The fair secretary sat at a card table, running the scale, meting out official weights, which would be used for market class placements and sale prices. She wore old jeans and rubber boots. Her hair was bobbed and graying. She was efficiency. She was rules. She'd been the secretary as long as I could remember, and she was flanked by volunteers who'd been running weigh-in just as long. They were former exhibitors and the fathers of exhibitors; eventually, they'd be the grandfathers of exhibitors, and they would mill around the scale house on the last Monday of August until they could no longer count on their bodies to hold back a foaming steer or drive a board between fighting hogs. All of them were fixtures, as though they didn't have lives outside the fairgrounds, as though they waited, frozen, for the year to pass and everyone to return. I saw the fair secretary in line at the credit union once. Her hair was styled; she wore polished shoes.

"Why, hello, Everett," she had said.

I nodded but couldn't for the life of me figure out how I knew her. It dawned on me later. Seeing her apart from the fairgrounds had turned her into a stranger.

When it was our turn, Dad backed the trailer up to the scale house. The onlookers were still there, now including the MacGowan girls. I told Katie to open the trailer door when I had my lambs haltered. I'd chosen a roomy pair with Curly's fullness through the hip and leg. When I put my hands on their melty hides, the flesh gave way to a tense shelf of muscle. One of them walked with a little more pride than the other. That was the one I wanted those chatterboxes hanging around the scale-house door to see first. I bunched the lambs in the back of the trailer and swept a nylon rope halter over the lamb's ears and under his chin.

"Let me and Fluff go," Katie said through the trailer door.

"I already got mine haltered."

"I don't need a halter."

She opened the trailer door.

"Katie! Wait!"

Fluff shot past me straight into Katie's open arms. The other lambs followed, including mine. They jumped off the trailer, cresting high like the lambs they still were despite their large bodies, and swirled into a tight cream-and-black whirlpool inside the pen that led to the scale house. They turned faster and faster, led by Fluff, and at its center—with her head tossed back, laughing, in pink athletic shorts and my old black cowboy boots, holding out her fingertips to the thundering hides—was Katie. The sun blinded off the top of her hair and she looked like some conjurer raising sheep from the dust.

The men in overalls came to life, picking up boards and pushing the lambs back onto the trailer. All but Fluff. Katie draped an arm across Fluff's back. Side by side they left the sunshine behind and walked through the dim light of the scale-house door.

I put my hands on the sides of the camper door and leaned inside. Mom skimmed grease from a Crock-Pot of sloppy-joe meat, expertly tilting the spoon into an empty Manwich can on the counter. There were hamburger buns on the table, potato chips, a jar of pickles, some veggies that needed chopping. The air was thick with the smell of browned burger.

"Take Katie down to the playground for a while," she said. "I need a half hour, that's all."

"Can't Jay?"

But he and Chase were gone again. They'd left their empty pop cans on the picnic table. Katie slouched in a lawn chair, swinging her boots, poking a stick in the empty firepit. I hoisted her onto my shoulders. It wasn't as easy to do anymore. She was getting heavy.

Mom came out and wrapped her arms around my waist and Katie's legs, boots and all, two of her kids in one totem. She looked up at me. "Thank you."

The metal slide, the cube-shaped jungle gym, the ring of riding animals bolted to springs—all of them glinted in the August sun, searing to the touch. The black swing seats sucked in the heat, waiting to release it on some poor little kid's ass.

Katie slid down my back and ran to the swing set. Jerks

thought it was funny to wrap the rubber seats around the crossbar like yo-yo string. I batted one of the swings down and tested the temperature.

"This side's fine."

She scooted onto the seat and demanded an underdog.

"You asked for it."

I pulled her back, holding her there just to tease her, and she squealed as I ran forward, pushing her high over my head and letting go. I turned in time to see her downy hair lift and flatten as she arced and dropped. She pumped herself after that, higher and higher. Each time she reached the high point, she made a chomping sound. "I'm eating the clouds!"

She pumped her legs and howled. One of her boots slipped off. Then she kicked off the other. She pumped and pumped until the swing stretched against the chains and her hair flew forward. I tried to remember the last time I'd felt like that, throwing back my head, shouting to the sky.

After a while, she dragged her feet on the ground, blackening her socks, and spilled out of the seat.

I sat down next to her while she caught her breath. The clouds passed overhead, full and soft like carded wool.

"How did the clouds taste?"

"Good." She leaned against me and gradually her breathing slowed. The sun poured on her head, and she needed a bath. Her kneecaps and the palms of her hands were the color of dust. But she didn't stink. Little kids never did.

"Are you moving away?" she asked.

"Why would you ask that?"

"Because after high school people move away. They go to college and get married and move away."

"I'm not going to college, trust me on that."

"What will your wife be like?"

"Jesus, Katie, I don't know."

"Don't say Jesus." She glared at me. "She'll be pretty."

"Of course she'll be pretty."

"But what if she wants to live downstate?"

"Then I won't marry her. She has to like it here. And she has to like you," I added.

"And sheep! She has to like sheep!"

"Yes," I said. "She's got to like sheep." I gathered up her cowboy boots and tossed them to her. "Let's eat."

On the morning of the sheep show, which was always on the last Wednesday of August, the sheep superintendent sprayed the show ring with water. But by the time the heavyweight market class started, the sun had burned off the moisture and the lambs kicked up a fine grit that made its way into my mouth. There were ten of us in the class, all dressed in blue jeans and long-sleeved western shirts. We led our lambs in a wide circle around the judge, a potbellied man wearing a bolo tie and a wide, buff-colored hat. As we passed, he stroked his mustache, a heavy white brush, tinged yellow like the shanks of a lamb.

Youth market-lamb shows, at least at the Chippewa County Fair, worked like this: The lambs were divided into heavy-, medium-, and lightweights, and a judge picked the top two lambs from each class. Out of those six, the judge picked the grand champion. Nine times out of ten, heavyweights took the grand champion title because they were the most complete and railed the most pounds of product. The grand champion got the top spot on the sale order and the best price per pound.

There was no easy way to get grand champion, even if, like the MacGowans, you threw your money at a fancy lamb from out of state. The lamb itself could only get you so far. You couldn't have a grand champion without giving that lamb the most attention, the most time, the most care. I'll just say it: You couldn't have a grand champion unless you loved it, whether you wanted to admit that or not, because if you loved it, then you'd do your damnedest to give it the best of everything—the best feed, the best hay, the driest bedding. You'd put your hands on that lamb every day, feel its ribs and rack and rump, and you'd know if you needed to push feed or hold back. You'd keep its water fresh. You'd clean the pen. You'd walk it, run it even. You'd get it out in the sun and let it touch the earth. And you'd do it all without anyone even telling you to.

Mom watched from the stands with Katie, and Katie waved at me, still beaming from her first show. She'd done well, taking reserve champion medium-weight with Fluff. It was a hell of a start to her showing career. Jay had placed fifth in the same weight class. Decent enough, I guess. Already, he'd put the lamb away, bummed ten bucks from Mom, and run off with Chase to the midway. We wouldn't see him again until dark.

Dad stood alone. You couldn't pay him enough to sit during the sheep show. He leaned over the top rail of the show ring, sucking on his Skoal like he was the one being judged, not the lambs. And maybe he was. Half the lambs in the ring came from his ewes.

The fair queen was sitting at the trophy table, waiting to pass out plaques to the winners of grand and reserve, and a puny ribbon to the poor bastard who would get third. Her hair was twisted Spanish-style at the nape of her neck, wet-looking and topped with a tiara. She wore a rose-embroidered western shirt, fringed to the elbow, under a pearly sash that read MISS CHIPPEWA COUNTY FAIR 1995. Her name was Stacy Harris.

Charlie had begged Kylie to enter the queen contest. We'd been at Mason's unloading the hay wagon.

"You're perfect for it," he'd said.

"It's old-fashioned," she'd said. "It's dumb."

"It's tradition," I'd said. "What's wrong with that?"

She'd turned to me. "OK, then you spend fair week passing out ribbons and trophies with a stupid crown on your head. I want to have fun."

It wasn't a beauty pageant. The contestants were girls who'd been showing livestock since they were Katie's age; girls who entered crocheted baby sweaters and canned green beans in the exhibit hall; girls who could mow a field as fast and straight as me and Charlie. But Stacy Harris could've won even if it was. I'd watched the speed and action show each year just to see her. She rode like no girl I'd ever seen. She pushed her horse fast and angry, hissing through her teeth, popping her whip. She would spin him tight in the waiting pen until the start gun cracked, then she'd unspool him and he'd blast into the arena, mane and tail wild and loose, her own hair—the same rich bay brown—flipping behind. She bullied him around the poles, leaning so hard her reins skimmed the sand. That horse would run to death for her. I'd never had the balls to talk to her. Not even Charlie had.

Stacy's eyes trailed the lambs lazily as they passed in front of her and I dreaded being seen like this, dressed in my western shirt, buttoned at the wrists—Mom insisted—and pulling across my shoulders. But she'd see me win heavyweight. And then grand champion. At least there was that. I let myself imagine it as I led my lamb in front of her. Me, standing in the center of the ring, Stacy watching, the MacGowans watching, Dad watching. Everything quiet and still. Then the judge would take the microphone and say, "Folks, this is your grand champion heavyweight market lamb." He'd shake my hand, everyone would clap, the MacGowans would start crying, Dad would be grinning ear to ear, and Stacy would come up with a big-ass trophy and say, "Congratulations!" And then she'd lean in and whisper, "We should hang out sometime." And I'd say, "Sure," like it was no big deal.

It only took two laps for the judge to motion the oldest Mac-

Gowan girl and her lamb to the middle of the ring. The ewe stepped with the girl in tow to the center, like a queen holding court, while the rest of us, even the judge, circulated around. The fullness and depth of her leg, the spring of her ribs, the lightness of her movements; it reminded me of these figure skaters I saw in Canada on a junior high field trip. *Nutcracker on Ice.* Boring as hell. All I could remember was how shredded the skaters were, the guys and the girls. The outlines of their thigh muscles and calves popped through the stretchy fabric of their costumes. They moved like gravity had no effect on them whatsoever. All that power bundled and released with no effort at all. Like breath.

I wanted to look over at Dad, to read his expression, but I didn't dare take my eyes off the judge. Any second, he would motion to me, and I didn't want to miss it. I rapped my fingertips on my lamb's back to keep him lively as he moved.

The judge signaled us to stop, and I set up my lamb's feet in a neat rectangle, shoulder-width apart in front, a little wider in back, meant to accentuate the length and width of his hind-saddle, where all the most valuable cuts were located. I tapped his belly. He flinched and tightened.

A sheep show wasn't a quiet thing. No matter how well trained they were, the lambs cried out to each other. The people in the stands ate concessions, shaking the ice in their empty cups, opening wrappers. Visitors walked past, oblivious to what was going on in the ring. The sound of the midway bubbled up in a spray of shrieks and laughter and music. Dogs barked. But I didn't hear a lick of it; that judge was my whole world.

He moved across the ring, and I moved with him, keeping the lamb's body before him. He wanted to see the lamb's ass, not mine. He tugged at his mustache and flicked his eyes from one lamb to another. I locked my eyes on him. *Come on. Over here.* Eventually, his gaze settled into an alternating pattern between just two lambs: the younger MacGowan's and mine.

The judge draped his stringy tie over his shoulder and slid his hand firmly over the MacGowan lamb's shoulders and back, measuring the width and length of its loin between his meaty fingers. He wrapped his hands around the bulge of its leg and slipped his hands all the way down to its pastern, grunting as he bent.

I've heard that judges know the champion the instant it steps in the ring. That the hemming and hawing is all for show. That may be, but I'd be damned if I was going to let those MacGowans edge me out. I stretched out my lamb's rear legs and lifted his chin, raising him on the tips of his front hooves, just enough to tuck in his gut and soften the squareness of his shoulder. He danced in place. I tried setting him back up, but he kicked at me.

"I'm tired too," I whispered in his ear. "Just a little longer." The judge should have called me to the center of the ring by now. I couldn't resist looking back at Dad. He leaned forward, watching closely, his brows drawn together, his tongue playing with the chew tucked in his lip. Stacy propped her chin on her hand and scanned the crowd.

Heat rose off my lamb. That was the thing about showing sheep. Where your body ended, theirs began; your breath was their breath. Charlie never got any closer to his hog than the end of his show cane. But I was so close I saw myself in the dark slash of my lamb's pupil.

So, when the judge placed his hands on my lamb, I knew he would bolt before it even happened. I felt his hide stiffen. Saw his nostrils widen. I registered it all in a fraction of a second but couldn't do a thing to stop it. He ripped his head out of my hands and knocked me on my ass. Dirt rained in clumps on my head.

I wanted a pit to open up in the middle of the show ring and swallow me down. I would have jumped in, gladly, and pulled the soil over top of me. Lambs got away from seven-year-olds, not seventeen-year-olds. I was too old, too strong. I got up slowly and dusted off my shoulders, the weight of a crowd of eyes on me, including Stacy's, the MacGowans looking at each other with small smiles. The superintendent caught my lamb easy enough and led him back to me, but the judge had already motioned for the younger MacGowan to join her sister in the center of the ring.

The judge considered the two lambs. He stood back and pursed his lips, turning his mustache into a puckered mess of bristles. Then he ran his hands over them, confirming something to himself, and took the microphone from the trophy table and addressed the crowd. Stacy got up and stood beside him.

"We've got some beautiful heavyweight lambs here today, folks, but these two"—and here, he turned his back to me and gestured to the MacGowans—"stand alone in the class." He talked about their balance, their long hind-saddles, how tight they were in the shoulder. "From a carcass standpoint, they're both going to rail more of your pricey cuts, but of the two, this ewe is fresher handling, the most expressive, and she's going to be your heavyweight champion."

The older MacGowan rose quickly to shake his hand. She was grinning so hard her pasty face looked like it would crack. Stacy gave her the grand champion heavyweight plaque. There was applause. The judge shook the other MacGowan's hand and Stacy gave her the reserve champion heavyweight plaque. Then he turned to me just as I was shaking dirt from my hair. He lifted the microphone to his lips again. The ancient PA system thinned and sharpened his voice, so that over the sound of the excited crowd, all I heard was: ". . . shorter-bodied . . . softer handling . . . the market is looking for a trimmer lamb with more volume of leg."

Mom stood and clapped. Top three was good in her book. That's how she would see it. Third out of ten wasn't bad. But there was no way I'd get grand champion market lamb now. Stacy gave me the thin, white third-place ribbon. The instant I took it from her, I soiled it with my hands. "Thanks," I said. She smiled politely.

There was no leaning into my ear, no mention of hanging out later.

I looked back to where Dad had been standing. He was gone.

I stuffed the ribbon into my pocket and led my lamb back to the barn, an enormous, whitewashed structure that sat unused most of the year, housing only pigeons and their shit and a few camper trailers.

Charlie was waiting at my lamb pen, already showered and changed from the hog show that morning.

"Hey man, I heard the fair board voted to open a new sheep class this year. Big special meeting in the bingo hall last night."

It was a setup, I could tell by his smirk, but I bit anyway.

"Oh yeah? What's that?"

"Mud wrestling. Your lamb gets away and you roll around trying to catch it. Dirtiest wins."

"You come up with that yourself? Or did a first-grader help?"

"Thought of it myself."

I opened the pen and steered my lamb inside. I slammed the gate closed.

"What are you pissed about?" he said. "You did better than I did with my hog."

"I know."

"You'll get a damn good price."

"I know."

I threw the lamb a flake of hay. Who cared about a hay gut now?

"So, you're crying over not getting a little trophy? Because you don't have that sign over your pen?" He gestured to the pens along the center aisle of the barn that were set aside for grand and reserve champion market lambs. Decades ago, someone had hand-chiseled the words "Grand Champion" and "Reserve Grand Champion" onto planks of soft pine, varnished them, and hung them above those pens. All fair week long, visitors milled through the barn and stopped beneath those signs to see what was considered the best. And not only that, but to see who *bred* the best. "You know how much money those MacGowans spent on those lambs, don't you? Christ, they bought grand and reserve. The same thing is happening with hogs. Fuck them. You should be glad you didn't win."

I lifted the water pail out of my lamb's pen. "The MacGowans didn't have anything to do with me having a shit lamb."

"Third heavyweight's not shit."

I looked my lamb over. He pawed at the hay and spread it around the floor of the pen. This was Lindt Lambs' best. Two days ago, I was proud of his wide body and generous finish. His square shoulders were a minor flaw, an indication of his heavy bone structure. Now he looked over-finished and stale, loose-bellied, short.

"What they're looking for now, Dad's way off."

"My dad's got the MacGowans' breeder's number. If you want to play their game, you can buy one of his lambs and give him every red cent you earned from Mason. And whatever you make off of this one."

I wasn't interested in a single show lamb though. I wanted something more.

The fair was all about tradition. That was right in the mission statement, passing on agricultural traditions to future generations. The livestock shows happened on the same days each year. The demolition derby, the mud runs, the stock-car race, the harness racing—they always came to the grandstand. You could count on the same vendors sitting in the same stalls, selling the same products every year: maple syrup, honey, clocks, leather belts, and knives. Each year, old-timers set up antique equipment across from the poultry barn so that visitors could feed corncobs through an old shucker, run their knuckles against a rusted washboard, or twist the knobs on the whistle machine, an engine connected to pipes and whistles that puffed and tooted and made the very soundtrack of the fair. And every year after the hog and sheep shows, Dad and Mr. King had the same conversation: They were right, the judge was wrong, unless their animals won. Nothing changed. Not even the style of animal they produced.

This year was no different. Mr. King and Dad were at the camper, leaning back in lawn chairs under the awning. Charlie and I sat beside them, listening to them talk. I waited for a chance to speak, afraid that Dad would laugh at me or worse, tell me my idea was dumb. Katie played with her Barbies on a mat of grass carpet. Mom moved inside the camper, opening drawers, turning the water pump on and off. The camper moved with her, creaking a little, and swaying, as though she were its heart, making it thud. She'd arranged crackers and sliced cheese and sausage on a tray. Mr. King held a cracker sandwich in one hand and an Old Milwaukee in the other.

"Your lambs were lookers, Rob. No doubt about it." Mr. King rocked the beer bottle on his knee. "But that judge liked them lean. Real lean. Not an ounce of fat on them. But when I eat lamb, I want a little fat on it. Softens it up. Gives it that flavor."

"Makes you wonder if that judge ever even ate lamb," Dad said. "Not one ounce of fat on them."

Charlie's dad tilted back his head and emptied his beer. He had plenty of fat himself, concentrated mostly in a round, heavy stomach. He hunched his shoulders around it when he walked, leaning forward, trying to conceal it, stilting his forward motion with the constant hoisting of his pants. The beer had done it, was my guess, and spending his days behind a steering wheel, his evenings in a recliner.

Dad was no stranger to beer or steering wheels, or even to his recliner, but he was a good ten, fifteen years younger, and his gut was hard and trim. It made me proud to stand beside him. How he could leap into the show ring at an instant to snag an ornery steer. How he could swing more bales than me and Charlie combined. When I followed him into the feed store or the gas station, women turned to look at us, snapping their eyes quickly from me—too young—and coming to rest on Dad. If he noticed, he never let on. And I never did either.

Dad turned to me. "What happened out there? Your last year in the ring; I thought you'd have something to show for it."

"I'll tell you what happened," Mr. King said. "That judge couldn't tell ass from head. All he was looking for was dollar signs. Who forked out the most cash. Which one's feeding the industry that's feeding him. Lot easier to go buy a slick animal than grow your own."

I untucked my shirt and rolled up the sleeves, releasing the pull across my back. "Maybe the judge has a point," I said.

Dad and Mr. King looked at each other.

"The hell are you saying?" Dad asked.

"I'm saying maybe he knows what he's talking about."

Mom leaned out of the camper door. "Are you guys staying for supper, Tom?"

"Nope, nope, just heading out." Mr. King motioned to Charlie and rocked his body out of the chair. When he was upright, he took a final cracker sandwich from the tray and held it up to Mom with a nod of appreciation.

Dad and I watched them leave; Mr. King bowlegged and hoisting his pants, Charlie all straight lines and ease. I sat in silence for a moment, thinking about how to say what I wanted to say. I'd never before questioned the way Dad did things. Every success we'd ever had in the show ring was because of him. The money he got for lambs in the spring kept the family afloat. If my life looked anything like his when I was thirty-four—married, kids, a job, a farm—I'd be a happy man. In the end, I just said what I wanted to say.

"We need a new ram."

Dad tilted his beer to his lips. "Is that right?"

"You heard what that judge said. Curly's lambs are out of style."

"Curly's just fine."

"None of our lambs placed for shit."

"Katie did all right. I'm not buying a new ram just because you kids don't know how to show, and one judge doesn't know good lambs when he sees them."

"I showed the hell out of that lamb."

"You did, now? The last thing I saw was you sitting on your ass in the dirt while the judge handed the plaque to someone else."

I looked away. My face burned, but Dad went on.

"Where's that judge from anyway? Iowa? He doesn't know what people here want."

"He knows trends."

"Trends! Trends make people start breeding animals that don't make sense. And taste like shit. Those tight little tubes he picked today: no finish. You cut them up and put them on a plate next to your lamb and then tell me which one is better. I know which one I'd pick. Yours'll melt in your mouth like butter. Those others you'll be chewing till next week."

"We've been using Curly's lambs for three years, Dad, and they haven't placed. They're fine for the smaller fairs, but not here. And definitely not at the state fair."

Dad leaned over the arm of the chair and pointed his bottle at me, an extension of his index finger. "People know Lindt Lambs. They can afford Lindt Lambs. They're good-quality lambs. Never have problems with disease. Always make weight, good temperament, correct feet."

"They're too Suffolky."

He laughed. "Too Suffolky. That's a new one."

Suffolks were big eaters with excellent rate of gain, but they could get gutty, dumpy. I wanted to cross some Hampshire into the herd to get taller, longer lambs. Hamps had that flashy leg shag the show kids had started blowing out. I wanted that too.

And then, before I could stop myself: "All right, *I* want a new ram."

"And how are you paying for that?"

"I got my hay money. And some money left from the fair last year. Let me breed a new ram with some of the ewes. You keep the best ewes. I'll take the yearlings."

I waited for him to scoff, but he didn't. He was quiet for a moment and then he tossed his beer bottle into the paper bag Mom was using to collect cans.

"Hell, it's no skin off my nose. All right, if you get a ram, I'll house him. And I'll let you breed the yearlings."

"And I sell the lambs."

"You sell the lambs."

Dad had taught me how to shake hands the first year I had sold a lamb at the fair. He'd squatted down in front of me, eye level, his Lindt Lambs hat right in my face. The auctioneer's cries filled the air. "This is what you do, Everett. You go up to that buyer and say, 'Thank you, sir,' and you put out your hand. Just like that. Keep your elbow straight. Firm grip. He's forking out a lot of money for this lamb and you show him that you know it. You look him in the eye and you say—?"

"Thank you, sir."

"That's right."

That was nine years ago. Dozens of lambs later, I knew how to shake a man's hand. I held my hand out to Dad, elbow straight, and looked him in the eye, man-to-man. He took it and I said, "Thank you, sir." Just like he taught me.

Charlie stretched out next to me on the grassy bank alongside the horse arena. In the ring, a black-and-white paint trotted through the poles like he was on a Sunday stroll, no matter how the girl riding him kicked and hawed. But as soon as he rounded the last pole, he tore toward the gate, flinging sand. Something inside him told him he was going home.

"Time to clean pens," Charlie said, rising.

Pens had to be cleaned every day by five PM or the barn superintendents taped a note on your pen that said "Clean Me Please," and then they shamed you at the exhibitor's meeting at the end of the fair. Jay never cleaned them. Even if Dad tried to make him, he'd just sprinkle some fresh sawdust over the old and cover the shit with hay. Katie did her best but couldn't do it alone. So I usually cleaned them myself.

"Hold on." I pointed over to where Stacy Harris was sitting on her horse near the holding pen. "I want to watch her."

Charlie eased back down. "A guy can dream."

She wore a red western shirt with beaded cuffs and collar, black jeans, and the queen's sash. Instead of the tiara, she wore a black cowboy hat with side brims steamed up like wings. Her glossy bay stepped foot to foot, unable to stand still. Stacy leaned forward in the saddle and said something into his ear, which flicked forward and back, and then the feet stilled.

She entered the holding pen and spun the horse in tight little circles, his energy and hers pent up, waiting for the sound of the gun. They exploded into the arena and Stacy held on, hunched over his neck, hissing in his ear, popping her whip. They ripped through the poles like a zipper. She leaned out of the saddle and the horse leaned, too, so tight his shoulders sheared each pole, rocking them but not knocking them over.

I didn't breathe. I couldn't look away. And when it was over, the horse wheeled in the holding pen, panting, dripping. Stacy raised her whip when the announcer broadcast her run time. First place.

Her hat had blown off before she'd reached the first pole. She rode out to it and swung off the horse with a single motion, landing like a cat with a little puff of arena sand. She kicked up the hat with the toe of her boot, dusted it against the side of her leg, and popped it back on top of her head. All that, a fluid little trick to save the effort of bending over, and the spectators went crazy. I was one of them. I stuck two fingers in my mouth and whistled, a long, low note that rose sharply at the end. Dad's sheep call. Stacy bowed, aware of every single eye on her, climbed back on the bay, and jogged off.

"What'd your old man say about the ram?" Charlie asked.

"He's not getting one." I paused a beat before adding, "I am. Ram sale's next month if you want to come."

"I'll be there."

We walked back to the livestock barns and Charlie split off to clean his hog pen. I found Katie in the sheep barn with Fluffernutter. She held a cup of fountain Coke under Fluff's nose. Fluff dipped her lips in it and sneezed, splattering Katie's shirt with brown droplets. Then Fluff took long, deep slurps. She rolled an ice cube in her mouth, pressing it against her hard palate before dropping it back into the cup.

"Remind me not to share drinks with you," I said, opening the pen.

Katie wouldn't look up.

"Hey," I said. "What's up?"

I sat beside her. Fluff sniffed my hands, my shirt, then dunked her nose in the cup again.

Katie couldn't speak. She drew in ragged, ugly breaths.

"Jesus, Katie," I said. "Whatever it is. It's OK."

She shook her head and pressed her eyes and lips closed. Fluff brushed her nose, sweet and wet with Coke, against Katie's forehead, and Katie leaned forward, pressing her face into Fluff's shoulder. The Coke tipped over and seeped into the bedding.

"I don't want Fluff to die!"

So, here we go, I thought. The moment we'd all been waiting for, and where was Dad? Where was Mom? I rubbed her back. She felt sharp and small under my hand. "I know, Katie. I know you don't. I know." I said it over and over. It was all I could offer her. Just words. And not even good ones. There was no way to stop the compartments from smashing together. The fair was terminal. Fluff had crossed the scales. That couldn't be changed.

Katie's voice was thick with mucus. "I'm never showing sheep again. Never."

"You will, Katie. You love sheep. This is part of it. It sucks, but it is. You got to be proud of how you raised her and what good care you took of her. She was never lonely. She was never sad. Never sick. Or hungry. Or thirsty. Even when her mom ditched her, there you were, right? And look at her, Katie. She's beautiful. She's one of the best ewes Dad's ever had. The best of Curly, the best of her mom. All she's going to have is one bad day, all right? One bad day in her whole beautiful life."

I couldn't get her to lift her face. And Fluff just stood there and let her cry on her. She nosed the Coke cup, checking for more.

"Never," Katie moaned. "Never, ever again."

And then I did what I always swore I would never do. I told Katie there was a family with a giant field of red-top clover that keeps sheep as pets.

"They come up for the sale each year," I said. "Maybe they'll buy Fluff."

She lifted her head. Her face was bleary and pink. She sniffed.

"Really?"

"Really."

Chapter 4

Sale day was as dusty and hot as show day. Flies circled around the pale mash shit left in the show ring by the hogs, the black splats left by the steers. The trick would be to avoid it when I led my lamb into the sale ring. Buyers sat shoulder to shoulder in the stands, some sat in camping chairs, some stood at the fence. They fanned themselves with their sale lists, circulating the clingy smells that rose from animals' shoulders and their own sun-blanketed bodies. 4-H kids wove between them, balancing bottles of water and bags of popcorn on cardboard pallets, offering them to the buyers no charge.

Steers sold first, then hogs, and then sheep. In between, there were pens of meat chickens and rabbits, turkeys, a jug of maple syrup, some butter and eggs. The hog sale was nearing the end. The MacGowan girls and their lambs stood at the front of a chute made of wire cattle panels waiting for the sheep sale to start. The rest of us were jammed in behind them according to sale order. I was right behind Katie. Jay was farther down the line. The chute was meant to move the sellers and animals through the sale as quickly as possible. It shunted us from the barn to the show ring and deposited us at a white-and-green photo backdrop that said CHIPPEWA COUNTY FAIR 1995. The 9 and the 5 were tacked on with pushpins.

Stacy waited there in her tiara to take pictures with the kids and buyers and animals. A waxy slab of a hog grunted at her feet, lured to the spot with a pan of feed, and the boy who sold it blinked up at Stacy like she was honest-to-goodness royalty. But she just smiled under that sparkling headpiece like she didn't see the hog or smell the shit, like she alone had caught a cool breeze on her face.

The auctioneer sat at a folding table on a riser and held the microphone against his teeth. His chant moved the animals in and out of the ring. It was monotonous and ancient-sounding, layered with the brass cries of "Yep!" whenever the ringmen spotted a bid. This crescendoed and accelerated until the auctioneer paused, and the crowd leaned in, holding their breaths, knowing what was coming. "Sold!" he said with the sound of a stone dropping into a stream, and the crowd could breathe again. They sat back. The auctioneer sipped a glass of water, and the next animal stepped into the ring.

Bidding on the grand champion MacGowan lamb started at $5. The bidding came so fast, the ringmen sounded like a pack of coyotes, throwing their plaintive yelps into the air, a frenzy of sound that excited and sickened me—each yelp was another dollar per pound. The lamb spun like a music-box dancer, stepping lightly, rapidly to the auctioneer's rhythm, while the bids rained down on her back. At $11, the frenzy eased, and the auctioneer dropped the bids to half-dollar increments, eking out six more bids. The lamb walked away at $14 per pound. It looked about 145 pounds, and I did some figuring in my head. Just over $2,000.

Katie and I inched forward in the chute as more lambs sold.

"Do you see them?" she asked.

"Who?"

"The people with the farm downstate. With the clover."

"Katie—" I started. Then pretended to scan the crowd. "I don't see them yet either."

"What if they didn't come? What if they're not here?"

The auctioneer called Katie's name. He announced Fluff's weight.

"You got to go out there, Katie."

She didn't budge.

"It's the rules, Katie. She's a market lamb. This is what market means."

"I got to wait for those people!"

"There are no people! All right? It was just something stupid I said to make you feel better. If you don't get out there and sell her, they'll get someone else to do it for you."

Mom was back at Fluff's pen waiting for Katie, but I spotted Dad's blue Lindt Lambs hat on the other side of the ring. I craned my neck and waved him over. He stood and started threading his way through the crowd toward the chute. The ringman came over. He was a shaggy-haired man who rolled up the pages of the sale order into a tight baton and used it to point at bidders.

"It's your turn, honey."

He opened the gate and motioned with the baton for Katie to enter.

She looked back at me, stunned into silence. I don't know how she did it—I guess the same way I did when I was her age—but she put one foot in front of the other and led Fluff into the ring. Fluff's ears flopped up and down puppy-style.

"Two dollars," the auctioneer began. "Now three, now three, will you give me three?"

The ringman scanned the crowd for bids: a wave of a hand, a nod, a wink. He hovered near a woman in a purple blazer who didn't look like she had any business at a livestock sale. Her nails flashed like jewels and her short gray hair was brushed back in waves. Her black shoes were still shiny. But the camping chair next to her overflowed with buyer's gifts, baskets and bags given to her by the kids she bought from. I squinted at the emblem on her blazer. Mom's credit union. Slowly, almost imperceptibly, she touched her nose.

"Yep!" the ringman barked.

Katie froze and looked around the crowd. Her eyes pooled. She tried not to blink, because if she did, she'd shear off those two big fat tears.

"Go on!" I yelled at her. "You have to keep moving!"

She led Fluff around the ring and the tears spilled over, leaving two shiny snail trails down her cheeks. This shouldn't have happened. I looked for Dad. He should have talked to her. I shouldn't have lied to her.

"Hey!" I called to the ringman. I'd read the fair book cover to cover; there wasn't one rule against sellers bidding. "I want to bid."

He pointed his baton at me, waiting. Except I didn't actually know how to make a bid. Touch my nose like the buyer from the credit union? Pull my ear? In the end, I did what felt familiar; I raised my hand like I was in class.

The ringman jabbed the air with his baton. "Yep!"

Katie looked at me like I was some kind of savior. I couldn't even explain to myself what I'd done. All I knew was that it made Katie happy. And I couldn't take the bid back.

But then the buyer from the credit union touched her nose again.

"Yep!"

Five dollars per pound. She folded her hands in her lap and watched to see what I would do next.

I raised my hand again.

"Yep!"

Six dollars per pound. At 125 pounds, that was $750. There was just over $1,000 in my account at the credit union, money saved up from haying and last year's fair. I'd make more on my lambs today, but I needed cash for my ram. I couldn't go much higher. But then the buyer from the credit union touched a glittering fingernail to her nose again.

"Yep!"

Seven dollars per pound. And the ringman spun on his heel and pointed at me, eyebrows raised, the baton extended like he'd just completed a magic trick: ta-da. Everyone turned with him. The buyer in the purple blazer, the auctioneer, and Katie. She and Fluff stopped turning in the ring, and faced me, as though awaiting a verdict. I was a judge suddenly, deciding Fluff's life by raising my hand or keeping it down. The next bid was $8. But $8 was $1,000. It was everything I had.

Dad pushed his way through the crowd. He leaned over the chute, and I was glad it was there to separate us.

"Are you stupid?" he shouted. His whole face was twisted up like a wet washrag.

Behind him, Stacy watched from the photo backdrop. She held a green buyer's ribbon in her hand. Her mouth was in the shape of a plush, pink O. She had never looked at me before, even when I walked right in front of her in the show ring. And now she waited with everyone else, to see what I'd do. My arm was frozen at my side. Raising it would feel wrong. Raising it would feel right.

Dad shouted again as I lifted my hand into the air: "Are you stupid?"

"Yep!"

Fluff was coming home.

I drove to the credit union after the sale and withdrew ten $100 bills. The envelope should feel heavier, I thought, since it contained so many hay bales, so much hot sun, so much sweat. So much stupidity. But it was feather-light. Ten brand-new bills pressed and smooth, as though they had been freshly cut from a sheet of money that very morning. The fair secretary parted them with difficulty.

"Which processor?" she asked.

"I'll be taking her."

She considered this, then wrote "self" on the bill of sale and handed me a receipt. Just like that. A thousand bucks here and gone, handed over so easy like it was nothing. I felt sick. Combined, my lambs had gone for about $1,000, but I wouldn't see the money till the following week. The fair held on to the checks until the exhibitor put up thank-you posters by the pen, wrote thank-you notes and turned them in to the fair office, and helped out at the work bee. I understood the policy, but waiting on that money would be hell.

Mom and Dad were arguing in the camper. Mostly Dad. The door was closed but I could hear everything through the thin aluminum siding.

"You don't buy livestock at a market sale, Shauna. And you sure as hell don't buy a bottle lamb for breeding stock. I sold her mother off months ago because she wouldn't nurse her. Tried to kill her. You saw. Damn near stomped her to death. And he wants to keep that trait going? Start a brand-new herd with it? Fluff's not even proven. And he's spending God knows how much money on her, like he's got money to burn?"

"Robert, he felt bad for Katie. And then the sale—the excitement."

"I understand that, Shauna. But, Christ, where's his judgment?"

"If this is the worst thing he does in his whole life—"

I turned around and went back to the barn. I didn't want to face them, and I didn't want Katie looking at me like she had in the ring, like I was some kind of hero, because I definitely was not that. I was an idiot.

A stillness had fallen over the barn. The chutes were down. The buyers had folded up their camping chairs, paid their bills, and left. The auctioneer had packed up his riser. Now there was only the sound of pigeons shuffling foot to foot on the rafters above as they peered down over their chests. The sheep were napping, chewing even in their sleep. The steers stood almost motionless in their stanchions, swinging their tails leg to leg. It felt like a Christmas afternoon, the great letdown after a morning of anticipation. Katie had leapt in the air, shouted, "Yes!" when I raised my hand for $8 per pound. There might have even been applause. Jay held my lamb when I got my picture taken.

I'd stood between Stacy and Katie, holding a buyer's ribbon—my first—feeling like I'd swallowed a frog. Katie kept looking up at me. Her face was flushed and shiny. Even Stacy seemed electrified. Up close, her tiara dazzled, her teeth and eyes shone when she smiled. I noticed that the bridge of her nose was splattered with freckles the color of mud. "Hi," I said. Our elbows touched when the photographer said, "Cheese." Then there was Fluff, the only one who was ready for the picture. She stood in that way she had, with her hips squared and strong, her head high. *Look at me*, she seemed to be saying. *Look at me.*

Fluff got up when I approached the pen, reaching her nose to me. I ran my hand over her head.

"What'd you get me into?"

She nuzzled my hand and directed my fingers where she wanted a scratch. I worked from behind her ears, along her jaw, under her chin. If she were a dog, her back leg would be jumping. But sheep don't do that when they're happy, they burp. I could smell them leaking out of her. One loose, sweet pillow of gas after another.

"We'll get a nice little flock going. You and some of those other yearlings. I've got a few in mind." I leaned in close to her. "And it'll be better than Dad's. A little fresh blood never hurt anything. And we'll come back here in a year and see whose lambs do better."

Fluff didn't need convincing though. Her mind was focused on the body, what it needed right then: how to get my hand back up behind her ear. She half closed her eyes, and I could tell that right then, the only thought in her head was the back-and-forth movement of my fingertips on her skull.

"Hey, Sheep Boy, you always talk to animals?"

I spun around. Stacy Harris stood there with one of the queen contest runners-up. She'd changed into a sweatshirt with the collar cut out and the sleeves pushed up past her elbows. She wore her tiara and so did her friend, although the friend's was smaller. She looked like she enjoyed catching me off guard. But it was the runner-up, a short girl with Cabbage Patch cheeks, who spoke first.

"Can I pet him?"

I led Fluff out of the pen and she squared herself up just like in the show ring. I held her head lightly against my thigh while the girl reached out, painstakingly, as though Fluff's hide had an electric charge. Finally, her fingertips made contact.

"Oh, my God, Stacy, it's like velvet!" She ran her hand along Fluff's back. "Does he bite?"

"Nibbles mostly."

"How did you get him so white?"

"It's a her, actually."

She squatted next to Fluff, her face right level with my crotch. I could see the crisscrossed bobby pins holding her tiara in place. An inch-long crease of cleavage peeked out of her V-neck. She was really getting into petting Fluff. I felt Fluff's body tense up. No more burps. Even she could only take so much.

Stacy looked at me over her friend's head. "You made your sister happy today."

"It was a dumb thing to do."

"A little," she said. "But not all the way. I remember selling for the first time. Wish I would've had a brother like you."

"Doubt I did her any favors in the long run."

"Maybe not." She was quiet a moment while she rubbed the tip of one of Fluff's ears. "The lock-in's tonight. Are you going?"

The fair board put on a barn lock-in for the livestock exhibitors each year. They played music and set up horseshoes in the center of the barn. Drove the animals nuts. The 4-H clubs brought pop and snacks. Mrs. Wheeler, a white-haired farmwife with giant blue glasses and a tiny nose, chaperoned each year. Even Jay thought it was lame.

"I was planning on watching the mud runs."

"Well, I have to go to the lock-in. Official queen duties. You should stop by."

"OK, yeah, sure. I could probably do that," I said. Casual, like this was all normal.

"Cool. We'll see you, Sheep Boy."

Cabbage Patch stood and Fluff relaxed. They started to walk away. Then they looked back at me, standing there holding Fluff, and they burst out laughing.

Charlie hefted scoops of his hog's damp bedding into a wheelbarrow. Rose, a flabby-cheeked Duroc cross, dozed in the corner of the pen, revving peacefully, with breaths noisy and rhythmic as a diesel engine.

"She asked you?" he asked.

"Yes, me."

"Bullshit."

"I'm not bullshitting."

It was the first time I'd seen him impressed, with me anyway. He kneed Rose in the ass. "If you'd move, I could clean the pen. I guess you like sleeping in your own piss." She didn't budge.

"Walk through with me at least."

Charlie stood the shovel on its blade and propped his chin on the handle. He smiled all smug. "Retty doesn't think the lock-in is so lame now. Here's the thing, Kylie's coming out for the mud runs tonight. Her and Fancy Pants."

I coughed. "Mary's coming?" My voice came out too high, like Jay's did now that it was changing. I'd worked hard to bury any thoughts of her, but now they came back: me, standing in the kitchen, the telephone in my hand, my hair wet from the shower, my heart exploding. Her number was still in my wallet. I cleared my throat.

"Does she know I'll be there? Like, is she coming because she knows I'll be there? That's what I want to know: Is she coming out for me?"

"Man, that city slicker is not coming out to the fair just to watch some trucks get muddy."

"What do I do?"

"What do you mean, what do you do? You go to the lock-in and see if Stacy's actually there waiting for you—which I guarantee she won't be—then you come over to the mud runs with us."

I shook my head. "I can't. That bridge is crossed."

"You called her one time."

"Yeah, and she said no thanks, so."

"So, maybe she changed her mind."

Rose sat up and pivoted on her rear end to reach the wall-mounted waterer, a metal nipple that she bit and drank from. She did this all without standing. "You lazy ass," Charlie said, but now he used the blade of the shovel to scratch her butt and lower back. She rolled her shoulders with pleasure and watched him as she slurped. Still, he couldn't reach the mess beneath her.

"What about Stacy?"

"You honestly think Stacy Fucking Harris is going to be waiting around the lock-in for you? I hate to break it to you, she was asking for that friend of hers."

It made so much sense. The small-eyed girl squealing as she moved her hands over Fluff's body, her tits tipped toward me, her face in my pants. How Stacy had stood back. How she'd laughed.

"So, you think I should try talking to Mary again?"

"What will it hurt?"

At this, Rose stood at last and rubbed the length of her body against the wall of the pen. Charlie slipped the shovel under her, quickly scraping the sharp-smelling sawdust down to the cement.

"See that?" he said, patting her rump. "You just got to keep at it."

I headed over to Charlie's campsite after dinner. He sat by himself at the campfire, holding a stick in one hand, a beer in the other. At the start of fair week, Mr. King had found a broken oak branch and used it to poke his campfire. He'd stripped it of bark and smaller branches, and now the stick was a foot and a half long, charred and blunted at one end.

"Where's your mom and dad?" I asked.

"Home for the night. I told them I'd stay back and keep an eye on things."

"That was nice of you."

"And Dad was nice enough to stock the beer fridge before he left."

I helped myself to the small refrigerator tucked under the camper awning. "When's Kylie coming out?" And by Kylie, I meant Mary.

"She knows the mud runs start at seven thirty. Why? You nervous?"

"Won't be after a few of these."

We plowed through a twelve-pack. I got a loose feeling going, and the sparks from the fire rose and fell like streamers, a fountain of thin orange arcs.

Soon we heard the wail of the mud runs, incessant as drills boring into wood. No girls yet. I stood and looked toward the livestock barn. It was blazing with light. I backhanded Charlie's chest. "Walk through with me."

"She won't be there."

"It'll take two seconds."

He stood. "Fine. You got gum or something?"

I held up my dip. "It's wintergreen."

Every light in the barn was on. A dozen or so kids stood around talking. Groups of four played euchre over hay-bale tables. There was a ring of metal folding chairs set around the perimeter. Someone had managed to hang a disco ball from the center beam and little white rectangles of light twirled across the floor. A radio played country. The animals shifted restlessly, tired from the sale and wanting rest. I felt sorry for them, honestly. Let them have some peace their last few days on earth, not a bunch of dipshit kids goofing around.

Mrs. Wheeler sat at a card table near the steer pens. She looked at her watch and wrote, "Charlie and Everett—7:45 p.m." on a list. Stacy's name wasn't on it. I looked across the barn, hoping for a glimpse of her tiara. I didn't see it.

"No alcohol," Mrs. Wheeler said.

"No, ma'am," Charlie said. His breath smelled like fire. I kept my mouth clamped shut.

"If you leave the barn, you won't be permitted back inside."

"Got it," he said.

She waved us in and I looked around.

"No Stacy," I said.

"Told you."

The thing was, I really thought she'd be there. All that talk about Katie and her own brother—something about it had felt real. I walked over to the corner of the barn where our lambs were penned. They dozed, unbothered by the commotion. Their water pail was still full and clear. This time, it was my lamb instead of Fluff that stood and came to the fence. I roughed his head.

"What do you want?"

He raised his nose to my face, and the wetness and warmth of his mouth startled me. I wiped my lips.

"You must be a good kisser, Sheep Boy. Get lots of practice, I see."

Stacy again, but without the tiara. I'd walked right past her.

"Your name wasn't on the list."

"I got here before the list. I helped set everything up. See the disco ball? That's me." She looked under my lamb. "A male too. Interesting."

Now that she was here, I wished I hadn't drunk all that beer. My arms felt like they were moving too much. I stroked the lamb's neck and shoulders. He rested his chin on the bar of the pen, loving every second of it. I didn't know what to say, so I kept petting him. I'd never petted the damn thing so much.

Stacy reached over and scratched his ears, then his neck. Her hand brushed against mine, the nails short and unpolished. I was surprised to see thin brown rims under some of them.

"I didn't think you'd actually be here," I said.

"I didn't think you would either." The lamb reached up and stuck his nose in her face. She leaned back in surprise and laughed. "He gets around, doesn't he?"

She had nice white teeth and she smelled like lemons. Lemons and pink flowers. Beneath that was the odor of neat's-foot oil, the smell of polished tack.

I held on to the pen to steady myself. My belly felt big. All that beer sloshing around in there. I remembered Charlie's breath and pressed my lips together.

"Now you don't talk at all? Or do you only like talking to sheep?" she said.

"Where is your friend?"

"What friend? Don't you want to talk to me?"

"I just thought . . . Charlie said . . ."

Someone turned up the radio. A dozen or so kids ran to the center of the barn and started jumping around. The poor animals. Stacy grabbed my hand and pulled me toward the dancers.

"No way."

"Yes way." She pulled harder and I followed, mostly because once I let go of the pen, I couldn't trust myself to stand upright. She stopped in the middle of the crowd of kids and turned to me, expecting me to dance. I stood there like a jackass while she swung my hands around. The disco ball and the movement of the other kids made it hard to focus on her face. I pulled her up close to me, something to hang on to, and she wound her arms around my waist, and we swayed left foot, right foot in a tiny circle while the song played. Every time I felt myself leaning a little, I tightened my grip on her and righted myself.

I felt a hand on my back. "Dude."

It was Charlie. He took it all in: me and Stacy moving slowly in the middle of the barn, our arms around each other. He shook his head in disbelief. "No way, man. No fucking way."

Kylie was there, too, and behind her, Mary, in her baggy jeans and hoodie, her bright Keds, everything loose and boyish except for the dark-brown lipstick and choker necklace. She looked cool and moody, just like in the field with the sunlight sparkling all around her. She gathered her hair over her right shoulder and stared at the ground, studying the spinning motes of disco light. Seeing her felt like two hands taking hold of my heart and yanking. It squeezed and ached, and it made me mad, how I still wanted her.

"Hey," I said.

She looked up briefly. "Oh, hey."

There was something I wanted to tell her, something perfect, but my mind was slippery with beer. The kids, the music, the mud runs. Everything was roaring around us. I had to think. It would come.

Kylie shouldered her way forward. "This is bullshit, Charles. You said there'd be four of us." She narrowed her eyes at Stacy. "What, did you lose your crown or something?"

"What's your problem?" Stacy said.

Charlie draped his arm across Kylie's neck. "There was only supposed to be four of us."

He looked sloppy hanging off her like that, his shirt collar gaping. How many beers had we each drunk? Five? Six? More than that? I straightened up, not wanting to look like him, but the disco ball churned, and the floor shifted. I caught myself and reached for Stacy's hand. She threaded her fingers through mine. I looked down at our laced hands and remembered what I wanted to say to Mary.

"Snooze you lose!" That was it. That was exactly it.

"What?" Kylie said. She looked to Charlie for translation.

I lifted our fused hands. "Snooze you lose!" And I pulled Stacy closer.

Mary turned to leave, but Kylie had a handful of hoodie, holding her in place.

"Listen," Kylie said to Charlie. "Me and Mary are going to the mud runs, like, right now. Are you staying or coming?"

He leaned into her neck, his fiery breath in her ear. "Coming," he said with a grin. "Definitely coming."

They moved off and I took a step after them, but Stacy held me back. She pressed her chin playfully against my chest and looked up at me. "I need to check on my horse. You want to walk with me?"

Charlie looked back at me. *Holy fuck*, he mouthed.

I looked down at Stacy. This girl inexplicably in my arms. Her eyes warm, her nose and cheeks sun-kissed and freckled. And Mary, the girl I'd looked for across the fields all summer long, now walking away.

"Yeah," I said. "I'll walk you."

We picked our way through the vendors that lined the path to the horse barn. My buzz made everything brighter and stronger. The lights streaked and throbbed. The air was scented with caramel apples and popcorn. The noise of the mud runs ripped overhead. Stacy slipped her pinky through my belt loop and tugged me along as we went. We passed the honey sellers, the ice-cream booth, the mini-donuts vendor.

"You want something?" I asked. A little food in my gut might not be a bad idea.

"Powdered donuts. That's what Bobby likes."

"Bobby?"

"My horse!"

"The horse eats donuts."

"Only when he's scared."

The donut stand was a small glass cube with stainless-steel equipment hanging from the ceiling. It reminded me of a giant claw machine. I returned with a steaming paper bag of powdered donut holes. Stacy popped one in her mouth and closed her eyes. "So good!" The donut left a rim of dust on the fine down above her lip. I stared at that powder trail, the cute upturn of her lip, and wanted to taste it.

I wondered what Charlie would do with that little trail of powder leading to Stacy's mouth. What would he do with Stacy standing in front of him with her eyes closed, savoring that ball of sweet fried dough on her tongue? With her pinky hooked in his pants? I knew exactly what Charlie would do, clear as a bell.

So that's what I did. Or the beers did. I kissed her right there in front of the donut stand. I cleaned her lip right up. The sugar was bright and chalky. I leaned in again.

"Sheep Boy!" Her lips curved up in a grin. "You've got moves."

I held the bag of donuts and timed it so that I reached in whenever she did and touched her hand. We neared the grandstand, and the noise of the place filled my whole body. People cheering. The announcer's voice high and buoyed by the tear and flap of truck engines as they dove into the mud. I'd never missed the mud runs in all my life but, glancing over at Stacy, I forgave myself.

The horse barn was constructed of creosoted wood that smelled dark and earthy. Bobby was pacing his stall, snorting, and shaking his head.

"I knew he'd be scared," Stacy said. She reached out her hands and he came to her. "What's wrong, baby? You don't like the noise?"

Bobby wrapped his head around her body and pulled her into an embrace. She scratched his cheeks, his neck, pulled on his ears, and rubbed his spongy muzzle. I handed her the bag of donuts and she balanced one on her open palm and held it out to Bobby. He ate it, then sniffed her hair and sleeves, looking for another.

"I'll be damned," I said.

"You should try it with your sheep. Here, you give him one. Like this." She stretched out my fingers one by one and placed a soft white donut in the center of my palm and guided it under Bobby's nose. He steamed it with his breath and his lips clipped across my skin. She was so close to me. I breathed the bright notes of her hair spray. Noted the layers of her freckles. The hint of shimmer across her lids. Bobby's body smell and hers seemed one and the same.

I let her put donut after donut in my hand.

When the bag was empty, Bobby hooked his head over the gate and watched us walk down to an empty stall. In the corner, I could make out some sacks of feed and some pails, a coiled hose, a bucket of combs and brushes, and a stack of hay bales. We were alone and it was getting dark. The beers made me ballsy. I lifted Stacy onto the stacked hay.

We started kissing. Just lips at first, but then she darted her tongue against mine and pulled out the front of my shirt. Her hands were cool and dry against my chest, her hair was scented with the fermented sweetness of Bobby's breath. I pulled her to the edge of the hay and slid my hands up her back. The palm that had fed Bobby was sticky from the donuts and caught on her skin. She licked the stickiness away.

"Better?" Her cheeks were rosy, her pupils wide in the dim light.

I nodded because I didn't have patience for words, only touch and movement. She was solid and strong. Everywhere my hands touched was firm. Two-tenths of an inch of finish, it felt to me. Ideal. I pushed up her sweatshirt.

"What do you want to do, Sheep Boy?"

What I wanted was for her to say my name. Long and slow, like Mary did. It was cute at first, the Sheep Boy thing—funny—but now I honestly wondered if she knew my name. They'd announced it at the sale. She knew it. Had to. I pushed those thoughts aside and focused. I'd made out with a few girls before but shyly, timidly. Now, with a belly full of beer, I was Charlie. I wasn't exactly sure what I wanted, just that the more of her I saw and touched, the closer I knew I was getting to it. I slipped my hand under her bra, and she leaned back on her hands and let me feel her tits. I filled my palms with them, eager. They were firmer and heavier than they looked. Beautiful in the white cotton frame of her bra.

"Gentle," she said.

So I kissed them. The smell of lemons and flowers and oil was stronger under her clothes, and I thought, I will smell this way too. This trace of her will be on me. I didn't hear the mud runs anymore or the midway. The horses in the stalls around us were calm. There was only Stacy's breathing and mine. Our jeans sweeping the stiff hay. I folded down the cup of her bra and licked the pink bud of her nipple. It hardened under my tongue.

"Oh God, Sheep Boy."

"It's Everett," I said, muffled, my mouth full, not really aware I'd said anything.

"Huh?"

My face was pressed against the humid skin of her chest. I didn't want to reenter the world apart from it.

"My name," I said. "It's Everett. You keep saying Sheep Boy."

She sat up a little and wiped her lips with the back of her hand. They were puffy from kissing. Her ponytail was loose. "I know."

"I mean, it's fine. Forget I said anything."

I bent toward her, eager to pick up where we'd left off, but she slid off the hay.

"Stacy, it's fine, really. I don't care."

I was blowing it. I knew I was blowing it. I stood there and listened to myself blow it. Already, I could hear Charlie's voice: "Are you dense? I would've let her call me Kris Kringle all night long or whatever the hell she wanted."

It was like I'd wakened us from a spell. She pulled down her sweatshirt and tightened her hair. "I should probably check on Bobby again anyway."

She left and I rubbed my neck and stared at the ground. "Fuck!" I was alone in the stall with the hay and the pails and the brushes and feed. The mud runs were over and the sounds of the horse barn came back. Her feet shuffled through the sand. The horses blew air through their noses.

"Hey, baby," I heard her say to Bobby. "You doing OK now?"

I tucked in my shirt and followed her. Bobby curled his head across Stacy's back; she crossed her arms around his neck. His eyes glistened in the darkness.

"I should be getting back to my camper," she said.

The temperature had dropped and there was a staleness in the air now that the rides were shuttered and the food vendors had closed for the night. We stepped over the webs of extension cords that had brought the fair to life earlier that day. The grandstand was silent. The lights were out, nothing moved. Stacy no longer pulled me along and I no longer needed her to. I was sober as a stone.

"I'll call you?" I said as she climbed the steps to her camper.

"Sure," she said. The door closed quietly behind her.

The moon was big and white above, pouring light on everything, crisping the edges of things. I heard thin voices from the campsites. Small groups of people sat around blackened fires, children dozed on laps, someone strummed a guitar. I shook out my arms and rubbed my palms on the front of my jeans, glad to be alone. It was strange how moments opened and closed, how a day could pivot on itself like a lamb midair, how yeses and noes pushed and pulled. That morning, I was $1,000 richer. That morning, I hadn't even wanted to go to the lock-in. Fifteen minutes ago, my face was buried in Stacy Harris's chest. My collar still smelled like lemons and flowers and tack. Now I doubted she'd ever talk to me again.

I needed to piss. Bad. The beers had done their job, and now they wanted out. I sidled up to the back of the rabbit barn and let it flow. A six-pack's worth. It took forever, but it was cleansing in its way, watching it pool and foam in the tall grass at the base of the barn. The day and all its worry and frustrations left me: Fluff, gone. Money, gone. Dad, gone. Stacy, gone. Mary—

I heard a shift of fabric, someone muttering. I finished up

and peered around the edge of the barn. A kid sat on the bench outside the barn entrance. The sodium halo of the security light shone off the sweep of her blue-black hair.

"You should get home, kid," I said.

"Wish I could."

It was Mary. "Oh shit. It's you." She'd heard everything. "Of course it's you."

"Never heard anyone pee so long. That's a real talent."

I sat on the bench beside her, my arms noodles at my side. "Where's Kylie?"

"She took off with Charlie."

I could guess what they were up to.

"She said she'd find me when they were . . . done."

"That's not right." I stood. "I know where they are. Come on. We're not far."

She walked with me, and I held my breath, not wanting to move too fast or talk too much, not wanting to scare her off. Her clothes bunched and swept as she moved, and I thought again of the strange ways a day unfolded and turned.

I banged on the side of Charlie's camper and tried the door. "Open up, asshole!"

"Move on, Lindt. Busy." His voice was gruff. I heard giggling. The camper squeaked.

I banged again and waited. Nothing.

I turned to Mary. "Do you have someone you could call?" I remembered the hard voice on the phone. "Your dad?"

She snorted. "That's not even an option." She sat in a chair by the cold fire. Our beer bottles littered the ground. "I'm fine here." She pulled up her knees and wrapped her arms around them. "I'll just wait."

"It's not fine. It's bullshit. I can drive you. My truck's just over there." I placed a hand on her arm. It was the first time I'd touched her. And it was mostly her hoodie, but inside, there was her arm, thin but solid, and I curled my fingers around it briefly, unable to pull away.

The camper began rocking steadily.

"Yeah, you know what? Let's get out of here," she said.

My truck was a bullnosed '84 Ford F-10 with a silver sport stripe. I'd bought it in 1993 with two summers' worth of hay and sheep money, but I was only fifteen, so I had to wait another nine months for my license. I'd been driving tractor for three years. It seemed stupid to have to wait, and it ate me alive walking past it every morning and getting on the school bus, a slow swallowing, like one of those snakes from the rain forest that ate goats whole. A guy had one on display at the fair once. It lay stretched out on two folding tables, calm and straight as a needle. I touched its mouth, and it didn't even flinch. But it blinked, so I knew it wasn't fake. The guy had a poster with pictures of the snake and its goat-shaped belly.

"It was still moving inside him," he said. "I could've killed the snake and saved the goat, but I was proud of him for what he'd managed to do."

Every day that year when I got home from school, I settled in the driver's seat and my body sank perfectly into the velvety light-blue bench. I squeezed the steering wheel and sometimes turned the key. I was only supposed to drive with Mom and Dad, but when they weren't home, I drove to Nine Mile and back, and sometimes to Charlie's. Once, I drove downtown, taking Ashmun all the way till it dead-ended at the Locks, then I turned right, and followed the St. Marys home. Every rotation of the tires, every stone striking the undercarriage, sent a vibration right into my core. I parked it exactly where it had been before, lined up the marks on the gravel and everything.

The previous owner was thirty or so with four kids. At least that's how many I counted running around in his yard. It was because of all those kids he was selling the truck. He'd gotten a minivan.

He nodded over at the van. "Hell of a thing. The kids all fit, the dog, camping gear, bikes. Easy to get in and out. You can take the seats right out of it."

"You camp?" Dad asked from the passenger's seat. He had come with me to look at the truck, getting under the hood, checking the tires, idling the engine, testing the blinkers and headlights, the radio.

"No, but maybe I will. Anyway, no use for a single cab now."

The man pulled his sleeve down over the heel of his palm and rubbed the chrome on the side mirror slowly, sadly, the way Dad handled the ewes in the fall that were separated for culling, letting them walk at their own pace up the ramp into the trailer. The man's eyes slid to the left, like he was looking at a memory, maybe the version of himself that bought the truck brand-new. Younger. Freer. The type of guy who needed a truck with a sport stripe.

"I'll take good care of it," I said through the open window.

He smiled, still half in the memory, and leaned on the door.

"You just promise me one thing, kid. Drive the hell out of it. That's what I want you to do. Just drive the hell out of it."

Being alone with Mary, with the highway open before us, the night alive with the eyes of stars, made me self-conscious. I turned on the radio, just enough to edge out the silence. The pines slid by. Then the land opened where it had been cleared for farming and it stretched away from I-75, wide and uninterrupted and disappearing into the blackness.

"I owe you," Mary said.

"Nah. That was shitty of them. I'll give him hell tomorrow."

We listened to music awhile. Too long, so I brought up my least favorite topic.

"You ready for school to start?"

She shrugged. "I'm a pro. I used to hate it. I'd get settled in, make friends, figure stuff out, and then, time to go. But I got used to it. And now, this is the last time. Next year, I'm on my own and no one can make me do anything."

She tucked her hands inside her sleeves and held the cuffs in her fists.

"You're holding your breath," I said.

She looked up, not sure what I meant.

"Like, you're underwater, holding your breath. Waiting."

"Exactly."

Mason's modular, where she lived, had been unloaded from a trailer and dropped in one piece onto its cinder-block foundation. It was Lego-shaped, a perfect rectangle right in the middle of the treeless field. New, but flimsy, as though the stiff winds that rolled across the fields could pick it up and blow it away. The narrow drive had never been blacktopped. Sections of it buckled and dipped. Dandelion rosettes pushed their way up the center of it like shirt buttons.

Her dad's truck was parked out front. If not for that, you wouldn't even know anyone lived there. At our house, you could always count on Katie's pink-and-white bike lying in the driveway; wind chimes waving over Mom's hosta bed; my truck or Dad's idling by the barn; Jay's music pouring from the window; and of course the sheep. Here, the only movement, the only sound, was the wind.

"Thanks for the ride."

She unbuckled and pushed open the door.

"I'm not with that girl, you know," I said in a rush.

She paused with her hand on the door.

"That girl at the lock-in. It's nothing."

She smiled. "Thanks again, Everett."

Then she climbed out of the truck and left me there, leaning into the space she'd just occupied, her voice hanging in the cab, heavy as smoke. I breathed it in.

Ev-er-ett.

Fall

Chapter 5

School arrived with a week of angry rain, as if it knew how I felt about it. The ditch spilled over onto the front yard and the ewes bunched together in the field, their shoulders tense under the falling water, their heads pointed north. Fluff stood a ways off, not yet accepted. She'd spent the entire summer apart from them and now she'd returned, shorn to the skin and smelling like Orvus soap and Lister oil. When the fair was over, Katie had walked her from the trailer right up to the herd, but when she turned back to the house, Fluff followed.

"Stay, Fluff." She held up her hand and Fluff stopped. But as soon as Katie took another step, so did Fluff.

"Just come on back, Kate!" I hollered from the gate. "She'll figure it out."

Katie jogged back to the gate with Fluff at her heels. The herd followed at a distance. I could see their brains working, trying to decide what to do with Fluff. They raised and lowered their heads, watching us, stomping their bony front legs. Then Caroline, an enormous white Columbia, tossed her head into Fluff's side. She was Dad's oldest ewe, one he'd bought when Jay was little and Katie wasn't even born. Any other ewe that old would have been sold off years ago, but her presence calmed the herd, and she was a good mother. She gave Dad two creamy, freckle-eared lambs each season. He'd keep her as long as she did.

Fluff staggered from the blow and Caroline nailed her again. Katie screamed and clung to Fluff's neck, but I grabbed her under the arms and set her safe on the other side of the fence just before Caroline drilled Fluff again.

"Stop her!"

"You got to let them work it out. They don't know Fluff anymore. They forget. They think she looks funny and smells funny. Sometimes sheep do this after you shear them. Just give them a few days, and it'll be like she never left."

"I want to put her back in the barn."

She started untwisting the wire that held the gate closed, but I pulled her back.

"Leave her! You can't keep her in the barn. She's got to be a sheep. She's got to graze. She's got to get bred."

"They'll hurt her."

"You'll get hurt. Now, leave her."

Katie watched through the gate while Fluff and Caroline tussled. Fluff ran off a few steps and Caroline rammed her in the ass.

"How long will it take?" Katie whispered.

"Caroline's too old to keep at it long."

"The herd's supposed to protect her."

"Fluff's strong. Look at her. She's stronger and faster than all of those fatties combined. You've been exercising her and feeding her really good. What have they been doing? Standing around all summer, eating." I squatted in front of her, eye level. "I got a lot of money into her. I don't want anything to happen either.

And you can see her from your bedroom. See? In a week or two, she'll be hard to tell from the others. Trust me. We'll make some beautiful lambs."

Caroline got a running start and plowed into Fluff. Another ewe got some knocks in too. Katie watched without a word.

"Trust me."

I steered her in the direction of the house, and she yielded to the pressure of my hand, shuffling her feet, looking back at Fluff. Her shoulder blade was sharp and light as a bird's wing and she trusted me.

Charlie pulled into the driveway the following Sunday, a little after one PM, and of course Kylie was with him. We were supposed to go fishing in Dunbar, just him and me. After the week of rain, the Charlotte would be stirred up and high, murky with leaves and bark, and the fish would be moving. Instead, my truck wouldn't start, and Kylie leaned under the hood, her curls draping on the engine block like she owned it.

"Someone's piece-of-shit Ford's got a problem?" Charlie asked.

"It's the starter," I said.

"You sure? Did you tap it?" He grabbed Kylie's hips. "I'm gonna tap you." His teeth were bright against his summer skin.

"You're an idiot," she said. They locked lips, steadying themselves against the bumper of my truck, not even caring that I was standing right there. I reached through the driver's window and laid on the horn. They smacked apart.

"Someone's pissy," Charlie said.

"Thought we were fishing, is all."

"We are. Put your stuff in my truck."

It was tight with all three of us in his cab, even with Kylie damn near riding on Charlie's lap. He traced a circle on the top of her knee with his index finger, around and around and around, and she giggled.

I stared at the window, my see-through face on the glass, watching the fields slide across my forehead. The starter alone would cost somewhere around a hundred bucks. That was on top of the money I'd already spent on Fluff. Plus, more on the ram next week. And how long would it take that parts store to get the starter in? A few days? A week? I'd be stuck riding the school bus with Jay until then.

"You still coming with me to the ram sale on Saturday?" I asked.

"Yeah," Charlie said. "And it looks like I'm driving."

"Where at?" Kylie asked.

"Just outside of Gaylord," I said. An hour-and-a-half drive. Two hours tops.

"The rednecks are crossing the Mackinac Bridge," she said. "Hope you survive."

The banks of the Charlotte were lined with trees leaning farther and farther, roots exposed, into the water. Deadheads bobbed with the chocolaty current; the water seemed slick, opaque. Over the years, people had worn trails down to the river's edge, just like the sheep did in the field, footstep after footstep in the same spot, leaving hard-packed and narrow paths. There, they set down their coolers, and opened their lawn chairs and tackle boxes.

I cast out into the cloudy water, reeled back slowly, then cast again. Charlie made some fishing motions for about a half hour then cuddled up on a blanket with Kylie. You couldn't have slid a piece of paper between them. Kylie's laugh bounced across the water.

I kept at it a while longer but got no bites, so I set my pole down and sat a few yards off, far enough away so that Kylie's voice was muted by the sweep of the current and the flutter of birch leaves. I lay back on my elbows. The air was getting the edge of fall to it, a quality that made you a little sad because it reminded you that change was coming, and time was passing, and you only had one life, and already one of its limited summers was ending.

Charlie called over, "Giving up?"

"Thinking."

"What about? Stacy? Man, you should call her!"

I picked up a birch branch and worked at peeling its paper skin, revealing the tree's damaged flesh. It was crisscrossed with blackened birch-borer burrows. No wonder the branch had fallen. Soon the whole tree would be dead. I tossed the stick into the river and watched the water ripple away.

"It was just a fair thing."

"You're fuckin' nuts. I'd be all over that."

"Hey!" Kylie said.

"Hypothetically." He smiled and buried his face in her hair, seeking the creased skin of her neck with his lips. Then he pried himself away and picked up his pole again. He cast the line a few times, reeling it in not too fast, not too slow. At the first tug on his line, he yelled for me to grab the net. A long, leopard-skinned fish breached the brown water, angry as hell, and flopped on its back before sinking again.

"Holy shit! It's big!" Charlie kept the tension on the line and drew it closer and closer to the bank. When the fish was close enough, I climbed out on a sagging tree and scooped it up. A steelhead. Seven or eight pounds, with a rosy blush running down its side. I could see just about every tooth in Charlie's mouth, he was grinning so hard. He took the fish from me and teased Kylie with it, pretending to make it kiss her. She screamed and pushed him away, so he dropped the fish to the ground, net and all, and pulled her into his arms.

The truth was, I had called Stacy. I'd found her home number in the phone book the night we put Fluff out.

"It's Everett," I said. "From the fair."

"Everett?"

"Sheep Boy," I said.

"Oh, yeah."

She'd sucked in her breath when I slipped my hands under her shirt, and her eyes had looked so dark and wet in that dim barn light. When I'd looked into them, I'd felt adrift, cast out into black waters. And with no earth to stand on, I knew I would drown.

"Sheep Boy? You there?"

Her voice drew my thoughts into focus: They weren't her eyes I was remembering. They were Mary's.

The next morning, so early it was still dark, I waited for the school bus at the end of the driveway with Jay. The cattails in the ditch had grown up thick and brown with their cigar flowers already balding and turning into down. A single mourning dove cooed from its perch on the electrical line across the road. It flew off, wings whirring, when the bus approached. Mrs. Caldwell slid open the doors.

"Well, I'll be," she said when she saw me standing there.

Her stringy gray hair draped limply on each side of her neck. The opposite of a snowbird, she spent her summers in Albuquerque and returned to Michigan every fall—her skin cracked into a hundred shards of suntanned pottery, a turquoise ring on every finger—just in time to drive the country kids to school.

"My truck's out of commission. I got to ride the bus for a few days," I said, stepping onto the bus.

"Can't say I'm sad." She nodded at Jay. "I see this boy every day, and that pretty little Katie on the elementary route, but I miss my Everett."

She'd been the bus driver since I'd started school and had probably been driving for a hundred years before that. I'd met Charlie on this same bus when we were five. His fine blond hair had clung to the pebbly green vinyl seat.

"Watch this," he'd said, and pressed a finger against one nostril and blew a shiny snot bubble out the other. It pulsed, frog-like, and I laughed despite the house and Mom getting smaller and smaller out the back window. We'd been best friends ever since.

There were only a handful of riders, a few junior-highers like Jay and some underclassmen. Jay dropped into a middle seat, and I headed for the back. Everyone was mostly asleep. First ones picked up in the morning, last ones to get home at night. Some of these kids had already been on the bus a half hour and it was only six fifteen.

I leaned my head against the window and watched the morning pass by. The sun was a glow in the east, bleaching the stubbly hayfields with its pale light. I tried to doze, but each pothole knocked my head against the glass, and I looked up each time the air brakes hissed. A herd of Black Angus pressed their noses to the earth, standing so still they could have been a photo. Roy Mason's house and silo, a silhouette I knew so well, came into view and the bus slowed. I sat up, curious why we were stopping, because Charlie had been picking Kylie up every morning for school. A slight, solitary figure stood near the road. Baggy sweatshirt and jeans. This time, I didn't mistake her for a kid.

Mary kept her eyes on the floor and spoke to no one as she walked down the center aisle. Each step closer made my heart beat harder. She slid her backpack off her shoulder and sat in an empty seat across the aisle from Jay, and I wondered if they sat by each other and talked every day. She kept her head down, hiding behind that curtain of black hair. She hadn't seen me yet and I could have kept quiet, dozed the whole way to school, but then I had that thought: What would Charlie do? No way in hell he'd sit there watching the fenceposts dribble by.

"Mary!"

She looked back and smiled. It changed her face for an instant, like an eggshell cracked open, revealing a quivering, uncontrolled yolk. She smoothed her face, but I'd seen what I'd seen: She was happy to see me.

I motioned her over.

The sweet, new smell of morning followed her down the aisle, caught in the threads of her hair. She sat in the seat in front of me and dropped her backpack between her feet. I told her about my truck while she pulled out a shiny blue textbook. I peered over the seat and watched her pencil hover over a worksheet of triangles and waves. She touched the eraser to her lip and twisted it, gathering her skin into a pink knot.

"What math is that?"

"Trig."

"Jesus." I didn't even have a backpack.

I sat back and let her work, but trying to doze was no longer an option. My eyes wouldn't stay shut. My mind spun, testing out bits of conversation in my mind, each as stupid as the last. For a while, I watched the colorless morning light slide across the crown of her head. Then she shifted in the seat and an inky ribbon of hair slithered over the back of the seat like a glistening baby snake. I coiled it in the palm of my hand, remembering the first time I'd met her in Mason's field, how I'd imagined her hair gliding between my fingers in just this way. I leaned forward, caught the smell of green apples, and bit the tail end.

"Hey!"

She turned, gathering her hair, and her mouth opened with a laugh. I saw the rise of her tongue, a pit of silver in her molar.

A slice of her opening up, and I felt myself shining back at her. I thought of how bus rides had a way of doing that, suspending you between one place and another, so that you could only do one of two things: look out the window or talk to the person next to you. I could have let her sit by Jay, and maybe I should have. Maybe I should have just kept my eyes on that herd of Angus. But if I'd have looked out bus windows all my life, I never would have been friends with Charlie, and I never would have loved Mary.

She sat beside me on the ride home, leaning into me whenever Mrs. Caldwell turned the bus, so that I found myself looking ahead for intersections, counting down the seconds until the bus changed direction and Mary's hoodie touched my Carhartt again. She'd drawn intricate roses and vines on the tops of the knees of her jeans, large-bodied birds with their wings outstretched. In ink.

"My mom would kill me if I did that."

"My mom doesn't care." She lifted her foot and started a repeating wave pattern along the arch of her shoe. "She'll never see them anyway."

She lived with her dad, I remembered that. I thought about Mom and Dad splitting up. One leaving the house and one staying. It would never happen. They'd never leave the sheep. They'd never leave us. The only solution I could think of was Mom staying in the house and Dad pulling a bed out to the barn, surrounding it with space heaters, and us kids wearing down a path between the two of them.

"Where is she now?"

"My mom? Florida. That's one of the reasons Dad picked this place: It's about as far from Florida as you can get." She added a setting sun behind the waves. "I'll see her at Christmas. That's the last mandated visit."

"That's harsh."

"What's harsh is walking out on your kid."

"Shit, Mary, I'm sorry."

"Don't be. She's not." She added some checks of ink next to the sun. Birds. "And I'm not either. Living with Dad is perfect. I don't cause trouble for him, and he doesn't cause trouble for me."

"Are you in art or something?"

The tiniest smile returned.

"Yeah, I draw."

"You're good at it."

"I'm trying to get into art school."

I didn't even know what art school was for. All I could picture was a roomful of people painting a naked guy stretched out on a couch.

"What do you do after you go to art school?"

Mary looked out the bus window as if she could see a wide sweep of futures there. She put the end of the pen to her lip and twisted again, considering. "I don't know yet. I don't have it figured out yet."

We spent the rest of the ride in silence, her drawing, me watching, our heads bent over her shoe, my hair for one shivering moment touching hers. I didn't want to ask any more questions. I had asked too many already. I sat still and let the bus bring her body close to mine, tip it away, and bring it close again.

All week long she sat with me. I perked up like a goddamned prairie dog, craning my neck when Mason's modular got close, straining for the first glimpse of her at the end of the drive. We sat in the back, our heads bent over her sketches, our knees touching.

"So, what really brought your dad here? Besides it being far from Florida."

"He felt called."

"Bullshit."

"I'm serious."

She told me how her dad saw a chunk of blue ice the size of a pickup bobbing in the Niagara River, dipping below the choppy gray waves and popping back up, pulled toward the falls from somewhere far, far north.

"And then he asked to be stationed here?" I asked.

"Yep. So here I am." She went back to her doodling.

I imagined the jagged and immense floe breaking from the side of Sugar Island, carrying a pair of ring-billed seagulls, and drifting slowly down the St. Marys River, curling around the northeastern-most corner of Michigan, passing the Straits of Mackinac, jostling like trailered sheep with other floes, shearing off its sharpest edges and sending the seagulls into the air like bursts of dirty snow. It would follow the current into Lake Huron, floating lazily, catching the early pink rays of sunrise on its melting back as it skirted the coast of the Thumb. Lake St. Clair would nibble at its belly, slick it down, smooth and polish it, until it arrived in Lake Erie and eventually Buffalo, where it would slide under the Peace Bridge, rocking dreamily, glinting in the sunlight, catching her dad's eye, calling him north.

The parts store called on Thursday to tell me the starter was in, and I cursed under my breath. No more bus.

The next morning, Mary rummaged in the front pocket of her backpack for a pen. The bag was covered with poems and sayings written in ornate lettering.

"Keep a green tree . . . ?" I couldn't read the rest. "What's it say?"

"It's from a fortune cookie I got once. It said, 'Keep a green tree in your heart, and one day the singing bird will come.'"

"What's it mean?"

"If you want something, you have to get ready for it, you know? You have to prepare. You can't expect a bird to show up if you don't have a tree."

"All right. What's your green tree? What's your singing bird?"

She thought for a minute and darkened the lettering absently. "My green tree would be getting good grades, practicing drawing, getting my portfolio together."

I wanted to ask what a portfolio was but didn't want to sound stupid. My English teacher, Ms. Weltzer, said to break words down into parts we knew. I knew port. Like harbor. Where the freighters were loaded or unloaded. But folio threw me. Not foal. Then I remembered foliage; the trees and their leaves. A harbor of leaves. Art school the harbor, her drawings the leaves.

"And my singing bird, the thing I'm hoping for, is art school; being on my own; going where I want, when I want." She paused. "I don't think I ever said that out loud before."

"What, going to art school?"

"No, going where I want, when I want."

"That's what everyone wants. That's all anyone really wants."

Her pen stopped moving and she looked at me. Christ, those eyes. "You do that a lot," she said. And the pen started moving again.

"Do what?"

"Say something really deep out of nowhere, like it's nothing."

"It's not deep," I said. "It's sheep. They know what they want. They're the most selfish bastards you'll ever see. They push each other out of the way shoving up to the trough for feed. They don't care if the sheep next to them gets any. They'll let another sheep starve if it means they get more. But it works the other way around too. I've seen a ewe shear her teats off jumping a barbed-wire fence to get to her lamb at weaning time. Nothing was going to keep her away from that lamb."

Her pen paused midair. "God, that's brutal."

"I shouldn't have said that," I said. "I'm sorry."

The pen started moving again. "Your turn. What's your green tree? What's your singing bird?"

"It's nothing."

"Tell me."

I hated these questions. People asked them constantly once you got into high school. They tried to act like they were really interested, but there was only one answer they liked: college. Better yet, college far away. The farther the better. They got starry-eyed if you said that. Like there was only success in leaving. Even Charlie was planning on welding school. Sometimes, just to avoid the looks on their faces, I said I was going to welding school too. But I wasn't going anywhere. I was planning on doing exactly what I'd been doing all along, minus the wasted hours spent at school.

"My dad's lining up work for me at the road commission. And I'll farm." I waited for her to nod and change the subject, which was what people usually did when I told them my plans.

"What kind of farm?" she asked.

"Sheep. Well, show lambs. I'm starting my own herd. I bought a ewe at the fair. She's really something. And I'm getting a ram this weekend. This spring, I'll have my own lambs."

"What do you do with them?"

"Breed them; sell them."

Sometimes Curly had to wait a day or two for a ewe to come around. He might weave through the herd licking others' flanks and growling at them. Sometimes he bred others and came back to her, thirsty and sweated up and determined. I could try again, I thought. I could bat her leg one more time.

"I could show you our farm sometime."

She took the cap off the pen and started sketching a tree just below the fortune-cookie quote.

"I'll have my truck fixed by Monday. I could pick you up for school and you could come over after."

She added a tiny bird, its beak open wide in song.

"And you could sleep in. If I picked you up, you could sleep in at least a half an hour."

"Now, there's an idea."

The bus was getting close to the modular. She zipped the pen into her backpack and swung her legs into the aisle. She stood.

"So, wait, is that a yes?"

It was the phone call all over again, waiting for her to decide. I saw my own wide sweep of futures, starting with Monday morning and me driving up the dandelion-buttoned drive and her trotting down the steps. I saw me showing her the ram, telling her he was my green tree. I saw me leading her across the field, and the ewes trotting toward me but drawing up sharp when they noticed Mary. I saw me pointing out Fluff and the other yearlings. See those ten? Those are mine. All I needed was one word from her.

"Sure," she said, sweet and high, with a shrug. "Yes."

I blinked. "Really?"

She smiled and lifted her backpack to her shoulder. "See you Monday."

She waved goodbye to Jay and Mrs. Caldwell as she passed. Outside, she checked the mailbox and pulled out a large, white envelope. She dropped her backpack and opened the envelope right there at the end of the driveway. She pulled out a letter. Mrs. Caldwell shifted into drive, and I twisted my body, wringing it like a rag, to keep my eyes on Mary as the bus pulled away. She'd said yes. *Thank you*, I breathed to God and Jesus. The sky and the wind. The St. Marys. The soil and sun. *Thank you.*

Chapter 6

Charlie's knuckles were white. The waters of three Great Lakes—Superior, Michigan, and Huron—swelled below us, the sky stretched above, and the Mackinac Bridge felt like a fine, five-mile-long thread suspending us inside the color blue. Dad's empty livestock trailer rattled behind us, and the tiniest gusts rising up from the water threatened to send us hurtling off the side. Leaving the Upper Peninsula was never easy. The Lower Peninsula waited on the other side of the bridge like the opening to another world. If we stayed on I-75 long enough, there were cities and suburbs and shopping malls. Some people couldn't wait to go. Me, I couldn't wait to head north again. My guess was Charlie felt the same way.

"You and your piece-of-shit Ford owe me," he said.

"Don't worry. The part's in. I'm fixing it tomorrow."

It felt like old times. There was no Kylie and I hadn't said anything to him about Mary. Whatever was happening with her was fragile and new and I wanted to give it space to grow. I held it with open palms and felt kind of jaunty and fresh with the secret of it. It was mine and mine alone.

Charlie looked over at me. "What are you grinning about?"

"Nothin'," I said.

I had exactly $300 in my wallet. I'd learned a lesson buying Fluff: You had to know your limit. I'd decided $300 was mine. I'd made just over $1,000 on my lambs at the fair. Out of that, I needed money for the starter (which I'd already used), the ram, hay for the winter and a little feed, gas for the truck, plus some walking-around money. Three hundred was enough to get a nice ram, but not enough to clean me out.

The ram sale took place at an auction yard with a sale ring and bleachers housed inside a large, red metal shed. Outside, a massive grid of pens spread out toward the parking lot and every pen contained a single ram. The racket they made was not like that of the ewes, who were brassy and explosive. Rams sounded deep and watery, like the undercurrent of a river, if currents made sound, or the rumble of a freighter sailing by. Buyers walked through the aisles and stopped when something caught their eyes: the height they needed, the length, the pedigree.

The way to pick out a ram was from the ground up. Dad taught me that. Don't even touch him at first or look past his pasterns. Look at his hooves, his stride length. Watch him move around his pen. Watch where he places his front foot and make sure he sets his back foot down in the same spot. You could feed or exercise out some flaws, but there was nothing you could do if an animal wasn't built right.

I picked up a sale order at the office and made my way through the pens one by one. The sale order listed each ram by lot number and gave his breeder, sire, dam, birth date, current weight, weight at sixty and ninety days. I couldn't keep my eyes off the showstoppers, the proud-headed ones with high shag, the tight bellies and long bodies. Some of them were as straight as a bullet casing and just as slick. A ram squared up to me, holding my eyes, his front feet set powerfully on the ground. I made a note on the sale order.

"You can't afford him, man," Charlie said.

"I can look."

The breeder came up to us, long-legged with aviator sunglasses. He wore a clean fleece vest over a collared shirt. New boots.

"See something you like, boys?"

"Yeah, but my broke-ass friend doesn't have the money."

The breeder smiled. "You know, I might have just the thing for you. Care to take a look?"

Charlie and I looked at each other. Why not? We followed him out to the parking lot to a beautiful black gooseneck, gleaming like the back of a beetle in the sun. Something inside it was raising hell.

"Have a look," he said.

I climbed up on the running board and peered between the slats. Inside, a hundred-pound Hampshire ram lamb climbed the walls, bawling because he was alone. I stepped off the runner.

"I need a ram that's ready now. I want lambs this winter."

"Now, hear me out. He was born late. May thirteenth. But he's off my stud ram Accelerate. Heard of him? I bet you have. Good genetics, bad timing."

"Thanks, anyway. Come on, Charlie."

"His half-siblings will sell today for six hundred . . . seven hundred, I promise you that. Maybe more. I can sell you this guy for four hundred."

"I don't have four hundred. And even if I did, he's no use to me."

I turned to go back to the sale.

"Hold on, we can haggle on the price later. At least take a closer look at him. I saw what pens you were looking at in there.

You got a good eye. Just a little light in the pocketbook, am I right?"

"Price doesn't matter if I can't breed him."

He held up his hands. "All right, there are plenty of run-of-the-mill rams here today, selling cheap as dirt. Hell, you can buy two. You could breed them tomorrow and have run-of-the-mill lambs in the spring. Or—and I'm hoping you'll see things my way—or, you could get a hell of a deal on a prime ram, advertise the hell out of his genetics, put Accelerate on everything, and take your flock to the next level."

I looked at Charlie. He raised his eyebrows. "Don't look at me. This is your deal."

The trailer thundered. I could at least take another look. I got back up on the runner.

The breeder opened the trailer door, and the ram went right up to him. He was a friendly little shit.

"Walk him up and down the length of the trailer." I felt like the judge for once, presiding over a mini show ring. He had a nice bounce to his step. I watched where his feet landed, how his front legs moved with his back.

"Can you set him up?"

"See that?" the breeder said. "He just wants to show. That's the genetics there. Accelerate's offspring have had more success in the show ring than any of my other rams."

I thought this over. The point of coming down here wasn't just to buy any old ram, it was to buy a ram with the qualities Curly lacked, to add some shine to the herd, a little star quality. This little guy had that and then some.

"Can I put my hands on him?"

"I wouldn't sell him to you if you didn't."

I got in the trailer, and I swear if the lamb had a tail it would wag. I ran my hands over his rack and loin and felt the width of his leg. I massaged his ballsack, feeling for symmetry and size, lumps or knots. He never flinched, only stamped his foot once at a fly.

I stepped back and looked him over again. His beautifully arched head, how it rolled into his neck and down to his compact shoulders. He'd never been sheared. I slid my fingers into the fine wool over his back and pulled it apart to expose the tender pink skin below. I spread open his ears and looked inside. They were clean and plum-colored. His mouth was clean too. I counted each tooth, checked for early wear or misalignment. I held a finger to each eye until he blinked. I lifted each foot and spread the cleft of the hoof apart, not even sure what I was checking for. An injury maybe. Some sore. But there was nothing. He was perfect. Just born at the wrong time.

"Two hundred," I said.

"Two hundred! I like you, kid, but I'm not going to let you steal him. Four hundred."

"I can't do that. I just can't."

"Three fifty."

"Sir, all I got is three hundred."

He thought for a minute, then held out his hand. And I took it.

The ram cried the whole way home. He never let up. We rolled up the windows and turned up the radio, and the highway wind washed over the truck, but we couldn't drown him out. Sheep are herd animals, born to move in groups. Alone they feel vulnerable, bare. In the trailer by himself, traveling God-knows-where, all he could do was back himself into a corner and cry.

A half hour into the drive, Charlie asked, "We got time for a pit stop? Feeling a little parched."

"Let's just get him home and bedded down." I wanted to give him a good drink of water; watch him take his first bite of

Chippewa County hay. Hay I'd cut myself going down into my own ram's belly. I wanted to hear his hooves touch Lindt soil. Mostly, I wanted to see Dad's face when I led him off the trailer.

"Come on. You need to celebrate." He held an imaginary glass to his mouth and tossed it back. "One beer. Another hour or two won't make a difference. Sheep can't tell time." He already had the blinker on.

I had to admit that a beer—if we could get it—sounded good. And he was right: The ram couldn't tell five minutes from fifty.

Charlie pulled off the highway and a few miles later turned in to the parking lot of a secluded bar made mostly of roof and low, narrow windows. Vinyl beer posters were tacked to the dark exterior. In the trees behind, I could make out a rotted boat draped with tarps, a stack of boards, a picnic table, a rusted-out fuel drum. The dumpster was near the front entrance. There were only two other trucks in the parking lot.

"Ain't she a beaut?" Charlie said. "I stopped here once with my dad. The bartender didn't even look twice at me."

I checked on the ram before following Charlie inside. Now that the trailer had stopped, he was silent. He watched me with wary, golden eyes, looking to me more like a milk-hungry lamb than the ram I wanted him to be. I understood Katie's need to thread flowers and grass, little pieces of comfort, through the trailer slats to Fluff. The ram took a step toward me.

"Listen, boy, we're going inside for a bit. Probably only ten minutes knowing my luck, but then we'll get you home, all right?" I reached inside and he raised his nose to my fingertips. With his head high like that, he was powerful again, regal. "There you are," I said.

I jogged after Charlie, and the ram started up his bawling again, louder now that the highway wasn't washing the sound away.

"Is he going to do that the whole time?" Charlie asked.

"Sounds like."

The bar had a low door, and we ducked to enter, standing fully upright once inside, as tall as we could, pulling back our shoulders and looking around. The little light the windows let in bounced off the glossy split pine walls and Bud Light mirrors. No one was smoking, but the air was murky, cave-like, stained with the scent of cigarette smoke. The only sound was a hushed buzz from the television mounted to the ceiling in the corner. The entire south wall was devoted to Polaroids of buck pole winners going all the way back to deer season 1975. Two old-timers hunched at the end of the bar, thin, in old jeans, with greased white hair. One wore a foam trucker's cap like Dad's.

We chose two hard-backed stools right up at the bar, like we were regulars. Right in front of the black-and-white sign telling us that our birthday had to be on or before today's date in 1974 to purchase alcohol, that it was a misdemeanor for minors to even attempt it. I'd never walked up to a bar and ordered beer before, but then I'd never needed to. It was all around me. And in two years, we could drive over to Canada if we wanted. This was bald-faced. Risky. And I felt a little jacked up with the idea of it; like I'd just stuffed my lip with a fresh pinch of chew, which we also weren't old enough to buy, even though we both had it in our back pockets. It all seemed so stupid.

With our faces reflected in the bar-length mirror, the dim light shadowed the undersides of our jaws, and I thought, This'll be me and Charlie. Five years from now, ten years. This'll be us. I looked down the bar at the pair of old men sitting at the end of it. Not speaking, just beside each other, their beers mostly gone. I thought of the one in the hat as me, the other as Charlie. I wanted to elbow him and point at them and say, "Look, there we are. That's us." I felt I'd seen the future and it shook me to see things laid out so plain. It was what we'd always told ourselves we wanted, or what others had told us we wanted, our dads especially, not so much with words but their lives—a beer at a bar, the silent camaraderie.

"You got a stupid look on your face again," Charlie said.

"Happy, I guess."

"What about?"

"Bringing home that beautiful ram. Hanging out. Getting served." *Picking up Mary on Monday.* But I kept that last bit to myself. I tapped my fingers on the thickly lacquered bar.

"We're not served yet," he said. "Barkeep!" And he turned his smile on high-beam, laid it on thick. Too thick, I worried, but she finally came over. She had Mrs. Caldwell's crackled skin; her thin, lined lips. But where there was warmth in Mrs. Caldwell's eyes, delight even, as if every kid on the bus was her own, the bartender looked burned-out, dried-out, like she'd breathed too much of the bar's stale air. She set two napkins in front of us, which seemed promising. There was a thin line of lipstick on her chin, which also seemed promising: She was distracted, she was human.

"What'll you have?"

I took a breath. This would go one of two ways. One, I ordered a beer, and she served me. Charlie too. And we sat in the company of our future selves, enjoying the easy pleasure of a cold beer. Or two, I ordered a beer, and she asked for my ID. Charlie's too. And she threw us out—or worse—when she found out we were underage.

I said the first thing that came to mind, quickly, so my voice couldn't betray my age, my nerves, anything. "Old Milwaukee."

And then, because I'd snuck canned and bottled beer my whole life, and because even keg beer was easy to come by at wedding receptions and graduation parties, usually bitter and flat, or warm, and dispensed in small plastic cups, I added, "Draft." You couldn't sneak a draft. You had to order it. It had to be served. I imagined cold white foam spilling over the lip of a tall, frosted glass.

She looked at Charlie. Somehow his smile was bigger, brighter.

"I'll have the same," he said.

I could taste the foam. I could feel the icy glass biting my fingertips. I cursed myself for ordering Old Milwaukee. There was a whole bar before me, and I'd ordered dad beer. I could have got anything.

"You boys have some ID?"

We looked at each other. Charlie's smile faded.

"Huh?" he asked, like her question was so absurd he couldn't understand it.

But I understood. There would be no beer, no icy glass, no foam.

"If you don't have ID, I can't serve you." She reached back and tapped the warning sign. Her eyes were bored as ever. She'd been through this routine before.

"I was just here a few weeks ago with my dad," Charlie said.

One of the old-timers, the one I thought of as future me, turned his stool toward us, listening. He drew his deep forehead lines into a knot. I thought maybe he would vouch for us. Like, maybe while I was looking down the bar at him, seeing myself in him, he'd been looking back, seeing a younger self in me. I half expected him to say, *Aw, give 'em a beer.*

Instead, he lifted his upper lip, exposing a line of square teeth. "Who else hears a sheep?"

We froze and listened. And then, we heard it too. The cries seeped through the walls, through the windows, until it sounded like the ram was at the door, the way the sound of a leaky faucet fills a room once it's noticed. Over and over he cried.

"What in the hell?" the bartender said. Her eyes were no longer bored. She walked out from behind the bar.

"Let's go," Charlie said. Then louder: "This place is BS anyway."

We bent under the door and stood up in the bright afternoon. I inhaled deeply the fresh air. The bartender followed us, blinking in the sun, raising her hand to her eyes, and coughing a little.

"What do you two have in there?" she said, but we didn't answer.

The ram banged against the trailer wall, and I banged back. "I told you ten minutes."

Charlie backed the trailer out of the parking lot like a pro and flipped off the bartender as we drove off.

"She was just doing her job," I said.

"She wasn't doing her job when I came with my dad then."

"It's different when you come in with another kid."

"Who's a kid?" he asked.

We pulled into the driveway like that, the ram crying and the trailer shuddering. Dad and Katie came out of the house to watch us unload. The noise and commotion didn't add up to the giddy little ram that trotted out beside me, happy finally to be on the other side of the trailer walls. I felt a little giddy myself.

Katie laughed when she saw him. "He's so cute!"

I walked the ram right up to Dad and set him up, holding him at arm's length, presenting him.

"Thought you were getting a ram."

"I did. A young one."

He crossed his arms. "I see that. Now tell me how you're going to start a herd with a ram that can't breed. I'm interested."

Charlie cleared his throat and started unlatching the trailer. The ram stood between Dad and me, his back straight and solid as marble.

"He will breed," I said. "Next season."

"Oh, next season." Dad nodded and smiled. "Meanwhile, he's eating feed and hay all winter long, taking up space in my barn, and he's not even proven. Between him and Fluff, this is quite the herd you've got going. I'm not even going to ask what you spent on him."

I leaned into the ram, and he braced against me, tensing his muscles and stretching out his rear legs beautifully. His balls swung heavy beneath him. I looked up at Dad.

"He'll be worth it, Dad. He's a good ram. A real good one. I checked everything. I mean, look at him."

"I'm looking. You know what I see? A kid who's fool enough to buy a ram just because he's pretty."

"He's a good ram and you know it! If any of your raggedy-ass ewes threw him, you'd be pissing yourself you'd be so happy."

He raised his hand to backhand me but stopped, and he held it there between us, a warning. He hadn't hit me since I was Jay's size, and I was glad he hadn't done it in front of Charlie. I stepped back but kept hold of the ram.

"The problem's not the ram," he said. "The problem's you not using the sense God gave you. First that stunt with Fluff. Now"—he gestured to the ram—"this!"

Charlie bent over the hitch, pretending he was busy with the safety chains. But Katie bit the side of her thumb and watched everything, her eyes huge and sliding back and forth between me and Dad.

"He's a good ram," I repeated, but quieter. I wasn't going to apologize or take back what I'd said. I was proud I knew what to look for in breeding stock. I was proud I'd had money in my pocket, my own money that I'd worked for, and that I'd used it to get what I wanted.

"You'll learn," he said. "If you won't listen to me, then you'll learn the hard way. Either way, you'll learn."

I hugged the ram's head to my thigh and watched Dad walk back to the house.

Charlie pulled his truck around. He leaned out the window. "He's not wrong, man."

"I know, but it pisses me off. He wants me to do everything his way."

"My dad would say the same shit. They got to second-guess everything. You know how it is."

I nodded. "I got to get this guy in the barn."

Charlie looked past me to Katie. "Hey, Kitty-Cat!"

Kitty-Cat was his name for her, something he'd called her since the day she came home from the hospital with her halo of white fur, like something from a nest hidden deep in the haymow. He'd sat next to me on the living-room couch, holding her. "She meows like a cat," he'd said.

Katie kept the side of her thumb in her mouth, but smiled at him and dipped her head, in love with him, I realized, just like every other girl.

"Call tomorrow if you need help with your truck," he said.

He drove off, and it dawned on me that he'd left out the "piece-of-shit" part for once.

I had a pen ready for the ram on the other side of the barn from Curly. I'd spread straw on the floor in great fluffy piles that I wouldn't have minded curling up in myself. Katie and I watched him wade through the straw, finding his hayrack, his water bucket. He drank loud and long.

"What's his name?" she asked.

"Roman."

"Why that?"

"The shape of his head. His shoulders. Can't you picture him on a coin? You know, like an old coin? They always put emperors and presidents on coins. That's how he looks to me. Noble, like a king."

"I see it," she said.

Curly bellowed darkly, deeply. He wedged his front hooves in the slats of the gate and pushed himself up until he stood on his back legs. Roman danced at the noise and called back, a sweeter voice, like polished wood. All night long, we could hear them from the house, calling to each other across the expanse of the barn, their chests pressed against the gates that held them apart, like freighters approaching each other and sounding warnings over the waves.

Chapter 7

The next afternoon was warm, and it didn't take long to replace the starter, so I washed the body of the truck knowing Mary would see it in the light of day. I wiped it down with a blanket from Mom's stack in the garage, the ones she used to wrap the lambs in, to sew them coats, to line the cardboard boxes we kept the bottle lambs in until they were old enough to go back to the barn.

I shined the windows and mirrors, even the door handles. Then I got inside, and the smell of the interior hit me—turned soil, wool, hay chaff, and road dust, the wintery cold tang of chew. This was the smell of me. I ran the damp blanket over the dash, then turned the key and closed my eyes. The engine turned over easily, and the rock station played loud the way I liked it. The bench seat curved warmly under the weight of me, the music pulsed in my ears, and everything around me was me.

In the morning, I drove to Mary's house and parked outside

her front door, not fully believing I'd woken up because there she was, just like I'd imagined on the bus, coming down the steps, opening the passenger door, and climbing in. The dreamy feeling stayed with me the whole drive. I kept looking at her to make sure she was really there. And every time I looked—like some prayer answered again and again—she still was.

I checked off each class until the school day was finally over. We met at the truck, and I pulled out of the parking lot before Charlie and Kylie even left the building. I wasn't hiding from them. There's a difference between hiding and protecting. Hiding means you're ashamed or scared. Protecting means you want to keep something safe. This friendship with Mary, or whatever it was, was something I wanted to protect.

I showed her Roman first.

"So, this is your green tree?" she asked.

"This is him."

She raised the back of her hand to her nose. It's hard to describe the smell of a sheep barn: the ammonia and oil, the shit and the sweet. The air feels solid. You have to stand there a minute and relax and allow yourself to breathe it in, sour and thick as it is.

"I've never been in a barn before."

"You can touch him. He's friendly."

But she kept her hands tight at her side and watched the ground where she stepped. "That's OK," she said.

"My dad gave me hell for buying him because he's young, but he'll come around."

I touched the side of my face. There was no mark, he hadn't actually hit me, but something there still burned, a stiffness if I pressed my lips or smiled. I'd been tucking in my chew on the other side.

"He's beautiful," Mary said.

"You see it too?"

She nodded. "He's proportioned and balanced. Totally symmetrical. And strong but sweet; being both makes him interesting. He's something I would draw."

Curly blared from the other side of the barn.

"That's Curly," I said. "My dad's ram."

"How come they're not together?"

"They'd kill each other."

Still, the rams had made a certain peace. Their voices didn't boom through the night anymore. The only ruckus over the past two days was when I gave Curly grain in the evening, something we always did the last two weeks before breeding season. He needed to build up his strength. We would turn him out with the ewes the third week in September and bring him in the day before deer season. He would come limping out of the field frenzied and fifty pounds lighter, his wool in patches, his shoulders poking up through his hide like coat hangers, having cared more about fucking than grazing for two months straight. Larry, our old ram, had put out his back during breeding season once and Dad had to borrow a ram from a farm in Pickford to finish the job. Then there was Grandpa Lindt's ram, Bucko. Dad liked telling the story: "He died right on top of the ewe. Heart just gave right out. Christ, that's the way to go."

I turned to Mary. "I'll show you the ewes."

We followed a sheep path through the north field toward the old foundation stones. I took her hand as she balanced across them and by the time she reached the end of the ruined wall, in my mind I saw us married, the homestead restored, children raised, and us grown old together, sitting side by side watching the eastern sky each morning.

"Your grandpa built this?"

"Great-great grandpa. Someday, I'm going to buy this land from my parents. I want to build a new house over these stones where the Lindts first settled."

We switched hands and she turned and walked back across the wall. "I can't imagine being in one place so long."

"I can't imagine not."

She stopped and looked at me, and I worried I'd said something wrong, but then she kept walking. "I don't want any ground under my feet. Not yet anyway." She stepped on another stone. "Where's your grandpa now?"

"He was gone before I was born. Young."

"What about your grandma?"

"She's gone, too, but I remember her. The house we live in now was hers. We lived there with her. Me and my mom and dad upstairs and her in the bedroom downstairs. That was before Jay and Katie came along."

"And your mom's parents are here too?"

"Well, they're in town." I didn't tell her how they didn't know me, how I'd never darkened the door of their house even though I knew exactly which house on Spruce Street was theirs. How these stones and the way I felt here, the voices of Lindts dancing on the heads of canary grass, was the closest thing I had to feeling a grandparent's love. Mom and Dad hadn't told me the particulars but I knew enough. Mom had me, and in their eyes, it was the worst thing she could ever do.

Mary stepped off the foundation, but her hand stayed in mine. It was only a little bigger than Katie's and softer. A few hundred yards off, the ewes grazed. They lifted their heads as we got closer. If I'd been alone, they would have come up and sniffed my hand or bit at my jeans until I scratched their heads, but with Mary there, they were wary, and she was too. She moved so that my body was between hers and theirs and clenched the back of my Carhartt. I liked the pull of her on my coat. Every nerve in my body was awake.

"Will they hurt us?"

"The sheep?"

I stuck two fingers in my mouth and whistled a long, low note that rose quickly at the end, the same call Dad used. It had taken me years to copy. I repeated it two more times. The sheep knew the sound and walked toward us, moving in their liquid, flowing way. Gradually, they surrounded us.

This gentle meeting of species always amazed me, how their trust in me overcame their deepest instincts. Caroline and the other old ewes approached first and stood shoulder to shoulder like ambassadors, bringing with them a sharp grease smell and the drone of blackflies circling their legs. The young ewes—and I already thought of them as mine—filled in the space behind. Fluff came last. She limped, still sore from Caroline's bullying, but her head and ears were up, so I wasn't worried.

I cupped Caroline's chin in my hand and pulled her ears playfully. I pressed my fingers into her unshorn wool. She was healthy, fat. Ready for breeding. They all were. Their dark faces were bleached red from the summer sun.

Caroline shoved her whiskered lips in Mary's hand, and Mary cried out and wrenched away. The motion sent the ewes running and Mary clung snug up against me like I was a life raft, her face deep in my chest.

The ewes came back, curious about Mary, smelling the newness of her, and she wriggled away, sometimes yelping, spooking them all over again. Eventually, the circle of sheep widened, and only Fluff stood nearby.

"Here, this one's Katie's. She's our gentlest girl." I petted Fluff's side to demonstrate, a good firm pat, but instead of pushing her head under my hand, she stepped away. Her queenly gait was gone. I made a note to talk to Dad about it. Maybe we should bring her in for a few days after all.

Mary peeked up from my Carhartt. "Can you make them go away?"

"You don't like the sheep?"

"I'd prefer a fence between them and me."

She was clinging to me and I liked that, but I didn't want her to ask to go home.

"Why, what is it?"

"The way they move together, like this force. How do you stop them?"

And then I understood: I saw each ewe, many with names given by Mom and Katie, each with her own temperament and history, her own genealogical relation to the others, mothers and daughters, half-sisters, and so on. Mary saw one single, heavy mass.

"Let me show you something else."

"No sheep."

"None."

We walked to the northeast corner of the field, where the fence jogged around a creek that had carved a deep wedge out of the ridge. We called this place the gully. It opened out below the ridge onto another field that Grandpa Lindt had bought from the Croft family. We still called it Croft's Place, even though the Crofts had moved away long before I was even born.

We climbed over the fence and skidded down the steep incline to the bottom of the gully, where trees leaned overhead, covering portions of the sky. Black-beaked starlings emerged from dark knots in the branches and croaked warnings to each other, so that the trek down to the creek bed felt like the crossing into a deep prehistoric world.

At the bottom, the earth was spongy and wet and left two brown circles on the knees of my jeans. I raked my fingers gently through the soft-moving water, stirring up pink and beige clouds of clay, feeling blindly under filmy, submerged layers of blackened leaves and twigs.

"Here's one," I said.

"One what?"

"Claybaby."

I dipped it under the water and rubbed it to clear off the soft layers of silt until its shape was revealed: a buff-colored comet, a hardened ripple of pink clay aggregated to another ripple and another, solidified in the ridge ages ago, and set free by the creek.

Dad had discovered the claybabies when he was a kid. He said he'd scraped his hands climbing on the old Lindt foundation and soothed them in the creek. He spent the rest of the afternoon pulling out one smooth stone after another. Except that they weren't stones exactly. They looked molded, like crude pottery. Grandma Lindt's the one who first called them claybabies. She said they looked like God started something but didn't quite finish. Like they were half-formed and tossed away.

Mary turned the claybaby over in her hands.

"Doesn't look like a baby."

"Sure it does. Like a newborn all swaddled up."

"Looks like a walrus."

"It's whatever you want it to be." I felt around in the water again. "The creek spits them out every now and then. The best time to find them is after a hard rain like we had last week. Me and Katie hunt for them all the time. She has a whole box of them."

My fingers touched something hard. It pulled easily from the sediment layer, and I rubbed it with my thumbs. It looked something like a bowling pin or a peanut in a shell.

"I showed one to Mr. Palinski, my soil-science teacher, and he said this whole place used to be covered with glaciers. When they retreated, they made a lake that left clay everywhere. He said all it takes is a little nucleus, a splinter of wood, a bit of shell or bone that attracts the clay and it grows layer by layer."

Mary slipped her hands into the water next to mine. The water was silky, a little thick. Decaying willow leaves bumped against my skin. I trailed my fingers across the soft, fine bed of the creek until they touched hers. I guided her hands into the soft silt. Plumes of pink sediment bloomed around her wrists. The cuffs of her sweatshirt were wet and her Keds were grass-stained but she didn't seem to mind. She moved a little farther down, gliding her hands along the creek bed, just how I imagined someone reading braille. Then she gasped. "I got one!" She lifted her treasure from the water. It was shaped like a songbird with a rounded head and deep chest sloping down to a pointed tail. She rubbed it clean with her thumb and held it up for me, glistening in the fleeting September sun, smiling, like she'd found gold.

Kiss her. It's what I'd wanted to do since I'd first seen her two months ago. But the way she was holding the claybaby up to the light made me tuck the thought away. She looked happy and free. The afternoon had been perfect, and I didn't want to mess anything up. She dried the stone on her sweatshirt and then pushed it into her pocket, and we walked together back to the house.

Katie stopped dead on the stairs when she saw Mary in the kitchen rinsing the claybaby in the sink. I'd never brought a girl to the house before. They'd come in tow with Charlie, but this was new. Jay had grabbed some lunch meat out of the fridge and said hi to Mary, but he was smart enough to take his sandwich back upstairs, and give us space. Katie would be different. She stood in the middle of the stairs, not coming, not going, just scowling down at us, holding her stuffed rabbit around the neck.

"This is Mary," I said.

Katie didn't move. The rabbit sagged at her hip. Mary left her claybaby in the sink and leaned on the kitchen counter. Her hands found Mom's shopping-list pad. She picked up a pen and began to move it over the paper.

"Mary's my friend."

"Charlie's your friend."

"Mary's a new friend." I lifted my arm, inviting Katie to come close. She came down slowly, hugging the rabbit under her chin. When she made it over to me, she picked at the fur around the rabbit's glassy brown eyes.

Mary smiled and slid a piece of paper across the counter to Katie. On it, she'd drawn the rabbit, roughly, with rapid, disconnected strokes, but she'd captured something essential about it, the tilt of its enormous round head, and—somehow—the wet sadness of its eyes, so that if it were back on the store shelf, lined up side by side with the other stuffed rabbits for sale, and you only had Mary's drawing to go by, you'd know exactly which one was Katie's.

"I like your bunny," Mary said, rising.

"He doesn't like you!"

"What the hell's wrong with you?" I said.

Katie's chest puffed up and she sealed her lips, like she'd taken a big bite out of a crab apple and was waiting for the pain, and I knew she would cry. She ran up the stairs, and the rabbit bounced at her side, looking back at us with his suffering eyes.

"Apologize, Katie!" I shouted after her.

"No!"

Her bedroom door slammed.

"I don't think she likes girls hanging around her big brother," Mary said.

"It's no excuse. I don't know what that was about."

She patted the claybaby dry and flipped it in her hands, looking at it from different angles. "My singing bird."

Katie pretended I was invisible all through dinner and she huddled in her room the rest of the night.

"You shouldn't have been like that to Mary," I said to her bedroom door. "It was rude."

"Good!"

I tried the knob. "Open the door."

"No!"

I'd never been so angry with her before. And never before had there been a locked door between us.

"We're not even going out or anything. She's just a friend."

"You showed her the claybabies! I saw you! That's our thing!"

"Will you just open up?" I leaned my head against the door. "Please."

No sound came from inside. I bunched the rabbit drawing through the gap under her door, a peace offering, and waited. I heard her unfold it, imagined her looking at the floppy face. Two seconds later, she pushed it back out.

I went downstairs, where Dad was watching TV.

"What's wrong with Kate?"

"No clue," I said.

I settled on the couch but didn't pay attention to the show. I could still feel Mary hiding in my Carhartt; I could feel the weight of her hand as she balanced along the old foundation. She'd been in this very house. The night felt open and wide. I couldn't wait to see her the next day, and I was annoyed with Katie, and maybe that was why I forgot to tell Dad how Fluff had been walking.

I drove Mary the next day and the next. On Thursday morning, I showed up without asking because by then chauffeuring her was routine. After school, with the leaves just starting to thin and change, I asked if she'd ever seen Lake Superior.

"There's a nice spot twenty minutes from here. You want to check it out?"

"It's not like anyone's dying for me to get home."

Whitefish Bay flashed through the trunks of the maple trees that crowded the north side of the highway. Their sleepy branches showered the road in our wake, dropping leaves like snow onto the ground behind us. I pulled off where the maples gave way to red pines—tall, thick trees with peeling, sunburned skin for bark. The ground was covered in their tiny orange needles and our footsteps made no sound.

We could hear the water before we saw it, no more than faint radio static at first. We walked toward it, and the needled carpet turned to sand. We skidded down a washout and the bay opened before us. A single seagull bobbed on the silky gray waves. I spread my Carhartt jacket on the sand. We sat on it side by side looking out at the water. It was dusted with golden disks of sunlight that reminded me of dandelions opening in the front yard.

A breeze came up from the west and touched our ears. The shadows of the trees on the shore stretched out into the waves. Everything—the sun, the breeze, the shadows, our eyes—was drawn to the water. And for the longest time, we didn't speak. The waves slid across the sand. The seagull rose and fell. Across the bay, Gros Cap Bluffs humped out of the horizon like a cloud-covered turtle shell.

"Have you ever seen the ocean, Everett?"

"This is as close as I've ever gotten."

"My mom lives by the beach. When I'm there, I head there in the morning with a notebook and some pencils and draw."

"Draw what?"

"Pelicans."

"The goofy birds with the necks?"

"I'm obsessed. They fly around in lines following the waves. They drop into the water when they feel like it and take off again. They hang out with the fishermen or go off alone. Anywhere they want to go. I have a whole notebook of them."

Something tinkled behind us. Like glass bells. Previous visitors had slid mini liquor bottles on the tips of the branches behind us. Jack Daniel's Tennessee Honey and Five O'Clock Gin. Smirnoff. Some had been there so long the labels were worn white and illegible and the tree's summer growth had curled up inside them. I got up and touched one, turning it in the warm beams of the sun.

Mary stood up, too, and it felt magical, standing there with her under the tree, with the music of the glass in the breeze, the waves shushing the beach, the sun melting away. That's when we kissed. And everything felt right: the warmth of her body next to mine, the pale September breeze swirling around us, the water—just a few months from freezing over—soaking the sand just yards from our feet. I wanted to stop time and never move again, but she whispered, "Let's go in."

"Hell, no."

She pulled off her Keds and socks. "Come on."

"That water's, like, sixty degrees. Probably less."

"Fine, just our feet."

She balanced on my arm as we stepped in. The sand gave way to pea gravel and then to rounded beach stones as it rose above our ankles, our knees.

"It's freezing!" she shrieked. She splashed me, and I caught her and kissed her again. She was out of breath. I felt her heart pounding against my chest. The seagull lifted itself from the waves.

"All this water flows to the St. Marys," I said.

"And now we're part of it too."

But we couldn't stay out there long, even with the sun clear overhead. The water was cold, the air was cool, too cool for the beach. I wished it were still summer.

We went back to my Carhartt. Mary pushed her toes into the sand. She was shivering. I was too. I put my arm around her, and she laid her head on my shoulder.

"Mary," I asked, "are we going out?"

She shrugged. "I don't know. Are we?"

A smile played on her lips and I leaned down and kissed them again.

Chapter 8

Dad's lips made tiny movements and his eyes flicked left to right as he counted the sheep. He did this every morning, every night, and a hundred times in between, asking himself the question shepherds have asked for a thousand years: Have I lost one?

It's hard to count animals. They move, dip their heads, blend together. Just when you think each one's accounted for, the shape of the herd shifts, and you start back over again.

"Everett, how many ewes we got?" Dad asked, not turning from the window. Mom and I were in the kitchen eating pancakes; Katie lay with her rabbit on the floor in front of the TV like she did every Saturday morning. She'd decided to forgive me for hunting claybabies with Mary, and we'd watched the early-morning cartoons together. Jay was still sleeping.

"Thirty," I said. But he knew that as well as I did. I got up and stood next to him. The sun, just risen, cast red light over the field. It lit up the webs strung overnight between the stalks of timothy. The ewes were bunched, asses touching, looking east, ears frozen forward. Their backs were painted pink with daybreak. I followed their gaze. About two hundred yards off, a pair of coyotes hunkered in the grass.

"Get the four-wheeler," Dad said.

I pulled up to the house just as he fired a shot from the back porch. The sound streaked like lightning across the sky. The ewes took off running like a cream-colored stream. They flowed to the southernmost fence line, stopped, veered east, and stopped at the fence again. Dad raised the rifle and fired another shot.

"Did you get them?" I called.

"Just run them off."

He climbed behind me and balanced the rifle between us on his thighs. The heat from the barrel curled up my back. I drove to the spot we saw the coyotes and cut the engine. Not far off, a dark head rose from the grass and flopped back down.

Fluff.

She pawed at the ground and dragged her body toward us, one inch, then another. There wasn't much left of her back half. The coyotes had snagged her belly. Her pearly intestines spilled out like a necklace dropped to the floor.

People think sheep are noisy. They can be. Especially at eight AM when they're used to the grain bucket at seven. But when they're lambing or hurt, they don't make a peep. Parts of Fluff lay all over, but the only sound came from the stalks of bromegrass folding over themselves in the wind. I looked over her body, hollowed-out and purple, her teats torn away and carried off. I didn't understand how she was still breathing.

"She was limping," I said. "I saw her and I forgot."

Dad handed me the rifle. "She's yours."

I thought back to the sale ring. Katie's eyes had begged me to bid. Eight dollars a pound to make her happy and start a herd of my own, a better one than Dad's. Now all that money lay writhing at my feet and Katie's heart would break anyway.

I made an X with Fluff's eyes and ears and aimed right at the center of it. Her body hopped then turned to rubber. A garnet puddle seeped out from under her head. Dad took hold of her back legs and I took the front. We hoisted her body onto the back of the four-wheeler and piled her guts on top. Neither one of us had thought to bring gloves.

He didn't need to tell me where to take her. Every farm had a place for the dead. Ours was the far corner of Croft's Place. There was a pair of sun-bleached jawbones, a junked-out washing machine, and a doorless sedan I used to play in, jerking the peeling steering wheel left and right. A stand of tag alders and chokecherries screened it all from the road, at least in the spring and summer.

As I drove, Fluff's head bobbed heavily at the end of her tapered neck. I slowed mercifully at each dip in the hard-packed track until Dad leaned forward and said: "Let's go, son."

We lifted Fluff off the four-wheeler rack, trying to keep her together as we walked. We arranged her on the hard, threadbare earth. I'd come back with a shovel to bury her later. It was wordless work. In the face of death, we, like sheep, were silent. We wiped our hands on our jeans when we were done.

Katie was on the front steps, pulling apart a leathery milkweed pod, when we got back. She split it with her thumbnail and pried it open, dropping silky parachutes from her fingers so that the wind picked them up and carried them off. There were six more pods on the step next to her.

"Fluff's not in the field." She picked up another pod and worked her nail into its flesh. This one was still green. The seeds were matted and heavy and dropped to the sidewalk around her feet.

It wasn't even nine AM and already her fine yellow hair was slipping out of its braids. Dad squatted in front of her and looped a piece of hair behind her ear. His hand was streaked with gore.

"Well, Katie, I think she run off. The coyotes scared her, and she took off just like a bolt of lightning. Right over the fence. She's probably halfway to Barbeau by now. Trying to join a deer herd or something. They're cousins, you know. Deer and sheep."

Katie studied his face. She was old enough to question this, but young enough to believe it. Then she looked at me, and I couldn't hold her eyes. I stood there, red streaks down the front of my jeans, and said nothing. She split another seedpod and watched the fluffy white seeds drift lazily away, snagging themselves on the lawn.

Dad went into the house, and I went to the barn for the shovel, but when I came out, Katie was waiting for me by the four-wheeler. I felt like a crook caught red-handed, standing there with the shovel in my hand, my jeans stiff with blood.

"Did Fluff run off?"

"Oh, hell, Katie. I don't know. That's what Dad said."

She looked calm, the way she had when I brought Roman home, quietly watching Dad tear me a new one, but I sensed panic inside her, the way the river current still flows beneath the silent ice.

"Do sheep join deer herds?"

I looked to the house. This would have been a good time for Mom or Dad to come out of the house. Even Jay. Anyone. But the door remained closed.

"Katie, just go talk to Dad, OK? I got to do some stuff."

"Where's Fluff!"

I saw the cracks in the ice then, the terror she'd been trying to hide. And I thought about Mary being scared of the sheep and how people were afraid of what they didn't know. It would be better, I thought—maybe it would be better—if she knew the truth. No more fairy tales. No more downstate fields of red-topped clover.

"The coyotes this morning. She got hurt really bad."

"Where is she?"

I stabbed the shovel into the ground. I made my voice gentle. "She's dead, Kate. All right? Fluff died."

"Did they eat her?"

"Some of her."

"Where's the rest?"

"Dad and I took her away."

"Where?"

"Don't worry about it, Katie."

"I want to see her."

"She doesn't look like Fluff anymore."

"I want to see her!" Her fists were tight. Her body as straight and sharp as a blade of grass.

"You won't like it. You won't like what you see."

"I don't care."

I pulled the shovel out of the ground and laid it on the four-wheeler rack.

"Get on," I said.

Red and yellow Indian paintbrushes warmed the edges of the track and the sun drizzled a strange fall heat on our forearms. Katie sat behind me on the four-wheeler with her arms wrapped around my belly. I could feel her bony little chin pressing into my back. Every rut we hit made me wish I'd put her in front.

I stopped the four-wheeler at the ridge just above the gully.

"Wait here," I said.

I walked down to where Fluff lay and carried an old lambing blanket with me. No critters had messed with her yet and it hadn't been long enough for her to bloat or smell. I shook out the blanket and tucked it tightly around her back and over the mess of her haunches and guts. I positioned her front legs over the blanket, so it looked like she was napping on her side, legs out, like you do on a hot summer day. There wasn't anything I could do with the hole in her head.

I headed back up the ridge and waved for Katie to come down. She pulled up buttercups and black-eyed Susans, some goldenrods, and a sprig of Queen Anne's lace as she came. I took her hand and walked with her the rest of the way.

She added some red and white clover to her bouquet and laid it at Fluff's nose.

"All your favorites," she said.

She fiddled with Fluff's ear tag and stroked her glossy black legs. Her shoulders were shaking under her purple T-shirt. She was crying good now, wiping her nose on the backs of her hands and on her kneecaps.

I sat off up the ridge a bit and looked out past Katie and Fluff and the junked-out car. The sun was at its highest point and the sky was empty of every seagull and cloud. In the east, the St. Marys gleamed like a gold-plated thread. I dug my fingers into the damp soil, felt it lodge under my nails.

I'd cried like that over my first show lamb, too, once Charlie went back to his camper and I was alone on the side of the packer truck, looking down at my lamb and all the rest of the show animals. The next Sunday at church, I'd asked the pastor if animals went to heaven. He looked me right in the eyes and told me no. His wife pulled me aside later and quoted scripture to me. "'And I saw heaven opened, and behold a white horse.' That's Revelation, Everett. Now, if God has a horse in heaven, why can't He have a lamb?"

Rosedale Church with its peaked, wood-paneled ceiling, the picture of the Last Supper on the wall, the half-empty pews—I didn't feel God there at all. I looked out the window and saw Him there instead. The wild roses were climbing up the shaded banks of the Charlotte River, the fields were dense and living, bursting with nourishment. Everything out the window was God. The crows spiraling. The sun dripping off the cool green leaves of the lilac bushes. All of it beautiful, and free to anyone who would open their eyes and look.

One of the pastor's sermons stuck with me though. He told us the story of a kid who buried his cat but left the tail sticking out. Every day he'd check on the grave and couldn't resist pulling on that tail, yanking out the cat. The point, I guess, was how hard it was to resist something that was right in front of you.

Katie was sitting quietly, too quietly, looking over Fluff, and it dawned on me what she was thinking.

"Katie, don't you touch that blanket!"

I scrambled to my feet but couldn't reach her before she jerked the blanket off Fluff's body. She screamed through her hands, taking in what I hadn't wanted her to see. The edges of the wound cavity had blackened and shrunk. There were flies. This was not sleep. This was death.

I spun her around and shook her shoulders. Her head bobbled back and forth like Fluff's on the four-wheeler.

"What were you thinking?" I hollered. "You weren't supposed to see that!"

Her cheeks and nose were all wet and she was still holding some clover stalks in her hand.

"You're a liar!" she screamed. "You said she'd be OK!"

She tried pushing away from me, but I had a good hold on her.

"I put that blanket there for a reason."

"You just wanted her for lambs. But I loved her!"

She wrenched away and ran up the ridge. Her braids caught the wind and blew out behind her like kite tails. I watched until her head disappeared over the lip of earth, leaving me and Fluff alone.

Red clovers lay everywhere. I picked one up and plucked out

a few tiny purple flowers with my teeth. The familiar thin, earthy syrup filled my mouth.

I'd wanted Katie to remember Fluff the way she was. Her smooth white hide, slick shorn like suede to the touch. Now she would remember this. I'd bought Fluff, I'd brought her home, I'd done everything to stop this hurt. It wasn't enough. Fluff had needed the herd to protect her. They'd let her down too.

I draped the blanket back over Fluff and sat beside her while the sun moved across the sky and my shadow stretched out farther and farther in front of me. The breeze and the sound of the waving grass wrapped around me. The sky was enormous. I got the shovel off the four-wheeler and dug the grave, but I didn't put her in. Not yet.

There was something I needed to do first.

I took Dad's rifle back to the gully at nightfall. Those coyotes had a taste of Fluff's flesh. They'd be back and I'd be ready for them. I stretched out on my belly at the top of the ridge where I could look down on her body and take aim at anything that came close to it.

The moon was crisp and cool in the empty sky. It washed the land in blues and purples. The katydids, hushed during the day, now emerged with their ratchet wrench of a song and even the St. Marys, shimmering and golden just hours before, looked like a matte track of slate now that the sun was down.

The last time I'd waited around to kill something was last year's deer season. I took Dad's rifle to Mr. King's hunting camp for the weekend. While he and Charlie's uncles were bullshitting and playing In-Between, Charlie and I finished off a bottle of coffee-flavored brandy. There was early snow that year and we left caramel-colored puddles of puke all over the smooth, white ground.

The next morning, I stood on the back steps, sucking on the icy air to soothe my gut. Mr. King clapped me on the shoulder. The smell of fried meat followed him, a smell that normally made my stomach dance. He looked out over the mess we'd made in the yard. "The hell happened back here?" He was laughing, but his eyes were as leaky and red-rimmed as mine. "The best medicine is eggs and venison," he said.

I shook my head. "I'm going to head out to the blind."

A bone-cold breeze combed through the roots of my hair as I walked. It woke me up and made me feel tight and light, like I'd never need to eat again and that I could walk the half mile to the deer blind and just keep on going.

The blind was a plyboard shack hidden in a clump of poplars and Scotch pines. Mr. King had cut a large rectangle out of the wall facing the bait pile. Old Milwaukee cans littered the floor. I sat on an overturned five-gallon bucket, blowing into my fists and listening to my stomach clench and shrink. I loaded a shell in the rifle and aimed at the bait pile. Without warning, my face got pinprick hot. Spit poured into my mouth.

I hustled out of the blind and doubled over, but nothing came, so I rubbed a handful of loose snow over my face and neck. I shivered, hot and cold all at once, and went back into the blind. The tree branches, warming in the sun and shedding the morning frost, made the sound of rain. I closed my eyes for a moment and peered through the pink screens of my eyelids, listening. When I opened them, a spikehorn stood in the middle of the bait pile like he'd just stopped by to say hello. He buried his mouse-colored snout under the layer of snow and browsed the apples.

"Hello to you too."

Silently, I lifted the rifle, eyeing the sweet spot right behind his shoulder. I leaned forward to balance and kicked an Old Milwaukee can. It clattered across the floor of the blind. The little buck leaped but I pulled the trigger anyway and blew a dime-sized hole in his neck. He toppled. Then with that strange dying-animal strength, he bolted a hundred yards away and dropped again. He sat there, drooping, like a little boy nodding off in church, until he couldn't hold up his head anymore.

Blood gurgled out of his neck and steamed up from the snow. His liquid black eye followed me as I approached. I saw myself in it—my pasty skin, the sickle-shaped shadows under my eyes—so I stepped back until the sky filled it again. A single cloud drifted across the eye, then a crow, each wingbeat an effortless escape. Then the eye rolled white, and the sky was gone. I felt the pin-pricks again. The spit. And this time, there was no stopping it.

Fluff's body, stretched out under the bright, moonlit sky, was a different sort of bait pile, and it wasn't long before the coyotes loped out of the gully like shadows. They quivered and danced, never still, circling, circling, until they closed in around her body like a brown whirlwind with yellow eyes and spiky scruff. The larger of the two limped badly. A dark smear of blood ran down its shoulder. Dad had got it after all. But the shot was high. A few inches lower and it would've been dead. I was happy for its suffering.

I nestled the rifle butt into my shoulder. The coyotes' noses were on the barn blanket, lifting it, licking. I pulled back the lever and felt the casing slide into place. There was the tidy sound of a machine doing exactly what it was supposed to do.

I focused my attention on the small coyote. The big one was as good as dead anyway with an injury like that. They had the blanket off now and were tearing at Fluff's back leg, biting, shak-ing, and then slipping away to chew and swallow. I waited till the small one filled the scope and squeezed the trigger. It was easy. I caught it just behind the shoulder and it dropped to the ground, arched its back and stretched its mouth in a wide, final gape. It ran on its side for a moment and then was still. Fluff and the coyote nested like spoons and looked waxen and white under the light-blue spotlight of the moon.

I jogged down the ridge, the rifle in one hand, the shovel in the other. I deepened the hole I'd dug earlier in the day and dragged the coyote inside it. I pulled Fluff on top of it, and the blanket too. A strange grave, the lion and lamb together. In the end, I thought, the dirt gets everything.

Chapter 9

It didn't take Charlie long to find out about me and Mary. Mary told Kylie and Kylie told him.

"It's bullshit you didn't say anything," he hissed. "How long have you been going out?"

"We're not going out."

We were in Dumbfucks English, the remedial class the school put together for seniors to get the credits they needed to graduate.

"Questions, boys?" Ms. Weltzer asked.

Charlie folded his hands on his desk. "I'm good," he said.

"Everett?"

"No, ma'am."

She turned back to her overheads and slid a transparency titled "Coordination and Subordination" onto the projector.

"The independent clause becomes dependent with the addition of just a single word."

Ms. Weltzer was youngish and chubby, with crunchy brown hair as wide as her shoulders. She wore filmy, flowery scarves. Her cardigans were magenta or teal. Everything about her was bright and happy. Even her voice curled up at the end of every sentence and sounded like a grin. But not even she could make the class bearable. The room was in the interior of the school and had no windows. It was carpeted and the drop ceiling was low. All sound was deadened except for the chucking of the second hand of the clock. It was the second-to-last class of the day. Then soil science with Mr. Palinski and I was free.

"I wasn't hiding it."

"Sure seems like it."

"I took a shit this morning. Sorry I forgot to tell you."

"Boys!"

The room was silent. Every eye was on Charlie and me. The projector fan whirred. For once, Ms. Weltzer had everyone's attention.

"Is there something you need to share?" She looked from me to Charlie and back again.

"No," Charlie said. "Everything is peachy."

"Let's try an exercise," Ms. Weltzer said, and the eyes of the class turned back to the screen. She slid a new sheet onto the projector. A list of short sentences. "Which dependent words could you add to these independent clauses to make them dependent?"

No one looked at her. No one spoke. I slumped with my feet out in front of me like two clumps of turned-over sod. I bounced the eraser end of my pencil on the top of the desk. The second hand clunked ahead notch by notch. The heat from the projector filled the room with the smell of Styrofoam thrown into a fire.

"Think of it," she tried again. "A single word that changes everything."

My eyes snapped up at her, so quickly she looked startled.

"Yes, Everett?" She was gleeful. "Do you have an example?"

Everyone looked at me again. Charlie sniggered.

I shook my head. "No."

"Are you sure?" For a long time, she looked at me. Her lips twitched, trying to form words for me. It reminded me of fishing. Coaxing that fish out of the water, not too fast, not too slow. Willing it, more than anything.

"No," I said. "Nothing." Know-nothing. Dumbfucks.

She sighed and turned back to the overhead. The fish had slipped the hook and sunk out of sight. "OK, let's see what happens when we try a word like 'because.'"

The words projected on the screen bled at the edges, swallowed in backlight. Ms. Weltzer's voice blended with the blowing fan and the ticking clock. The smell of heated vinyl made the air thick and warm. Usually, my eyes would get heavy, but today I turned over Ms. Weltzer's question in my mind, marveling at how simple it was.

Mary.

A single word that changes everything.

Charlie didn't stay mad for long. The four of us sat around a bonfire in his backyard that Friday night. He and Kylie were already loaded. The cooler was open and icy, but I didn't reach inside and Mary didn't either. Even then, when it was just the beginning, I wanted every moment with Mary to be sharp and clear, every sensation black and white, bold, slowed down. I wanted to remember everything.

Mary and I perched on logs close to the flames, our knees touching, leaning into the heat because she said it burned away the pig smell. We could hear the hogs in the shed, their grunts bubbling up like air through mud. They could hear us, too, talking right outside the barn walls, and it made them restless. Every once in a while, a sharp squeal shot up through the barn roof and Mary sucked in her breath and looked around. I touched her fingertips. They were stained with drawing charcoal.

“What’ve you been working on?”

“You’ll find out,” she teased, then leaned into my ear. “Why do we have to be so close to the pigs?”

“Does it bug you?”

“Can’t you smell it? I can feel it clinging to me.” She picked up a chunk of her hair and held it under her nose, testing. She dropped it and picked up another.

Honestly, I didn’t smell a thing. I could smell the pigs when we got out of the truck, but after a few breaths, I was used to it. Charlie smell. The smell of the Kings. It was like my brain recognized it, registered it as unpleasant but familiar, even good, and then stopped paying attention. I worried about the sheep, their grease ground into my Carhartt and jeans, their shit in the tread of my boots. I always showered before I saw Mary, but what if it was still on me, clinging, like she said?

Mary studied the hog shed. “At least we can’t see them.”

I nodded like I agreed, but the firepit at my own house was right by the barn. The flames and the chatter, the smell of food, made the ewes curious, and they stretched their necks against the wire fence to get closer. Katie broke pieces of graham cracker off her s’mores and laughed when they nibbled. We didn’t push them away. They were part of us.

Charlie and Kylie were stretched out on the ground, sprawled against each other, looking like a two-headed calf. I couldn’t tell where one body ended and another began, so I focused on the legs. The denim leg that ended in a work boot was Charlie’s; the one that ended in a tennis shoe was Kylie’s. I wanted to be loose and easy like them, how Charlie trailed a lazy finger up and down Kylie’s arm, but I also wanted to slide out from under their gazes, and go back to the time on the bus, before they knew about us, when Mary and I were like two seeds dropped in rich, black soil with nothing to do but grow.

Charlie turned his attention to Mary. "So, Everett finally wore you down, hey?"

She kept her eyes on the flames. "If you say so." She never gave him more than a few syllables in a row. I could tell it drove him nuts, never getting a rise out of her.

I folded her blackened hand in mine. "Nobody wore anybody down," I said.

"Well, if it weren't for me, you wouldn't be together. I had to give Retty a shove in the right direction. Then he put his mind to it. Me, I had my goals. I locked in on Kylie, and next thing you know, boom!" He slapped her thigh. "Of course, I had a little help from my buddy Vulcan here." He kissed his biceps.

"You are such a crock of shit!" The alcohol made Kylie even louder than usual. She sat up and their bodies peeled apart down to the waist. "Like you had anything to do with it. Why do you think I was bringing lunch to the field? For the fun of it? Have I ever done that? In all your years haying for dad? Have I ever brought lunch to the field?" Charlie wouldn't answer, so she turned to Mary. "Mary knows."

We all looked at Mary, and she raised her eyebrows, surprised to be drawn into their argument.

"It's true," she said simply.

But it was all Kylie needed. She turned back to Charlie, triumphant. "See? I locked in on *you*."

Of course we knew she'd never brought us lunch before this year. Mrs. Mason always had, everything arranged neatly in the trunk of her car, including a tub of hot, soapy water for us to wash our hands. This was some game they were playing, each trying to prove who'd wanted the other more, their desire wide open. They were just *saying* it. I looked down at my fingers entwined with Mary's. She was still trained on the fire, the flames flashing against her smooth face, and I wondered if I'd ever know what was going on inside her.

Charlie pulled Kylie back and she shrieked and sank into him again. He scooped her hair away from his face. "All I know is I saw what I wanted, and I got it." He kneaded her hip.

She leaned in about an inch away from his face. Now, they shared even the same head. "So did I," she said.

A hog screamed, high and womanly. Others joined, and the racket lit up the barn. They knew we were outside and they wanted to know why. Pigs were smart like that. Smarter than sheep. I hated looking them in the eye. It felt like something human was staring back.

Mary stood up. "I'll be in the truck."

"Hey, wait up," I said.

"Fancy's too good for the hicks!" Charlie called. His face was painted with firelight. The flames etched his smile deeper, wider. "You be careful, Lindt, or you'll start thinking you are too."

I jogged back to the truck. Mary was already inside, and I got in and closed the door.

"I couldn't listen to him anymore," she said. "I couldn't stand the pigs. It was like any second they would break through the barn walls."

If they did, I'd have helped Charlie get them back in, guiding them with gates, trotting beside them with a hand on their shoulders. Kylie would've helped too, and I was glad for how we were raised, not fearing animals but knowing them.

It was peaceful in the truck, the hogs and Charlie suddenly far away, but her face was still hard, holding on to that anger like her brow was stone and it was carved in. I traced my thumb across her forehead, smoothing one dark eyebrow, then the other. The grooves returned.

"Why do you hate him so much?"

She brushed my hand away.

"He's so in love with himself it makes me sick."

"You just haven't given him a chance." Though I could say the same to him about her. They were like magnetic poles and I was drawn to them both. "I know he loves a lot of things. Kylie for one."

She sat up, her face changed. No more furrows. "He told you that?"

"No, but look how whipped he is. It's embarrassing."

I could still make them out by the firepit, completely horizontal now, shameless. Mary saw them too and I felt something unspoken between us—the knowledge that we were not like them. Not yet anyway. The truck keys were still in my hand and I wanted to get out of there, fill the windshield with a different view. But I waited. I wanted to say or do something bold and raw too, ask her plainly why she was with me that very second, right there in my truck. I wasn't looking for declarations like Charlie's and Kylie's; I just wanted a hint at what was going on behind the planes of her face that she worked so hard to hold in place.

"Mary?"

"Yeah?" She fastened her seat belt and looked up at me, her brows lifted, waiting. It was a chance to say with words how I wanted her just as much as Charlie wanted Kylie. Her eyes were wide, expectant. But I was afraid. Asking meant knowing, and what if she didn't want me as much as I wanted her? So, I laughed it off and held my jacket collar to my nose.

"Do I stink?"

She laughed too and pressed her face into my Carhartt, inhaling dramatically. "I think I'm used to it."

At the end of September, we brought in the ewes from the field to worm them and vaccinate for tetanus, overeating disease, and blackleg. Jay worked the gates, pressing the ewes tight against the barn wall like a wedge of packed snow. They rolled their eyes and moaned because they couldn't move anything else. Curly pressed against his gate and rolled his upper lip, tasting the females in the air. Roman paced, too, adding his bright voice to the din. The noise was maddening. You could torture someone with angry sheep.

Dad and I waded through their bodies, dosing one at a time. I tented the skin behind the ewe's shoulder, slid in the needle with a pop, and pushed the plunger. It was mechanical for me, easy: tip up the bottle, measure the dose, push out the air, and jab in the needle fast, so that she barely felt the penetration. It took three seconds, at the most.

I waved the syringe at Jay. "You want to learn?"

Dad gave his OK and Jay made his way over. I caught another ewe and held her for him. I walked him through drawing up a dose.

"Their skin's tougher than ours. You'll feel a pop."

He tented the skin and held the needle there.

"Go on," I said.

"I don't want to hurt her."

"Oh, for Chrissakes," Dad said. "You won't hurt her. You just got to do it one time. Then it's easy."

I held my hand over his and guided the needle through the skin. I pushed on his thumb and forced the plunger down. The ewe bucked a little and I pulled out the needle. Three seconds.

"See?" I said. I rubbed her shoulder, working the medicine in. Dad handed me the drencher, a syringe fitted with a long metal nozzle. He'd filled it with ivermectin, a clear, bubbly wormer. I held the ewe's nose to the ceiling and pushed the drencher in her mouth and squeezed the liquid down her throat. She gagged and tongued the drencher but had no choice but to swallow. Dad drew a stripe down her back, and Jay pried open the gate to let her into the larger pen. She bolted, coughing, and we moved on to the next ewe.

When they were all striped, Jay slid open the bay door and the ewes ran toward the light. They packed themselves in the corner of the corral, almost as tight as Jay had packed them in the barn, until Dad opened another gate, and they flowed back into the field. Curly was next, which took all three of us. Then Dad opened his pen door and Curly galloped after the ewes like a bloodhound.

"That boy doesn't need a job description," Dad said.

Ram-release day required some backward calculation, beginning with the date of the fair, which was always the last week of August. We wanted the lambs to be at least six months old at the fair, so they needed a February birth date. Any older, they got big and rangy. Any younger, they were under-finished. Then we factored in a five-month gestation. That meant the ewes had to be bred in September.

Curly caught up to the ewes and got right to work, snaking through the herd, picking out who was ready, who wasn't. The three of us leaned over the fence watching. Dad's lower lip bulged with chew. The sky was empty except for the contrail of a single plane. The sun was distilled and pure, forcing our focus down on the sheep and the dirt.

Curly was oblivious to his audience. He'd singled out a ewe in minutes. He walked up on one side of her and lowered his head like, *Well?* He waited. We all did, but she acted like she didn't notice, tearing up mouthfuls of grass, chewing, tearing up more. He crossed to the other side of her and repeated his moves. I wished it were Roman and Fluff, but Roman would spend the fall in the corral and Fluff wasn't getting fertilized by anything but earthworms.

"Everett, you taking notes for Mary?" Jay said.

"Shut up, dipshit."

Dad eyed me. "Who's this?"

"Mary," Jay said.

"Mary who?"

For all the times I longed for Dad's full attention while he studied the shade of the clouds, counted the ewes, or rubbed a lamb dry at three AM, I wanted nothing more just then than for him to go back to watching Curly.

"Williams," I said. "Her dad's Coast Guard. They moved here this summer."

"You like this girl?"

"It's nothing. We're just friends."

Jay coughed "Bullshit!" into his fist.

"Does your mother know?"

"There's nothing to know."

"He takes her to school every morning," Jay said. "He brought her here."

"I swear to God, Jay—"

"Has this been going on long?"

"Couple of weeks, I guess."

I turned back to Curly, but Dad kept his eyes on me. "You be careful, Mr. Big Stuff. You hear me?"

"Dad, yes. Forget it. It's nothing."

Curly rubbed his front leg against the ewe and licked her shoulder. He made a sound like a pop can rattling down the road on a windy day. Then he mounted her.

Chapter 10

In October, you could wake up to find the ground covered in snow as though someone had draped a threadbare cotton sheet over the lawn. But it never stayed. It would be washed away by days of bitter cold rain that would fill the ditches and septic lagoons with light-brown water. Then the sun would come again, and you could let yourself forget, for a few days anyway, that it was late in the year, and that the kind of snow that wasn't washed away by rain was on its way. You let yourself be lied to, lied to yourself, even, turning up your face to the sun, absorbing the weak warmth into your skin, because you knew it would be such a long time before you felt it again, and you desperately wanted it to stay.

As the temperatures dropped and the sun hid more and more, Mary and I spent more time in my truck, driving the long, paved county roads that barely rose or fell, flat as the open fields around us. There was no destination. We just wanted to be together and didn't want to be home.

"If you could go anywhere," she asked, "where would you go?" There were dreams in her throat. By now I was used to this tone: singsong, high. Her favorite thing to do was dream.

She wore a maroon-and-gray flannel shirt. In the morning, when I picked her up, it was buttoned like a jacket, protection against the frigid morning. Now, in the afternoon warmth, it was tied around her waist. She had her feet on the dash. Her Keds were half tattooed now. A wave of interconnecting blocks ran along the soles. The back of the left heel was almost completely colored in. I liked the way she looked, sprawled out, like she owned the place. I reached over and held her knee at that hollowed-out spot around the tendon. It made me giddy, how I could do that, and it barely made her blink. I had access to every part of her. I could pull over right now and park the truck and pull her toward me. She'd let me. And if she wanted, I'd let her.

Mom called it making yourself at home. She said it whenever Charlie came over and threw open the refrigerator doors and rummaged around inside. That's how being with Mary felt. Like there was no hers and no mine. Just my hand on the inside of her thigh and it being so natural she barely noticed.

"Like, if money or school wasn't an issue, no restrictions at all—where would you go?"

"I don't know."

"You don't have someplace you've always wanted to go?"

I shrugged.

"No strings attached," she said. "Where would you go?"

She sat up and leaned toward me, her elbow on the back of the seat, readying herself to extract some wild ambition from me, like Ms. Weltzer begging me to come up with a right answer, or at least try. The sun was big and orange and getting bigger and heavier as we drove. Soon it would be too heavy for the thin cloud netting that seemed to be holding it up. The black line of trees at the horizon was ready to catch it when it fell.

But it wasn't in me. I knew what I wanted. The sheep. The foundation stones. Mary's hand as she stepped across them one by one. What I wanted was here. "Where should I go?"

"I don't know," she said, falling back against the seat, disappointed, just like Ms. Weltzer. The sun flamed in the center of her eyes. "Everybody has someplace."

"I like it here. Right here. Right now. With you."

I tugged at her knee, and she unbuckled and scooted over to the center seat. I lifted my arm and she slid into my side. That was where I liked her best. Curled against me like a kitten, the scent of green apples rising from her hair. Her shoulder jutted into my side. It hurt a little, but not enough for me to say anything or move an inch because everything else felt so right.

"I think you're scared."

I laughed. "Scared of what?"

"Leaving."

"Not wanting to leave isn't the same as being scared to. I know what I want."

"I'm just saying, you could—"

"Why is it so wrong to want to stay?"

"It's not wrong."

"It's what I want. You said yourself you want to go and do what you want. Why is it different for me?"

"It's not. Forget it."

The truck was going fast. I was gripping the steering wheel hard. I took a deep breath and loosened my shoulders. I lifted my foot off the gas a little. The trees had caught the sun and the flames were gone from her eyes. I exhaled, wanting to start over. "What about you?" I looped a ribbon of her hair around my index finger. "Where would you go?"

"California," she said, no hesitation.

"No shit."

"And not just to visit. To stay."

"Why there?"

With a smile, she turned my own words on me. "Because it's what I want."

"But you must have picked it for a reason."

"Art school, I guess. But you know what it really is? A place where I can find myself. All by myself. I'm not even sure I'm that great of an artist."

"You are."

"It's a doorway. And once I walk through it, everything starts."

I understood that. Dumbfucks English. Soil science. Doing the bare minimum until I was free. In that sense, we were alike. One stupid year to get through until our real lives could begin.

I tightened my arm around her. "But we're both here now. I'm glad your dad brought you."

She didn't say anything.

"I mean, aren't you?"

"Yeah," she said. "I am." But she didn't look at me when she said it, and I wasn't sure I believed her.

"Mary?" My voice slid up into Jay territory. I cleared my throat. "Why are you even with me?" Once the words were out, I wanted to swallow them back down, but there was no unsaying them. The tips of my ears burned and I didn't dare look at her. I watched one yellow stripe after another disappear beneath the truck. "I mean, why do you even like me?"

I wasn't in the habit of asking people why they liked me, if they liked me. Mom was a no-brainer. I couldn't leave the house without her yelling out, "Love you!" But the rest of them, Dad and Jay and Katie—all that was automatic, wasn't it? Your family loved you because they were stuck with you. Charlie was stuck with me too. There was hardly a day over the past twelve years when I hadn't heard his voice, hadn't worked beside him, hadn't driven, drunk, or just sat with him. The body got used to things.

I remembered after our old dog Petey died Mom saying, "I miss his head. He was always right here." And she'd moved her hand at her side, and it was like I could see him there, pressed up against her thigh, his blond tail beating the linoleum. Was that love? Or was it habit? Mary was the only one who was with me because she chose to be.

"I'm serious," I said, feeling stupid suddenly, and needing even more for her to tell me she liked me.

She took my right hand, leaving the left to steer, and tilted her chin up to look at me. It was smooth as river stone. Her bangs fell away from her forehead, and I had a hard time watching the road with her looking at me like that.

"I like you because . . ." She held on to each word for a long time, stalling. "I'm afraid you won't like what I say."

I pulled my hand away from her. "You don't have to say anything."

She took it again. "Because I didn't like you at first." It came out in a gush, a hot potato she had to get rid of before it seared her hands. "Like, at all. Hick. Never been anywhere, never going anywhere. The way you let Charlie push you around."

"He doesn't push me around."

"But Kylie was the only person I knew. And then she and Charlie got serious. And I was alone."

"I get it," I said, putting both hands on the wheel. "You're bored."

"Don't put words in my mouth. You asked, now you can listen."

She was right. I closed my mouth.

"When Kylie asked me if I wanted to meet up with you at the fair, I was like, Why not? And there you were with Stacy. But after, when you drove me home, and on the bus, I thought, This guy keeps showing up. You don't know my dad. Or my mom. They don't show up. And that's how it is. It's fine. Really, I can live with it. But all of a sudden it was nice for someone to show up."

I could feel her eyes on me. She took off my baseball cap and threaded her fingers through my hair. Five butterflies nibbling my scalp. It felt electric. "You don't even know you're hot, do you?"

I snorted.

"The muzzle of your face . . ."

"My muzzle? I'm a dog now?"

"It's a portraiture term. See the hollow of your cheeks? The line of your jaw. So strong." Her thumb grazed each part of my face. She twisted the rearview mirror. "I mean, look at you."

"I'm trying to drive."

Her lips were at my ear. "Maybe we should stop driving."

Sometimes I tell myself that if I had been smart, if I had known then what I know now, I would've turned the truck around. I would've taken her to the modular and walked her to her door, turned around, and walked away, taking only that handful of memories with me. But I wasn't as dumb as I'd like to tell myself. I knew everything right from the start. I walked into it eyes wide open and kept right on going. She'd tipped her hand the first day I met her: "Far away from here."

And yet, her knee. Her shoulder. The way she slid in next to me and fit just right. How there were dusty streaks on the dash from her shoes. What's mine is yours and what's yours is mine.

So I said, "Down the road a little ways, there's this spot I think you'll like."

A colorless, abandoned hay barn in the middle of a field on Riverside Drive was all that was left of the Bonner farm. A long dirt track with tufts of grass growing up the center led out to it. It was a massive structure, unused and sagging. We picked our way inside, ducking under cobwebs. Old halters hung from the gray bleached walls.

“Why don’t they use this barn anymore?” Mary asked.

“Pole barns are easier to put up, and cheaper. They don’t rot.” Our own barn was a combination of old and new. Dad had added a metal addition years ago. He stored the tractor and haying equipment there. We called it the shed.

Mary lifted a blue glass canning jar from a window ledge littered with papery fly bodies. The jar looked about a hundred years old. I steamed it with my breath and wiped it on my Carhartt, removing years of dust and fly shit. She held it up to the light and the sun kissed a turquoise jewel of light on her face.

“Can I keep this?”

“Doubt anybody’s looking for it.”

She popped the wire bail clasp. “Cool. I’ll put all your love notes in it.”

“My what?”

“All the ones you’re going to write me.”

“Don’t hold your breath. I got Dumbfucks English for a reason.”

“Don’t say stuff like that.”

“It’s true.”

“It’s not. You’re not dumb. You just explained to me about barns.”

“No one cares about barns. Obviously.” I gestured around us—the rusted tools, the warped wood. I leaned against the wall and played with the ends of her hair.

“Then just tell them to me.”

In junior high, girls passed notes to me to give to Charlie. They would fold lined paper into complicated shapes and shove them in my hand. The girl who had written the note would hide behind her friend, red-faced but brave. Then her friend would say, “Give this to Charlie.” And I would carry back his response. So many intermediaries: the paper, the friend, me, and back again. But Mary wanted no intermediaries. She only wanted my words.

"Dear Mary—" But I stopped. "This is stupid."

"Just try. Please."

I thought for a minute. "Dear Mary, I think you're cute and smart and I'm glad I got stuck on the bus with you. Love, Everett."

She smiled. Her teeth were white in the grimy barn light. "I'll keep that one." She pretended to pluck the words out of the air and stuff them in the jar. She snapped the lid closed. "Give me another one."

"Dear Mary—" I started. The light from the open roof struck her lashes and cast shadow feathers on her cheeks. I kissed the shadows, her lips. I could see my face mirrored in her eyes, dark disks that reflected what they saw.

"Dear Mary," I said. "You're beautiful. Love, Everett."

She reached into the air and caught my words and put them in the jar. She closed the wire clasp.

"That's a good one," she said.

"This way." I started to lead her to a ladder of two-by-fours nailed to the wall, ten feet straight up to the hayloft, but she stopped me.

"Hold on. My turn." She thought for a minute, grinning playfully. I waited like a birthday boy while everyone sings, loving the attention, hating it.

"Dear Everett," she said. "I'm glad it took a week for that truck part to come in." Then her face grew serious. "You see me. Love, Mary."

I didn't have a jar, so I shoved the words in my Carhartt pocket. Then I kissed her, and I wanted to get her in that loft even more.

"Come on."

She watched me climb, her hands on her hips and the Ball jar swinging like a miner's lantern at her side.

"You sure that's safe?"

"I've been up here a million times."

I waited for her at the top and reached under her arms and pulled her up the rest of the way. She set the jar down and looked around. I saw the place through her eyes: the loose, dry hay; the hand-hewn beams strung with pulleys and ropes. Pigeons and sparrows, long used to solitude and silence, swooped from beam to beam, unsettled by our presence. They moved through sheets of sunlight streaming through the shrunken slats.

"It's beautiful," she said.

"Charlie and I used to swing on those ropes and drop in the hay. Jay still comes with his buddy Chase sometimes."

"But they're not coming today, are they?" she asked, tucking her chin coyly, looking up through her lashes.

"No," I said, pulling her close. "Not today."

We lay down on the hay, ignoring the mustiness and how it scratched and poked as we reached under each other's clothes and warmed our fingertips against each other's skin. I kissed her belly.

"Everett, have you brought other girls here?" She had the same expression on her face as when Katie asked me about sheep joining deer herds, wanting to know the truth but scared of it all the same. I was scared to tell her the truth, but I had no other answer to give.

"No, Mary. You're the first."

I'd had the same condom in my wallet for months, and now I rolled it on, hardly believing its time had come.

Her body was like mine. A promise of what it would be. Straight and sharp and needing a little more time and feed. There was no beer this time. It was just me and Mary and the sparrows shuffling above. The sounds we made startled me at first, and I probably did everything wrong, but the whole time she called me *Ev-er-ett*. The only person I knew who said it that way. No rush.

All time and breath. Each syllable lush and promising a future. *Ever, Ever*, over and over.

Her dad's truck was in the driveway when I dropped her off.

"Should I come in?"

"I thought we weren't doing parents."

"We're not. I just don't want him to think I'm not honorable."

"Honorable? Are you kidding me?"

I shrugged.

"It's your funeral."

The kitchen was beige and spare. There was a row of cereal boxes on the mauve laminate counter and a radio near the sink. The floor sagged with each step, and I walked slowly like on an old dock, touching with my toe first, testing. The wind shook the house. The walls hummed.

Her dad sat in a recliner in front of the TV. It was shiny on the arms, and in the dimness, I made out a dark smudge behind his head.

Mary held out her hands to me game show style. "So, Dad, this is Everett."

His eyes were Mary's—no pupil, no iris, just black and swimming. His hair was hers, too, but buzzed, the only military thing about him, as far as I could tell. He was older than Dad, at least ten years, and his pillowy body made him seem even older. The TV flashed green and gold against his face. He didn't turn it off.

I reached out my hand, elbow straight, and looked him in the eye.

"Nice to meet you, Mr. Williams."

He kicked the footrest down but didn't rise or take my hand. He mock-saluted me, then laughed. "You just keep your pants up, kid, and we'll get along just fine."

Curly had caught me in the gut once, a headbutt right to the softest part of my body. Standing there with my hand out, I felt like Curly had done it again.

"Sir, I—"

But that was it. He was done with me. He leaned back in the recliner and the footrest rose. He turned back to the TV. A man was running down a sidewalk, running for his life. His arms and legs pumped like *Looney Tunes*, spinning and getting nowhere. A grin played up the corners of Mr. Williams's mouth, his trigger finger hovered over the remote.

Mary pulled me out of the room, across the saggy kitchen floor, out to the driveway, and back on sturdy ground. I leaned against my truck. The wind, still roaring, cooled my face.

"See? That's why I didn't want to do parents." She saluted the tiny new stars above, laughing. "'You keep your pants up!'"

"Too late," I said simply.

This made her laugh harder. "Too late, Dad!" she shouted at the closed door behind her. "Too late!" The wind carried her words over the yard. Her body shook with laughter and she sat on the steps. She dropped her forehead in her hands. Her hair flowed all around. My impulse was to shush her. I didn't want Mr. Williams to hear, but instead, I sat beside her and watched her give in to the laughter. She toppled into me, vibrating, and I gave in to it too. We were strong and alive, laughing at Mr. Williams, shrugging him off. I felt drunk on the night and the wind and the feel of my body inside of hers, a warm, deep hug that loosened the borders of her and me. I threw back my head and shouted up to the sky. Being with Mary made me feel new.

Sex changed things. Deepened them. Like we'd waded out into the river and kept going until the water covered our heads. Every time I was with Mary, I couldn't get enough. And when I wasn't with her, I couldn't wait until I was. I'd get a hall pass just to walk past her class and see her sitting up front, listening hard, raising her hand. Then I'd go back to my class, sprawl in the back row, shift my eyes from the clock to the door and back again until the bell rang, and I'd slam my book shut and slide out of my seat before it was even done ringing.

I was like a fresh ram tearing through the field humping a ewe's shoulder, chest, whatever he bumped up against. We used her room when her dad was gone, a blanket in the bed of my truck when the weather was mild, the cab of my truck when it wasn't.

"Sit back."

She wedged herself between the steering wheel and me. We started moving in rhythm to the spruce boughs as they bobbed up and down under the weight of heavy white crusts. There was snow then. The kind that stayed. It erased the driveway to the Bonner barn, but I knew it was there. I shifted the truck to four-wheel drive and watched in the rearview mirror as the tire tracks followed us from the road.

I laid my head back against the seat and slid my hands over the smoothness of her back, the sharpness of her shoulder blades. Her hair poured down her back and skimmed my arm. I gathered it all in my hand, a thick, healthy cord, and held her. The instrument panel silhouetted her face with dim green light and put strange, pin-sized sparks of jade in her eyes.

"Oh God, Mary." I touched the damp strands at the nape of her neck.

We rocked, foreheads touching, until she tossed her head back and laughed.

"Roy Mason said he saw your truck out on Riverside. At the old Bonner place."

"Roy Mason needs a hobby."

"What were you doing there?"

"Hanging out."

Dad snorted. His breath rose around his face for a moment before disappearing into the bitter air. "Hanging out? With this Mary girl? You think I'm stupid?"

We were setting up the area where we'd house the ewes over winter. The rams watched us work from opposite sides of the barn. Roman thumped his gate. I'd had to reinforce it once already. He was growing into everything I'd hoped for: showy, proud. He demanded your eye, wanted to be seen, knew that he was beautiful. Each time I looked at him, I saw his lambs: leggy and tight, circling the show ring with their shining bodies shouting, *Look at me, see me.*

"Let me tell you something, big man," Dad said. He fished his Skoal out of his pocket and tucked a pinch in his lower lip. I could have used a dip myself. That metallic taste of a bit lip; molasses and wintergreen and salt. The juices flooded my mouth, and I ran my tongue over my bottom teeth, wanting it.

"Your mother and I used to 'hang out.' Guess what happened?"

I didn't answer.

"Go on. Guess." His spit landed on the barn floor.

But I wouldn't. I couldn't meet his eyes.

He jabbed a finger into my chest. "You. All right? You happened."

I'd done that math a long time ago. It wasn't hard to figure out. They were married in May, just after they graduated; I was born in August.

"So don't come crying to me when you get that girl in trouble. Because you know better. You got that?"

His finger was still in my chest. He poked me, hard. Looking at him was like staring into my own face, my own eyes, only harder at the edges, thickened from years of squinting into the horizon, gauging the height of hay, counting the backs of sheep. I knew already what I would look like at thirty-four.

"I said, you got that?"

"Yes, Dad!"

"I just don't want you making the same mistake I did."

His arm softened and he pulled me toward him in a rough, one-armed hug. His jacket and shirt were open and his collarbone glowed, still brown from the summer. His neck was warm. The smell of him, the mint, the shit. I almost laid my head on his shoulder, I almost cried. But then he straightened his elbow, holding me at arm's length again. The fingers of his leather gloves creaked against each other.

"All right, then."

He carried over a gate and I held it in place while he bent to wire it. We worked under Roman's watchful eye, shoulders touching, hands moving in unison. We didn't need words for this work. Dad had said enough anyway. He'd made a mistake. And that mistake was me.

When the pen was done, I sat in my truck awhile. The heater and radio blasted my face. I took my own can of chew out of the glove compartment and whacked it against my palm a few times, packing it. I took a pinch, a big one. The effect was immediate, the loosening in my arms, the warming of my gut. I rubbed my neck, still feeling Dad's hand there. I leaned against the headrest and closed my eyes. As the nicotine worked its way through my body, I thought about Mary in the hayloft of the Bonner barn, sunlit motes floating around her like gold dust. She was working a timothy flower out of her long black hair. And then I was there, kissing her gilded shoulder, the softest thing I think I'd ever touched.

Winter

Chapter 11

In the second week of December, five feet of snow fell over a three-day period. A record. Sault Ste. Marie was on the news. The snow filled the windows like water rising and made the living room dark. Mom opened the kitchen door to a flat stack of snow filling the doorframe. She took a picture of Katie and her rabbit standing at the door, the snow up to her middle, looking like a shadow with the sunlight and snow sparkle behind her. The yard was smoothed and perfected under the snow, and we crowded around the door of blinding light and tried to understand what we were seeing.

School closed for a week, and the road commission worked nonstop clearing roads. I barely saw Dad. But what was worse was not seeing Mary. I kept myself occupied with moving snow. The first day after the storm, I scraped the driveway down to the gravel with the tractor, pushing the snow into great mountains in the backyard. I spent the second day digging out the barn. When I punctured the tomblike interior with the first streaks of light in two days, the sheep blinked at me, snug and dozing. The hayracks still had plenty of hay and the barn was sealed so tightly with snow, their breath and body heat kept the water from freezing.

Roman called to me.

"Hey boy." I rubbed his back. And because no one else was there, and because I missed the feel of another body, I touched my head to his and stood with him in the stillness until Katie came out looking for me.

"Want to play with me and Jay?"

We dug a tunnel in the base of one of the snow mountains, a spot Katie would use as a fort for the next few months, bringing out cups and ladles from the kitchen, her rabbit and her claybaby collection, turning it into a snowy second home.

The three of us climbed to the top of the snow hill and sat there looking around. Everything was white. The land, the sky. There was no up, no down.

"It looks like we're inside a cloud," Katie said. "Or heaven. This is what heaven would look like."

"Heaven better be warmer," Jay said. He scooped up the snow in his hand and licked it. The skin of his face was red. "I think it's more like a desert. A snow desert. Imagine if you got lost in it."

"You could bury yourself in it," I said. "I heard of people doing that. And sled dogs doing it. The snow insulates you and you can survive like that."

"Bury me," Katie said. She started digging. We hollowed out a basin at the top of the snow mountain and Katie curled up at the bottom of it.

"Now cover me."

We pushed the snow over her red jacket and bibs, a snowsuit Jay and I had both worn years ago. She tucked her face under her arms.

"Do my head."

"Can you breathe?" Jay asked.

"Yeah," came a muffled voice. "Can you see me?"

"No," I said. "Are you warm?"

"Yeah."

We sat quietly and the top of the snow mountain was smooth. It convulsed every once in a while when she moved inside. But we got bored of the game and told her to come out. She burst out with an explosion of snow, her arms wide. She looked around.

"Am I dead?" she asked. "Is this heaven?"

"No," Jay said. "It's Sault Ste. Marie."

We slid down the hill on our asses. Jay found an old sled in the garage and I piled up some snow for a jump. We took turns hitting it, clattering across the driveway, and spilling out inches from the barn wall. The sheep called to us from inside, hearing us, but not seeing.

Eventually, we got cold. We stomped into the house and tracked snow through the door. Mom was home because the credit union was closed. Everything was. She put on the kettle and lined up three mugs on the counter. She spooned hot chocolate mix into them and dropped a fat marshmallow in each. She handed us the steaming mugs and kissed our heads.

"Just look at my babies," she said. "I love you so much."

That night, with Dad home, we made a pretty picture, the five of us sitting around the dinner table, Mom and Dad at the ends and us kids at the sides; me by myself, and Jay and Katie across. The table was full and we took our time eating. The sheep were happy, there was nowhere to go. Jay didn't slink upstairs and pull his headphones on, Katie didn't drift away to the TV, the roads were still too bad to get to Mary's. We all helped clean up and Mom ran water in the sink. Dad squeezed her waist and kissed her temple. Katie crooned, "Oo-oo-oh!" and Dad held Mom while the water warmed.

We talked almost every day, but the roads didn't open up enough for me to get to Mary's until Wednesday.

"Feels like I haven't seen you in forever," I said. We kissed and her face was cold against mine. Seeing her again and the bite in the air energized me.

I squeezed her hand. "Where do you want to go?"

"Anywhere. Way too much quality time with Dad."

The roads were white except for two pitted tracks on either side of the center line where tires and salt had eaten the ice and snow down to the asphalt. We drove past Charlie's and down Mackinaw Trail, witnessing the snow, walls of it pushed away from the road. The closer we got downtown, where the storm had hit hardest, the higher the walls were. We passed a caravan of sand-colored National Guard trucks hauling snow away.

"Buffalo got hit by the same storm," Mary said. "Did you know that? Buffalo and the Sault. Isn't that crazy?"

"The storm followed the water," I said.

The radio was low, but suddenly, Mary turned it up.

"I love this song!" She sang along to "Bohemian Rhapsody," even the high parts, scraping along under the melody, shouting, getting louder instead of higher. "*I don't want to die! I sometimes wish I'd never been born at all!*"

I made a big show of plugging my ears and she sang harder. She was goofy and open. I'd never seen her like that before.

"I danced to a Queen song at a ballet recital in fifth grade," she said when the song was over. "I've loved them ever since."

"Ballet, hey?"

"Yeah, just a few years. But then we moved. Of course."

"I wouldn't mind seeing you in a little tutu."

"OK, Charlie."

"Which song?" I asked.

"'Love of My Life.'"

"Don't know it."

She hummed the beginning, four slow, sad notes. "I saw Mom and Dad dancing to it one time in the kitchen. I can't even remember where we were living. But that was the first time I'd heard Queen. And I picked it for my recital because I thought it would help or something. Like, they would come watch me and hear it and it would remind them of . . . I don't know. You know how kids are. They think they can change things." She squeezed the cuffs of her winter coat and looked out the window. "Kids are stupid."

"Kids can change things," I said. "My mom says that. Her and Dad didn't have an easy start, but she always says whatever good they had between them made—" My voice caught, and I swallowed. "Whatever good they had between them made me." I touched Mary's knee, ran my thumb over the bold outline of a drooping rose. "Whatever good your mom and dad had between them, it made you. And they put that good out in the world."

She pretended to gather my words from the air and put them in her coat pocket, the way she had done with my love notes and the Ball jar.

"You always say the right thing."

"Those are my mom's words."

"What's their story?"

"Mom and Dad's? They were young. Too young."

I didn't say how young. Mom and Dad never talked about it. No one did. Just like no one talked about Grandma and Grandpa Petersen. There were hurts there, like Dad said. No one wanted to bring up hurts. I rubbed my neck, remembering his gloved hand there. Dad said "mistake." Mom said "good." The truth, I thought, was somewhere in the middle.

I changed the subject. "My mom wants to meet you."

Mary sank back against the seat. "We said no parents."

"Just a quick hello. That's all. She's been asking. She's home now."

Mary pulled down the visor and looked at herself in the mirror.

"You're beautiful," I said.

We knocked the snow off our boots and left them by the kitchen door. The air smelled like sugar. Pillows of snow crowded the windows, and the house felt snug and protected from the outside. We hadn't done the tree yet, but signs of the holiday were everywhere: Christmas cards propped on the ledge of the living-room window; a Nativity scene on the coffee table.

Mom's housecoat was dusted with powdered sugar where she'd wiped her hands. Her hair was pulled back in a short ponytail at the base of her neck.

"Mom," I said. "This is Mary."

"I've heard so much about you!"

Mom's smile was enormous. I could tell she wanted to hug Mary or take her hand, embrace her in some way. That was Mom's nature. But Mary held her arms tight at her side, a little wild-eyed and stiff, like a sheep who's caught the first whiff of coyote in the air.

"Hi," she managed, but her smile was thin and didn't use her eyes. She looked around the kitchen—the mixer on the counter, the opened carton of eggs, the spatulas and spoons and baking sheets, rows of Russian tea cakes cooling on sheets of wax paper on the table.

"Oh, it's a mess," Mom said. "I do a cookie exchange each year." She brushed at her housecoat. "Everett, you could have told me you were bringing Mary over."

I popped a tea cake in my mouth and plopped down on a kitchen stool, chewing on the nutty, vanilla cookie, the very taste of Christmas to me. I held one out to Mary, but she shook her head. She perched on the stool next to me.

We watched Mom scoop the pastelike dough out of a mixing bowl and roll it between her palms. Expertly, she filled a new baking sheet with identical, ping-pong-ball-sized tea cakes. She slipped the sheet into the oven and set the timer, then began rolling a batch of cooled tea cakes in powdered sugar, coating them twice.

"What sort of things does your family do for Christmas, Mary?"

"Not too much really."

"Her mom's in Florida," I offered. "Mary's going to see her."

Mom turned to the window, where fresh flakes had started to whirl. "I can't picture a Christmas with no snow. What does your mom do in Florida?"

She was using her credit union voice. The syrupy tone that made customers feel welcome.

"She works at a restaurant. She does everything for them. Waitresses. Cooks. Does books. Bills. Everything. They're open on Christmas. That's our big Christmas tradition, I guess. She brings me home anything I want. I used to try to stay awake until she got home. Now, I just wait for the smell of onions and fryer grease to wake me up."

"You only see her a few weeks a year?" Mom reached across the counter and squeezed my hand. Her grip was strong. "It must be hard, being so far apart. I couldn't imagine not seeing this kid every day."

Mary shifted on the stool. She toyed with the cuffs of her sweatshirt. For a moment, the only sound in the kitchen was the click of the oven, the flakes flicking the windows.

Mary poked my side, mouthed, *Let's go.*

I nodded. "Mom, I got to run Mary home."

"You just got here. We could have tea. Or dinner later."

"My dad's waiting for me," Mary said. And that was the only time I ever heard her lie.

Mom wrapped up a plate of tea cakes and pushed them into Mary's hands. "From our family to yours."

"Sorry about that," I said on the way back to the modular. "All the questions. I know you didn't want to have to meet her."

"You want to know what Mom and I really do on Christmas?"

"Tell me."

"We take the food outside and watch planes. It started when I was little. She told me to look for Rudolph in the sky. She pointed out a plane with a red, flashing light. And then after the divorce, she moved closer to the airport because it was cheap. And even though by then I'd already figured out they were planes, we still lay in the lawn chairs in the backyard, like we were suntanning, only it was night, and watched the sky. We wrap up in blankets if it's cold. We make up stories about where they are going. The big planes are the best because you know they're going the farthest."

When we got to the modular, we kissed until the living-room light snapped on. Mary hurried inside out of the cold. I was already halfway home when I noticed the plate of tea cakes still on the seat. I ate them all so Mom wouldn't know.

Charlie and I climbed on his old twin Yamaha snowmobiles and nosed our way through the gate to his parents' back forty and opened up the engines. We streaked across the field, carving the unmarked drifts, filling the noontime air with the high whine of our exhausts. In the winter, the fields became byways, interconnected by tracks that threaded through open gates or over sagging fence wire, leading from one field to another until we could practically get from one end of Chippewa County to the other without ever touching a paved road.

I leaned to the left and the machine moved like an extension of my body. I dropped down the side of a depression and exploded up the other side. Behind me, Charlie did the same, emerging with a whoop from a spray of white powder.

We crossed onto his neighbor's property and entered a secluded patch behind a line of trees. There were carcasses scattered everywhere, the picked-clean spines of deer, rising up like the backs of fish leaping out of an icy ocean. Coyote hunters had dragged them there. Sometimes, the carcasses themselves hid snares. I motioned for Charlie to move on. We picked up a trail that entered the woods and slowed to a crawl as we maneuvered around stumps, rocks, and fallen trunks. The trail doubled back on itself, like a meandering stream, and spit us out at the opening of another shining field.

Charlie held up a fist; snowmobile for "stop." He lifted his helmet visor. "Gotta take a leak."

I walked with him back into the shelter of the trees. We stood in front of a perfect, untouched drift, dazzling with diamond dust, begging us to piss on it. I tucked my gloves under my arm and unzipped my coat and bibs.

"Shit, that's cold," I said.

Charlie swung his hips and dipped his knees, scrawling K-Y-L-I-E in wavering, yellow strands. He stood back to admire his work. "Dude, check it out."

"Wow, must be love."

"Do Mary."

"I'm out of ammo," I said, zipping back up. I'd drilled a steaming hole in the bank.

We walked back to the sleds. Everything was muted and still. Creamy, clean fibers of cloud stretched across the sky. The pines, with their branches coated in snow, looked like children in white oversize dress shirts, holding out their drooping sleeves. The peace of the place, the stillness, the warmth of our bibs and the cushioned sleepiness of the trees, made us drowsy, and we draped our legs over the taillights, rested our necks on the handlebars, and closed our eyes against the sharp light from the sun and snow.

"I been thinking about Kylie," Charlie said after a while.

"Yeah?"

"I think it's the real deal, man. All that crap I said about senior year—maybe there's more to it."

I rolled my head across the handlebars in his direction. He had my attention.

"It's like, everything's just so good. She's the first thing I think about when I wake up and the last thing before I fall asleep. You know what I mean? Constant. And it's not just me. Mom and Dad like her too. She came over and made cookies with Mom. You know, for the cookie exchange? I go in the kitchen because I'm smelling things and Mom and Kylie are up to their elbows in cookies. Like, trays of them. Frosting and sprinkles and shit everywhere." He propped himself up on his side. "And Mom goes—I shit you not—'I've decided whatever happens between you, we're keeping Kylie. You can live in the hog shed.' Even Mason's warming up to me. Hasn't brought up the bull snips the last few times I was over."

"That's progress there," I said. "You love her?"

He lay back down. "Christ if I know. I'm just saying it's going good right now."

A shelf of snow slid off the pine branches behind me and dropped with muted thuds into the drifts below. We lay in the silence, not ready to budge.

"What about Fancy Pants?"

"She's good." I scooped up a handful of snow and tried to pack a ball, but the snow was dry and disintegrated into icy grains.

"Just good?"

"Yeah, I mean, she's not baking cookies with Mom, but it's going good."

"You still think it's a senior-year thing?"

"What else could it be? She's not sticking around. No sense getting too hung up on her," I said, clapping my mitts together, brushing the snow crystals off my bibs. "Just keeping things light, you know? Keeping things real."

Though all I ever thought about was Mary. The sound of her. The smell of her. God, the feel of her. But I wasn't telling Charlie that. That would only make the thoughts more real, give them bones, put skin on them. And for what? I couldn't make her stay. The best I could hope for was to make her a little less eager to leave.

The cold had worked its way inside my coat and bibs, seeping in at my collar and sliding down my back. My fingertips ached. I kneeled on the machine and gave the pull-start a quick, hard yank. It didn't fire.

"You could always do what my cousin did."

"What's that?"

"Knocked up his girlfriend on purpose. They're married now. Bunch of kids."

"That is the stupidest thing I've ever heard."

I gave the pull-start a few more tries. Nothing.

"She was all wishy-washy about staying together, so he just went ahead and planted that seed. That's what girls all want anyway. They want to sink their claws into you with a kid. Kylie's already talking about ours. I'm serious. But I said that's not happening anytime soon. If you wanted her bad enough, that would change her plans pretty quick."

"She'd die here."

"I'm just saying, it worked for him. Try choking it."

I flipped the choke and yanked the pull-start again. The

engine bubbled and I pumped the throttle to give it life. "You ready?"

He started his machine and we gunned it, bent on shredding the pillowy field, crossing over each other's tracks, hollering, working heat back into our limbs. The field was endless and white. I would write her name here, I decided. Enormous letters carved into the snow, not with piss, but with speed. Acres tall. Legible from the sky but hidden on earth where no one, not even I, could read them. I worked my way across the field, leaning hard to the right at the peaks of the M, whipping the snowmobile around to make the A, easing into the simple, soft blip of the R, and then turning sharply into the first arm of the Y, which would be the hardest letter of all, looping back over itself like the trail in the woods. I squeezed the sled between my knees, and jerked the handlebars to the left, forming the second arm of the Y, and then dropped into a tail that underlined it all. When I was done, I was panting, ready to shed layers, and her name stretched the length of the field.

Chapter 12

The day before she flew to her mom's, Mary and I huddled in my truck outside the modular. Billows of exhaust rose around us. The leafless trees in the distance against Mason's snow-covered fields made the scene look like a black-and-white photo.

"I got you something," I said. I opened the glove box and handed her a thin, square gift, obviously a CD. "A going-away and Christmas present."

A few days before, Charlie and I had gone to Kmart to buy gifts for Kylie and Mary. I had thumbed through the Queen CDs until I found the one with the song I was looking for.

Charlie took it out of my hands and flipped the jewel case over.

"*A Night at the Opera*? What are you getting her this wacky shit for?"

Kylie was getting chocolate-covered cherries and Exclamation! perfume.

"It's got that song from the *Wayne's World* movie," I said. "She'll like it."

At the checkout, the cashier, youngish but no one we knew, smiled to herself as she rang up our orders: the perfume, the chocolates, the CD, and two packs of Trojans.

"Someone's having fun tonight," she said.

Charlie winked at her. "Better safe than sorry."

Mary took her time opening the gift. She studied the cover, the image of what looked like an open Chinese fan flanked by lions with wings, a giant swan hovering over them both, flames, Tinker Bell fairies. If there was meaning in these images, it was lost on me. She read the song list on the back but said nothing.

"I just thought maybe when you're down in Florida, you could play it and start singing and the guys down there would hear you and steer clear." She laughed a little but wouldn't look up. I leaned over her shoulder. "It's got 'Love of My Life.' See?" I said, pointing out the title. "Now I can listen to it too. Now I can know."

She nodded and rubbed her thumbs across the glossy plastic, but still she said nothing, and I worried she would cry. She dipped her head and her hair fell between us, shutting me out. "What did I do wrong, Mary? Tell me."

"Nothing," she said. She tried to say more, but stopped and shook her head, needing time. I waited. Finally, she looked up and tucked her hair behind her ears. "It's sweet. Really. It just surprised me, you know? You were paying attention. Not many people do." She peeled off the wrapper and handed the disc to me. "Can you play it?"

The truck only had a tape deck, so I'd fixed a CD player to the dash with Velcro strips and got a cassette adapter for it. I opened the CD player and waved the Queen CD over the open mouth. "Only if you do your ballet."

"Oh God, I can't remember."

"You want to hear it, you got to dance."

"Fine."

She left the truck door wide open and stood in the middle of the driveway, her arms high above her head, fingers almost touching, feet crossed heel to toe.

"This is fifth position."

I put the CD in the cassette adapter. "Ready?"

"Ready."

I pressed Play and she listened for her cue, nodding her head to the beat. She leapt and spun as the movements came back to her.

"And then I ran in like this," she narrated. "And pliéd." She slipped a little on the snowy drive, weighted down by her winter coat and boots. Color came into her cheeks, and she stopped trying to remember the routine. She just spun, laughing. "Come dance with me!"

I left the truck running and took her in my arms, in that stiff way I'd seen Dad hold Mom at wedding receptions, her right hand in mine, my left hand at the small of her back. We turned together, packing the snow under our feet. Then, I picked her up and twirled her around. Her hair fanned out, collecting the snowflakes in a net of inky silk.

"This song used to always make me feel sad," she said when I set her down. "But now I've got a new memory."

We moved slowly back and forth. Her nose was cold, her lips were cold, her tongue was not.

"I got something for you too," she said. "I made it actually."

She went back to the truck and pulled her sketch pad out of her backpack. She tore out a sheet and held it out to me. The fringed edge waved softly in the bitter air.

"I was going to frame it but—"

"It's Roman."

She nodded, watching me. She'd drawn his head and neck, captured him looking slightly to the side to show off the proud set of his head, the Hampy nap looping down the bridge of his nose and under his eyes. His ears were low and tranquil. I'd only seen the ballpoint doodles on her jeans and shoes and in the margins of her textbooks. This looked professional.

"I worked on it in art class this marking period. It was either Roman or your truck. Hard to tell which one you love more."

"Tough choice," I said. The truth was, I loved her more than them both combined.

I pulled her close, holding out the paper so it wouldn't wrinkle. The truck played the next song, one that was stringy and fast, about a dad's advice for his son to keep good company, and how the son marries a girl but ends up alone anyway. Still, we swayed slowly, kissing. And I tried to shush the countdown in my head that shadowed every moment we were together: seven more months with her, six more months, five.

"You know," she said, "dancing in the driveway is fun, but my dad won't be home for a while."

I laid the drawing of Roman next to the CD player on the dash, turned off the truck, and followed her inside.

Her bedroom was at the very end of the saggy hallway that ran like a spine through the center of the modular. The walls of her room were tan, a color less than a color, and papered with taped-up sketches of pelicans and surf. She had a table next to her spindled white headboard and on it was the blue Ball jar, the brightest thing in the room, maybe the whole house. She'd wreathed it with white Christmas lights and they cast a pool of watery light on the table. The bird-shaped claybaby she'd found at my house was inside.

We crashed into her tiny twin-size bed and crashed into each other because there was nowhere else for our bodies to go. The bed sagged beneath us and shook. The wind streamed around the house. We paused long enough for me to get the condom on and then we crashed into each other again. I kissed her neck, her shoulder. I wrapped my arms—still two-toned from the summer—around her and inhaled the dampness of her body. But it wasn't enough. She'd be gone for two weeks. I wanted to feel her. I wanted to feel everything.

"Mary," I whispered. I could only speak in fragments. "Can I take it off? The condom. I mean, just for a second."

Her face was flushed. She spoke in fragments too. "Only a second."

Sliding my bare dick inside her was like running through a barn with a torch, sparks flying, the dry hay stacked to the ceiling, dying to suck up the flame and burn the whole thing to the ground. I could only stand it for a few seconds. It was too much, white hot. It took every kernel of willpower I had to roll off her and blow it into the wadded sheets.

"Shit, Mary. I'm sorry. I'll clean it up." I lay back and caught my breath. Felt the sweet lick of air circulated by her ceiling fan.

She propped herself on her elbow, grinning, like she enjoyed the effect she'd had on me, but then her face got serious. "Let's not do that again," she said.

"No," I said. "We better not."

But the dazzling knowledge was there. The heat. Skin slick against skin. And I wanted it again and again. So I'd ask for it. Not every time. I knew the birds and the bees. Growing up on a farm there is no way you're ignorant in that department. I'd been keeping Dad's lambing books for five years and tracking which ram bred which ewe, when, where, and predicting birth dates. I waited till her period was over and usually she'd let me. She knew how it worked too. She'd say, "But this is the last time." And I'd say, "Yes, it's the last time." I'd say, "Nothing's going to happen." I'd say, "Trust me."

I thought about Charlie's cousin planting his seed, working his claws into that girl's flesh, keeping her at his side. This was nothing like that, but I understood his motivation: If you wanted something bad enough, you'd do whatever you could to get it.

Charlie threw a big New Year's party at the hunting camp but I stayed home. The thought of standing around the hunting camp at midnight without Mary while everyone else swapped spit kept me away. I'd been a third wheel long enough. We watched Dick Clark on TV like usual. Dad was in his recliner and Mom perched on the arm. Katie and Jay sat on either side of me; Katie kneeling against me, an arm draped loose around my neck; Jay holding a bag of Doritos. The lights were off, and our faces were washed in pale white light. The people in Times Square bristled and waved under the glittering crystal ball, like stalks of hay stretching and bending under the sun. The ball shone in each and every one of our eyes, and we leaned forward, waiting for it to drop. The numbers "1996" sparkled. They looked ten feet tall. When the camera zoomed in, I saw they were covered in row after row of bulbs waiting to burst into light.

Beneath Dick Clark's radio-station voice was the roar of five hundred thousand whistling, screaming people. I felt that roar inside me. A brand-new year yawned, and yet, my chest— It felt like the suck of water that follows a stone heaved into the river. Every second Dick Clark ticked off was one less second I had with Mary.

I lifted Katie's arm from my neck. It was too tight, her little body too warm. I felt pent up and big, like a wild animal. The house was small. My family too close. By now, everyone would be shit-faced at Charlie's party, and I regretted not going. I craved noise, people. I wanted a beer.

"One minute and thirty seconds to 1996. Hold on to your hats!" Dick Clark said.

Dad rubbed his hands together. "We're getting close!"

We stared at the TV, flickering with the flashes of thousands of photos. The ball started its descent, too slow, I thought. It should fall faster. Sixty seconds until the New Year. Katie held a horn to her lips, one that would unroll like a frog's tongue when she blew.

The phone rang, interrupting our trance. We sat up tall, looking at each other. Who would call now? Charlie at the camp, piss drunk? But there was no phone there.

Mom got up. Whoever was calling didn't know her eight PM rule, but they would soon. How many times had I heard her tell a caller, "Are you aware it's after eight PM?" But when she answered, her voice stayed bright. "Yes, dear. He's right here."

Then she held the phone out to me, her eyebrows raised. *Mary*, she mouthed.

The sucking dread turned to elation. A fountain. The change was instantaneous. On this night of all nights, with the whole time zone focused on that goddamned ball, she'd thought of me.

"Thought we could watch the ball drop together. There's not much time."

I heard the giddiness in her voice. I huddled as far from the family as possible while keeping the TV in view. The countdown began. *Ten, nine, eight, seven.* Katie crouched, ready to leap. Awake for her first ball drop. Mom and Dad stood. Even Jay set down the Doritos bag and focused his attention on the shining crystal ball, its awkwardly slow descent.

Mary joined the countdown. "Six, five, four . . ." Mom and Katie and Jay did too. I plugged my room-facing ear to keep out their voices, the TV, the horn. I only wanted to hear Mary. "Three, two, one!"

Mom and Dad kissed, and Jay made a show of gagging and running upstairs. But I watched them for a moment, struck by the familiarity in the way they moved toward each other, Dad's head tilting down, Mom's tilting up, their hands resting at each other's waists. They'd been kids together. That's the thought that came to me. They'd been the same age as me and Mary, and they'd grown up and into each other. They danced to "Auld Lang Syne" in their relaxed, rocking way.

"Happy New Year," Mary said in my ear. "Mwah!"

I pressed my lips into the receiver, a hard substitute for her, and looked around to see if anyone had seen. Mom's head rested on Dad's chest, and they moved in a slow, small circle. Katie danced, too, blowing the horn until her spit softened the paper and it couldn't retract. On a normal day, I would have knocked it out of her mouth. But I had the phone, Mary's kiss in my ear. The knowledge that in all this big, old, wide planet, I was the person she wanted.

"I love you, Mary." My voice was low but sure.

The words slipped out before I even thought to catch them, and then they were there, solid between us. I'd never said them to her before, only felt them. Only said *Love, Everett* in her love-note game. I felt bold for having said them, brave.

I hadn't been worried about her saying the words back. That's not why I said them. I said them because I felt them, and I wanted her to know how I felt. How I missed her. How everything was better when she was around. For once, I just said what I felt. There was freedom in that and simplicity. I didn't need anything in return.

But once they were out, the weight of them struck me. They were big words. A girl had said them to me in ninth grade and I hadn't said them back because they meant something to me and maybe she didn't. A second clicked by, and then another. A whole new countdown.

But then: "I love you too."

A warmth spread through me, starting in my center and seeping into my limbs. A loosening, like tucking in the first pinch of snuff. Three beers, but not four. Not thinking about anything, free of distance and dreams and futures, just feeling, operating in the here and now, laying ourselves bare in a whole new way.

Chapter 13

She came back on a Sunday and I was in her driveway first thing Monday morning to take her to school. Tiny morning stars, just pinpricks in the frosted dark-blue sky, blinked silently. The engine hadn't warmed yet and the clouds of our breath filled the cab. Her hair was wet and stiff in the raw, early air. Hungry for her, I pressed my nose against her neck, and she squealed and squeezed her shoulder to her jaw.

"I missed you," I said.

"I missed you too."

I backed down her driveway, twisting to look over my shoulder, and waited for a plow to pass. It kicked up a wake of sparks as it sliced down the icy road. Grains of salt flew up and popped against my truck as I drove.

"Tell me all about the trip."

She described the house, a tiny bubblegum-pink stucco with a tiled roof supported by decorative white metal columns at the front door; a short driveway of crushed shells and limestone; a hibiscus with enormous red flowers; the shadow of a solitary queen palm playing chase with the sun in the yard.

She described mornings with her toes touching the tide, the waves pulling the sand out from under her feet; how sandpipers crowded the incoming waves, bopped and scurried just beyond the foam and pressed their long, thin beaks into the freshly turned sand; how the surf casters with their twenty-foot-long poles and coolers full of ice made her think of me.

"They haul all their equipment in these little wagons with huge, wide wheels, and rake up sand fleas for bait."

"Sand fleas?"

"These tiny insect crab things in the sand."

"Jesus."

But I liked that she was thinking of me down there on a beach in Florida, more than a thousand miles away, her thoughts pulled north.

The truck was warm now, blowing hot air against our faces, drying the ends of her hair. We were getting close to school. We were early.

"I drew too," she said. "Almost every day."

I parked the truck and left it idling while she pulled a sketchbook out of her backpack and spread it over the dash. She leafed through a few pages, pausing at some and flipping hurriedly past others until she stopped at a sketch of four pelicans gliding just above the water's surface. She used her finger to blend the delicate line of charcoal that formed the crest of a wave.

"I watched this group of pelicans one morning," she said. "They flew in a line, just like they were being pulled along by a thread. They followed the waves all the way down the beach. It looked like they were flying just for fun."

I took the notebook so I could see it better. "Looks like a bunch of seagulls on my windrows."

She snatched the notebook out of my hands. "Only you."

"That's what it looks like!"

She studied the image. "OK, the waves do kind of look like raked hay." She put the sketchbook back in her bag. "Anyway, that was my Christmas. I got fifty bucks from Mom, which I already blew on art stuff."

"Did you do your airplane thing?"

She smiled. "We did."

"You got to wonder where people are going on Christmas Eve," I said. "You'd think they'd want to be home with family."

"Not everyone's family is perfect like yours."

"It's not perfect, trust me."

"Seems it! I mean, your dad teaches you all this stuff. Katie and Jay worship you. And your mom looks at you like she can't even believe you're her son she's so proud. Then there's mine. My mom never really knew what to do with me. Then my parents realized they hated each other—you've met my dad, no surprise there. They stuck it out as long as they could." A parking car illuminated her face for a moment, capturing it in a rectangular glare of headlights. She arranged her face into planes of indifference: chin up, eyes glued ahead. The driver turned off the car and her face slid back into darkness. "Anyway, we're all better off now. They're a thousand miles away from each other and Mom only has to mom a few weeks a year."

"We get ewes like that. Fluff's mom was one. That's why Dad was so mad I bought her."

"What do you mean?"

"They drop their lambs on the barn floor and walk away. The crying doesn't bother them. They've got no mothering instinct."

She sighed. "Not everything is about sheep, Everett." She traced her knee. The inky flowers crept up her thigh. "What do you do with them?"

"With who?"

"The bad ewes."

"Sell them off. You don't want that trait passed on."

We stared ahead for a while, thinking, watching the thin, dry snowflakes fall.

"Maybe it's not their fault," she said quietly. "Maybe you just shouldn't breed them in the first place."

"But they're sheep. That's what they're for. And she made Fluff. Fluff was one of the most beautiful ewes I ever saw."

At the end of January, the barn became the focal point of the entire family. In less than a month, the rafters would ring with the bleating of sixty newborn lambs. We spent weeks preparing for them: The lambing jugs were set up; heat lamps strung; feed bought; buckets washed; lambing kit restocked with clean rags, iodine, nipples, milk replacer, selenium, and ear tags. Mom washed and dried each and every lambing blanket. Roman and Curly watched our activity from pens on opposite sides of the barn. The ewes inhabited the space between.

Close to lambing and in their winter coats, each ewe weighed upward of 250 pounds. Most of them carried twins, some triplets, and their bellies stretched like they'd swallowed basketballs. Their bodies generated so much heat, the air in the barn was so humid and warm that I didn't need my Carhartt.

One of the final tasks before lambing was crutch shearing, clipping away the fleece and shit tags from the ewes' rumps and bellies and udders, anywhere lambs were likely to put their mouths. They would suck away on dirty wool thinking it was a teat and end up with scours.

"Hold her, now," Dad said. "She's jumpy."

He had the clippers at Caroline's twist, that delicate intersection of leg and dock that was prone to nicks and cuts. She shifted her weight and snorted. Sheep didn't like their back ends touched. It stirred an action inside them, a whisper at the base of their ears, something I didn't think people could ever understand: the muscle-deep knowledge that they are prey. Coyotes went for the rear flank or the belly, and even in the steamy safety of the barn, with full stomachs and the snow gusting toothless outside, that fear opened inside Caroline, and she tossed her head and kicked at us as we worked. I tried to imagine Fluff milling with the other ewes, her belly tight and high the way first-time ewes carry their pregnancies, looking like they've got a single when they're actually carrying twins.

Part of me blamed Caroline for Fluff's death. She'd injured her with her ramming, bruised or broken something that slowed Fluff's pace and made her lag the herd. Easy pickings for the coyotes. But I couldn't fault sheep for their nature. Their instinct was to protect the herd and keep outsiders out. There was no one to blame for Fluff getting killed but me.

I crouched near Caroline's shoulders, just as if I were showing her, and placed a hand on her nose. "Easy now," I said. Her eyes were golden with a flat, horizontal slash for an iris. "Just cleaning you up."

I've said all sorts of crazy shit to ewes to get them to calm down, even cuss words, because it didn't really matter what I said, only how I said it. This time, I didn't know why, I started to hum. Four long, sad notes, "Love of My Life," again and again.

Dad looked up from Caroline's back end and shook his head. "You joining a choir?"

But it worked. Caroline rested her jaw on my shoulder, and I felt her mouth working, the cud sliding up and down her gullet. Her breath was warm and damp against my ear, the clippers buzzed, the wool fell away. I ran my hand along her oily fleece, the deep hollows at her hip bones. Already her belly was dropping; she would be one of the first to lamb.

By Valentine's Day, the barn was full of lambs, and I wanted Mary to see them. The ewes had scared her, and so had Roman and Curly—I could understand that; they were big and pushy and loud—but how could she resist the lambs: sweet-smelling and leggy, small, clumsy, and determined. So instead of bringing her to her house after school, I drove home and led her down the snow-packed footpath to the barn. It was dim inside and quiet.

The ewes shuffled slowly around the large open pen; some dozed in the corner. Roman looked up at me and called. I whistled to him, and when I did, a gang of lambs that were old enough to run around on their own but small enough to slip between the rungs on the gate surrounded us, nibbling our pants and butting our legs. Mary backed away from them and held my arm. I picked her up, bridelike, and she looked down at the lambs like they were a frenzy of sharks. Not even they could win her over.

"They're just saying hello." I laughed.

She gripped my Carhartt collar. "Don't put me down!"

It turned me on, saving her from the killer lambs. I felt strong, like I could protect her from anything. "I won't," I said, and kissed her. She relaxed into the kiss and let go of my collar. Her body felt heavier. She touched the side of my face.

"Get a room!"

Katie was sitting cross-legged on the stacked hay, scowling at us, and holding a sleeping lamb in her lap. Its freckled, white ears gave away its lineage: Caroline's.

"What are you doing in here?" I said.

She held a finger to her lips and pointed to a ewe standing by herself in a quiet spot, pawing the ground.

"What's she doing?" Mary whispered.

"Looks like she's lambing," I whispered back.

"Lambing?"

"Having a baby," Katie said, and rolled her eyes.

I set Mary on the hay next to Katie, high and dry and away from the swirling lambs.

"How long has she been at it?" I asked Katie.

"A while."

"Like, a long while?"

Katie shrugged.

"Are we going to sit here and watch?" Mary asked.

"For a minute. I just want to see where she's at."

The ewe lay down and arched her neck, once, twice, and curled her lip. Then she raised her body from the floor, struggling with the weight of her too-big belly, only to lie down again, the joints of her knees folding neatly beneath her. The other ewes, even the rowdy gang of lambs, steered clear, never crossing into the cushion of space that surrounded her.

"Isn't Katie young to be watching this?" Mary asked.

Katie and I looked at each other. The question made no sense.

"You mean birth?"

"Well, yeah."

The ewe stood again and turned so that I could finally get a look at her ass. She had strings of mucus all tangled in her legs. A single, thin black leg protruded from her swollen backside.

"Jesus, Katie, why didn't you say something?"

"I didn't see it!"

I climbed into the pen and Katie dropped the sleepy lamb into Mary's lap and followed after me.

"Try and hold her still," I said. "Hold her like you're showing her. She won't like this."

I tossed my Carhartt on the ground and pushed up my sleeve. Ideally, I would've washed my hands and coated them with Vaseline, but there wasn't time. I just wanted to get the lamb in position as fast as possible. I reached inside the ewe and pushed the lamb's body back far enough so that I could sweep my hand underneath it and bring the other leg forward. The ewe groaned and pushed against Katie. She staggered.

"Talk to her, Katie. Or sing."

She made up a little song with no real melody, just random

notes chosen as she went along, syllables stretched as she saw fit. "*We are all here waiting; waiting here for you. The barn is full of creatures who are waiting to meet you. Curly and Roman and Caroline. The mice and the spiders too. All of them are waiting, waiting here for you.*"

Once I had the lamb's legs and head in the right direction, I pulled its front legs straight down and out. It fell heavily onto the hay, wide and wedge-shaped, just like Curly. Steam whorled up from its slimy, black body and it jerked and kicked and sat up. I wiped away the mucus and afterbirth from its nose and mouth and then the ewe took over, licking and grunting, talking in that strange way ewes have, sort of like a coo, a sound I could never understand how they made, a sound that told the lamb who its mother was. I wiped my glistening hand on my pants and looked over at Mary. She had cradled the little freckled lamb in her arms and was rocking to soothe it back to sleep, which seemed to me even more of a miracle than the newborn lamb at my feet.

On the drive back to her house, she said, "That was crazy back there what you did."

"What, the lamb?"

"Yes, the lamb! You just jumped in there and, I mean, it was really gross, but you saved that lamb's life. And you were so calm about it. I would have been freaking out. I think I'm still freaking out. How did you know to do that?"

It was funny to see her like this, looking at me all starry-eyed, when pulling lambs was something we had to do every winter.

"Just been watching and doing my whole life, I guess. They're supposed to come out front feet first, but sometimes just the head comes out, or one foot like today, or their back feet, or they try coming out butt first. That's the hardest."

"You're unbelievable. You just reached inside a sheep's ass and pulled out a baby, and you act like it's nothing."

"Not her ass, technically."

She got serious. "Will the mom be OK?"

"She'll be good." I'd have to watch her though. I hadn't washed my hands. There hadn't been time, and I'd just reacted. There were antibiotics in the garage fridge, and I'd give her a shot if she started looking low. I took Mary's hand. "You looked good holding that lamb."

"He was sleeping. I can handle sleeping. It's awake and moving that freaks me out. Hey, Everett?"

"Yeah?"

"It was really cool what you did. No one back in Buffalo could've done that. I don't know anyone who could've done that."

"It's normal."

She shook her head. "It's not normal. Nothing about you is normal." Then she turned to me, one foot tucked under her. "I'm going to say something cheesy, all right?" She was bashful suddenly, picking at the laces of her Keds, letting her hair fall forward around her face. Then she looked up. "You're pretty incredible. I just want you to know that."

"Nah."

"Seriously," she said. "I mean it. You're not like anyone I've ever known."

And then she did that thing where she unbuckled and scooted over right next to me. It made it hard to talk for a mile or two. I kept swallowing and blinking and squeezing her hand.

A few days later, there were dead lambs in the kitchen. They were wrapped in a blanket and Katie knelt beside them rubbing their chests, humming, while Mom filled the sink with warm water.

"What happened?" I said.

Mom didn't look up from the sink. "I checked the barn at three AM and there were no lambs. None of the ewes showed any signs. I went back out just before six and these two were lying like bricks of ice on the floor. I had to pry them up with a shovel."

I peered over Katie's shoulder. "Nice-looking lambs."

Like all lambs, their legs and ears were disproportionately long, but you could already tell what a fine pair they would have been.

"They're Janie's," Mom said. "She always has beautiful lambs. Katie, keep rubbing."

Mom lifted one of the dark bodies from the blanket and slid it into the warm bath. She worked its limbs in circular motions, like someone riding a bike.

"Mom," I said, "if they were froze to the floor—"

"Ev, I've seen them come back. You've just got to warm them through. Katie, don't be afraid to rub hard." Mom manipulated the limbs, pressing the hind legs against the belly and relaxing them, curling the front legs up against the chest and out. The kitchen counter was arrayed with a gavage tube, a powdery trail of colostrum replacer, a whisk. Sometimes a little milk in the belly warmed them from the inside out. She shook her head. "I don't know why I waited three hours. It's too long."

I reached into the water and took the lamb from her hands. "Let me do it for a while."

"You got to get to school."

"I got time."

She sat at the table in front of a cup of coffee that no longer steamed. Her eyes were red. Her knuckles were red. She still had her barn boots on.

The lamb was limp and heavy in my hands. I swirled it slowly in the warm water, creating gentle waves that lapped up its neck. The fine black hair on its legs moved with the water. I loosened the frozen afterbirth on its pelt and moved its legs back and forth like Mom had done. The lids of its eyes were open a slit. Unseeing olive eyes.

Dad came in the kitchen, ready for work, carrying an empty coffee cup. He peered over Katie's head at the lamb in the blanket. "What's your mom got you doing now?"

"Warming up lambs," Katie said.

"Doesn't look like it needs any more warming."

She sat back, staring blankly at the motionless body. "Is it dead?"

"Just do it a little longer," I said. She nodded and went back to her work.

"I don't know why I waited three hours," Mom said again.

"You should've got me or Jay up, Mom. We would've gone out."

"Maybe you boys should've gone out without having to be asked," Dad said.

"We'll go out tonight, Mom. Every two hours. I promise."

I laid the lamb next to its twin and folded the quilt over them both. Katie, Dad, and I stood over them, waiting, watching. They looked asleep. They looked peaceful.

"Fluff will take care of them now," Katie said.

"Goddamn sheep are born trying to die," Dad muttered. He straightened. "All right then, I'm off." He filled his coffee cup and kissed Mom's cheek and Katie's head and left.

Mom walked to the sink and let the water drain away. She sprinkled it with Comet and began to scrub.

"It would've been nice if they could've stayed inside her just a while longer," she said. "Just a day or two even. It's going to be warmer tomorrow. If they could have come a little later, it would have been a different story."

I slipped on my boots and Carhartt. I'd carry the bodies out to the barn and toss them on the lamb pile. We'd lost five others already. Usually we didn't lose more than ten. When the weather warmed, coyote hunters would peel off the frozen carcasses one by one and use them for bait. I lifted the blanket and reached for a lamb.

An ear twitched. I waited, not sure if I had made it up. It twitched again. And then the olive eye widened.

"Mom!"

She got up from the table and took the lamb from my arms. Her face was joy. She kissed its glistening nose, inhaled the sweetness of its damp ears.

"You came back!" she said. It blinked deep, wet eyes at her, and she laughed. Katie leapt up and danced. The barn was already filled with dozens of newborn lambs, but this was the one we celebrated.

I was late getting to Mary's. Late, but happy. The lamb had lived. I couldn't wait to tell her. She stood outside the modular in the freezing cold. Her arms were crossed.

"You could've called. I could have taken the bus."

"Sorry," I said. "I had sheep stuff."

"We're going to be late. I know school's not important to you, but it is to me."

"I know. I'm sorry."

"God! Don't say sorry. You've already said that. Just drive. Please."

"I'm sor—"

She stared straight ahead, her face half hidden by hair. I put the truck in drive and drove as fast as the slick roads would let me. When I parked, she scrambled ahead of me over the icy parking lot to the school entrance. Eighteen minutes late. I sat in the truck, watching her go. I wasn't so incredible anymore.

What's funny is that I really thought she was mad about those eighteen minutes. I thought, if I had just gotten her to school on time, then things would have been fine. I thought, if those lambs had just come later, like Mom said, then it would have been a different story.

Chapter 14

It was getting toward the end of March, the time of year just before spring when you thought the winter would never end. You'd get teased with a day in the thirties followed by a day in the teens. An inch of snow would melt one day, another inch would fall the next. Crows would gather on a newly exposed patch of yard, pinching dried dead grass in their beaks for their nests; then the snow roared back, covering everything, and the crows would wait by their unfinished nests, watching the ground. Classmates went away for spring break. They came back with summer arms and faces and told everyone how they couldn't make it through winter if they didn't go on spring break. We never took spring break. Lambing consumed us. Birthing was done but that was only part of it. Sixty-some lambs needed docking, tagging, and vaccines. The ram lambs needed castrating. This weekend, Dad and I would gate off a corner of the large pen for creep feeding, an area where the lambs could learn to eat grain. The vertical openings in the gate were too narrow for the ewes but allowed the lambs to slip inside and eat undisturbed. They napped there too; piled up tight, their necks draped across each other.

I drove to the modular on Friday to pick Mary up for the movies. We'd planned it on the way home from school: I needed a few hours to work on the lambs with Dad; she wanted to get some homework out of the way. I'd pick her up at seven.

There was a truck in the driveway when I got there and it wasn't her dad's. I squinted, not believing what I saw until I pulled up right next to it. It was Charlie's. Mary's bedroom light was on. I saw movement behind the shade. I froze for a minute, torn between peeling out of the driveway and kicking open the front door. How could he do this? How could she do this? The lights were on at Mason's. Was Kylie home? Was she looking across the field to Mary's house while her boyfriend slinked around inside it?

I pictured him in there, telling her how good her drawings were, popping his pecs, smiling. He'd say something to let her know she was special. Then he'd lay her down on her little white bed and do everything better than me. The whole time she'd be thinking, Why have I been wasting my time with Everett? I'd never forget this. I'd never forgive him. Twelve years of friendship—done. I wanted to send him through one of the modular's paper-thin walls.

But then, Mary opened the front door and trotted down the steps. Charlie and Kylie came out behind her. Their breath billowed around them. The bitter air made their eyes shine.

Charlie came up to my window. "What are you creeping out here for?"

I opened my mouth but had no answer. Kylie pulled at his coat and dragged him to his truck. "First one there picks the show!" she shouted. They skidded out of the driveway, his tires pelting the back of my truck with a spray of snow.

Mary got in, laying a dry peck on my cheek before buckling in. She stopped. "What."

"Why'd you invite them?" I said.

"Kylie wanted to hang out. I didn't think it was a big deal."

"I thought we'd be alone."

"We don't have to sit by them."

It'd been eight days since we'd had sex. Not like I was writing it down, but I was used to keeping track of things. My body knew. The last time, we'd had another close call. We'd agreed on some ground rules. If I wanted to do anything without a condom, it was in and out one time, and only during the first few days after her period. Sometimes I could handle it. But there'd been times—and I can't really explain it—when I didn't stop, when I wasn't sure I'd even tried. I was shamefaced and buried my face in her neck, and she'd cried out and pushed me away.

"What were you thinking! How could you do that?"

She'd pulled on her shirt and underwear and locked herself in the hall bathroom. I heard water running, drawers opening and closing.

"It was an accident!" I'd said through the door.

I'd figured that was why she had been keeping her distance. I wouldn't even ask about taking off the condom anymore. It wouldn't even be an option. It was stupid. It was risky. We'd been lucky. I just wanted to hold her and kiss her. I wanted the weight of her in my lap. I leaned toward her. "Well, we're alone now. I don't care about previews, do you?"

That was her cue to unbuckle and scooch over, or invite me inside, but she didn't.

"They'll know what we're doing if we're late," she said.

"So?" Had she forgotten the night of the mud runs, when we'd waited by the campfire while Charlie's camper rocked?

"So, it makes me feel weird," she said.

I started the truck. "Fine."

We got tickets and the girls went into the theater to get seats while Charlie and I waited in line for concessions. It was a good-size line. Lots of classmates and underclassmen. There wasn't much else to do on a Friday night except bowl or rent a movie. Or find someone's garage and drink. I studied the menu. God-damn, popcorn was expensive. I took out my wallet and peeked inside, flipping through the bills as discreetly as possible, to make sure I had enough.

"Need a float?" Charlie said, reaching for his back pocket.

My ears reddened. Chastised, I snapped my wallet closed. "No, I'm good. Thanks, man." He could have ridiculed me, but his first impulse was to help me. Offering to pay for my girlfriend's pop-corn just to save me face, when less than an hour ago I'd wanted to send him through a wall. What the hell was the matter with me? This was Charlie. My best friend. He was an ass, but he was kind. Mary was wrong about him.

Charlie snapped his fingers in my face. "You're mumbling to yourself."

"I wasn't mumbling."

"Dude, your lips were moving. If you need money, I got you covered."

"It's not that." The line inched forward. There were five people ahead of us, a good ten-minute wait. "Let me ask you something. Do you and Kylie ever—" I looked around. I leaned toward him a little and lowered my voice, though the cavernous lobby was crawling with people and their voices bounced off the white walls and shiny floors. A group of junior-highers stood around the air-hockey table. Two little boys got bouncy balls out of the quarter machine and whipped them against the floor. They hit the movie posters, a few people. Their mothers started yelling. No one was paying attention to us. "Do you ever do it without a condom?"

"You're going in without a raincoat?" He was too loud, even for the busy lobby.

"I'm just asking," I hissed. I took a step forward in the line, but he stood square in front of me.

"Did you do something stupid, Ev?"

"It's just a question." I tried to walk past him, but he channeled his show hog Rose, who was packaged now and stacked in someone's freezer, and wouldn't budge. "There's been a few times, all right? But nothing happened."

"Oh my God, you idiot! What are you trying to do, end up like my cousin? 'Cause that's messed up." He put a hand on each of my shoulders. "You do not want to get chained to that girl."

"What's that supposed to mean? 'That girl.'"

"She's a fucking drag, man! It's like talking to a fencepost." He made his voice high and singsong: "'I don't like it here. It stinks. Come on, Everett, let's go.'" Then back to his own voice: "She doesn't belong here."

"You don't know her."

"No, but I know you."

His expression was hard to read. Angry, but soft around the edges. I looked past him. We were next in line and one of the cashiers waved at me. "I can help who's next," she called. I moved toward her.

Charlie grabbed my arm. "Listen, man, all I'm going to say is this," he said. "You do whatever you want, but if you're worried about paying for a fucking bag of movie popcorn, you got no business taking a rubber off."

I shook him off and got Mary's popcorn—extra-large, to prove I could. I found her in the theater seated next to Kylie, which pissed me off even more because she'd said we would sit by ourselves. Charlie came in a few minutes later and sat on the other side of Kylie. So, there we were, the four of us in a row. Me on one end, Charlie on the other, the girls in between.

When I put my arm around Mary, I could feel Kylie's hair brushing my skin, so I put my hand in my lap. A few minutes later, I tried again, but Charlie had his arm around Kylie and my hand brushed his. I jerked away. He looked over and mouthed, *ID-I-OT.* And I didn't look at him again the rest of the movie. I held Mary's hand, that's all. The little boys with the bouncy balls were probably getting more action in their G-movie in the screen next door.

After the movie, Mary's dad's truck was parked in the usual place and the living-room light was on.

Another dry peck. And she closed the truck door and went in the house.

I noticed other things. Small things. When she was in Florida, we'd gotten into a phone routine and stuck with it. We talked almost every night at a quarter to eight. That way, we'd already be on the phone before Mom's eight PM rule kicked in and Mary could wait by the phone and pick up before her dad did. Her number was still in my wallet. I'd never taken it out. I didn't need it. The seven digits were etched on my brain. My thumb punched the numbers automatically. But I liked knowing it was there. The paper was charmed. Like I already knew it was something I'd want to keep forever.

So, the busy signal was weird. A few minutes later, I tried again. Still busy. The high-pitched pulse flashed against my ears. I sat on the couch next to Jay and decided to use the TV as a timer. Two commercials and I'd try her again. I waited, then picked up the phone.

"Ev," Mom said. "It's getting late."

"I know. But we always talk now. She's waiting for me."

I dialed again, slower, intentional, pressing each button all the way down. Maybe I'd dialed it wrong before. Maybe I'd gone too fast. I heard the busy signal before the phone touched my ear. What the hell? Who was she talking to? I sat down again, staring at the TV. I'd wait for the end of the show, I decided. At the end of the show, I'd try once more.

Finally, she picked up.

"Holy! Who were you talking to?"

"Hi, Everett." My name was a sigh, an exhalation. She sounded tired. "That was Jen."

Jen was the only friend from Buffalo she'd ever mentioned. She'd talked about her in the beginning, during one of our bus conversations. Jen had wanted Mary to stay with her senior year.

"It's the least Dad could've done," Mary had said. "Let me finish my last year of high school in peace. Jen's parents were totally OK with it. But no. He said no."

The information had barely registered at the time, but it returned to me now. There was a girl out there who had almost kept Mary from me. A family that would have opened its home to her, made space for her, fed her dinner, washed her laundry. A family that, if not for her dad, had almost had senior year with her instead of me. And now she was calling again.

"What did she want?"

"Nothing much." She didn't offer any more information, and I didn't press her. She was using the voice she used on Charlie. The one that wasted no words. The one that said, *You only get this little bit of me.*

"Listen," she said, "can we just talk tomorrow?"

"Yeah, we can," I said, and hung up. My own version of the voice. If she could use it, I could too.

A new day, a new start. I was early to pick her up on Tuesday. I wouldn't do anything to make her mad. I'd get her to school early, I'd give her space: No walking by her classroom door, no hanging around her locker. I'd give her a day without me. I could tell that's what she wanted. Maybe I wanted space too.

I shuffled from class to class, kept my eyes on the clock. But my brain was on fire. I worried where she was, what she was thinking, if she'd noticed I was leaving her alone, if she cared. And if that wasn't what she wanted, then what the hell was?

Charlie sat across from me at our usual spot in the cafeteria, opposite sides of a long, white table, our lunch trays between us. Since freshman year we'd sat at the same table every day: right near the end of the hot-lunch line, the trash, and the exits, and we usually had the whole thing to ourselves, except when Charlie was with someone, then she'd sit with us too. But Kylie had B lunch with Mary, which meant Charlie and I ate alone every day.

"Have you ever felt like Kylie wanted a break?"

"From what?"

"You, dumbass."

"Why would she want a break from this?"

I stabbed some carrots and green beans with my fork. They tasted like shit. Waxy, lukewarm. They always did. But usually I didn't mind because I was always starving by lunch and, honestly, I'd eat anything. Today, I forced them into my mouth, made myself chew, swallow, because if I didn't, Charlie would know that underneath the smooth surface, my insides were churning.

"Why? What's up?" he asked.

"I don't know how to describe it."

He shrugged. "Well, what do you have, like, two months left with her? It's got to happen sooner or later. Might be sooner."

"Good point," I said, as if he hadn't shrugged away my whole world. It's not like I could blame him. I'd never told him how I really felt about Mary. And even now, with that rabbit waking up, stretching its hocks against my ribs, pushing my innards up in my throat, I wasn't about to tell him. "Maybe it's better this way."

I slammed my chocolate milk. It was the only thing I could trust myself to get down. "Just remembered, I got to do something."

I returned my tray and ducked inside the bathroom by the gym. I closed myself in a stall and sat on the toilet, jeans and all. I held my head on my knees and listened to the blood in my ears. The stall got smaller and smaller. The tiles on the floor got huge. I could see grains of sand caught in the grout. A cold wave spread from the center of my chest and into my arms. It hurt, like someone had taken a shovel to me and scooped out the darkest, richest soil.

Were things ending? Was that what was happening? I thought of what Charlie's cousin had achieved. I should have tried harder. Really gone for it. The close calls and accidents that weren't really accidents. I hadn't wanted her bad enough. Because if I had, we'd have our whole lives together, not just two more months.

When school was over, I waited by her locker as usual. She filled her backpack, and I wound a section of her hair around my index finger and fanned the ends across my lips. How much longer would I be able to do that? We walked side by side to the truck and I slipped my arm around her waist, curling my hand around her belly, wanting to hold her while I still could. She twisted away.

"Cut it out!"

That night, I didn't call.

Chapter 15

Rotary Island is a make-out spot at night, but during the day, it's just a city park on the edge of the St. Marys next to the Sugar Island Ferry dock, where tourists feed French fries to seagulls and watch the freighters glide upbound to the Locks or downbound to the Straits. It was Mary's idea to go there.

I cut the truck ignition and lifted my foot off the brake pedal. Each movement felt weighted, like swimming with a coat on. The temperature inside my truck started to drop and an icy crust climbed up the windows.

"How many weeks late?" I asked.

"Three, I think."

I counted the vehicles loaded on the Sugar Island Ferry. Fifteen cars and four pickups, some pulling trailers. A lot for a Thursday afternoon. When the last vehicle boarded, the deck-hand raised the ramp, but the ferry bobbed in place, unmoving.

Mary nodded upriver. "It's waiting on that freighter."

The vessel approached so slowly, it barely seemed to move.

Curls of blue-black water broke against its bow as it forced its way down the river. I wondered for the thousandth time how something a city block long and full of iron ore could ever float.

"They just opened the shipping channel." She spoke to the windshield, trained her eyes on the mosaic of broken river ice that closed like a curtain around the ship as it passed. "I've always wondered what it would be like to jump from one chunk of ice to the next, on and on, before it sank."

The drivers on the ferry were getting impatient. Some were walking around the deck, smoking, visiting with other passengers despite the frigid air. They all knew each other. Most families had lived on the island for generations.

Two kids in matching knitted mittens and hats tumbled out of the back seat of a Jeep Wagoneer and scurried to the front of the ferry, snaking through rows of cars, climbing up the safety rails, waving at the freighter with all their might. Jay and I used to do that down in Dunbar, standing on the shoreline, killing ourselves hoping the captain way up in the pilothouse would look down and give us a master salute.

The kids dangled over the icy water as the freighter rumbled by.

I wiped the windshield with the sleeve of my Carhartt. "Those stupid kids are going to break their necks."

The freighter's horn split the gray afternoon air. A flock of blackbirds, early migrators, rushed from a leafless maple. Their dark, triangular bodies contrasted against the soft billows of exhaust that drifted south from the steel mill on the Canadian side of the St. Marys. The ship bellowed five times, three long, two short—the master salute. I leaned back in my seat while each blast moved through my body. The boom shook the kids from the safety rails back onto the deck, where they leapt to their feet whooping.

I looked over at Mary. "Three weeks isn't that long, really. Maybe it's something else."

She lifted a finger to the passenger-door window and scratched *3/21/96*—today's date—into the icy layer. The frost collected under her nail and she pressed it against her tongue.

"Maybe." She started etching a heart.

"We had this one ewe," I said, leaning a little closer. "She thought she was bred, we thought she was bred. She bagged up and everything, but she never lambed. It was all in her head." I touched her knee. "Maybe—"

She shoved my hand away. "I'm not a sheep, Everett!"

"I'm sorry, Mary! God, I'm sorry!"

"You're such an asshole!" She turned back to the window, sobbing, pulling in deep breaths that she couldn't seem to exhale. She wrapped her arms around her knees, leaned her forehead against the glass.

"I'm sorry. That was stupid."

I slid over and pulled her into my arms. She pressed her face so close against my neck I could feel her question on my skin before it reached my ears: "What are we going to do?"

But I didn't have an answer. There was only river ice in my chest, heavy, suffocating. I wanted to glide away on an ice floe or sink down into the cool and the wet and not leave even a single ripple behind.

We watched in silence as the freighter passed.

"I don't want anyone to know," she said.

I took her hands, rubbed my thumbs lightly across her silky knuckles. They were getting cold. I kissed them. "We don't have to tell anyone. Not yet."

The deckhands pulled in the lines and the ferry eased away from the dock. The kids with the matching hats and mittens leaned against the rails, watching the freighter disappear around the Point. Their mother stood out of the driver's-side door of the Wagoneer and motioned for them to get back inside.

I turned the key in the ignition and filled the truck cab with the heater blower and the sounds of the radio. I let the truck warm for a few minutes as the ferry made its way across the river. Mary pressed the side of her fist against the frosted window, added five dots. A footprint. Then the heat melted everything away.

We didn't speak on the drive back to the modular. I tried once, but she turned to me with eyes as black and flat as asphalt and said, "Don't."

She walked to the side door with her fists balled in the sleeves of her jacket, the wind lifting her hair like cormorant wings. I should have wrapped my Carhartt around her shoulders or carried her backpack, but my arms lay limp at my side, heavy and underwater again, and she closed the door without looking back at me.

I idled in the driveway as the sun slipped. It was after five and Mom was probably wondering where I was. I shifted into reverse but kept looking at Mary's house, waiting for her face at the door waving me in. But there was no movement, no lights, not even the strobe from her dad's TV. I backed out of the narrow driveway, hedged on each side by drifts tipped like Dairy Queen curlicues, and drove home though I didn't remember seeing stop signs or passing Rosedale Church. My hands moved the wheel and my foot pumped the brakes and gas until I got home. But I didn't go in. I didn't trust my face in front of Mom yet. She would take one look at me and say, "What happened?"

I headed out to the barn instead. I understood now why Dad went there for solace: the ewes never asked what's wrong or where have you been. Their demands were simple: food, shelter, a soothing palm on their heads. They jostled for position at the feed trough when they saw me. I tossed them some fresh hay, then climbed in the pen and rubbed their backs and shoulders as I weaved my way through them. I broke the frozen layer on the water pail.

The lambs filled the space with their bleating. At the noise, Roman lifted his head over his pen, wedging his front hooves into the gate. I slid my hand over his ears and pressed my forehead against his. Then I heard myself talking, not even recognizing the sounds at first: “Hey boy, you hungry?” My mouth moved on its own, remembering things from another life. Each movement was familiar and comforting, as though I were still a boy, as though the world had not just changed forever. And then, I can’t explain it, I smiled. All this time, I’d been worried she hated me, that it was over. But it wasn’t over, it was just beginning.

In the morning, I picked her up as usual. She walked to the truck, and I looked for differences in her. Any sort of sign. Something I alone could see. But in her winter coat and jeans, with her mouth drawn tight and eyes hard, she gave nothing away.

She closed the door firmly behind her. “I meant it when I said I don’t want anyone to know.”

“I know.”

“Not parents or Charlie or Kylie. Especially not them. No one.”

“I know, I know.”

“Everyone will talk about me. I just want to get through graduation. That’s only two months away.”

“OK,” I said.

I waited a moment.

“What then?”

She didn’t answer.

"What then, Mary? What then?"

She looked out the window, watching the houses and trees flick by in the gray morning light. She started to say something and then stopped.

"I don't know," she finally said.

So we said nothing. We did nothing. We coated ourselves in ice, frozen, waiting. And sometimes it seemed as if nothing had happened at all. The lambs grew, the snow melted, Roman got more beautiful every day. Walking down the halls at school, holding Mary's hand, hoisting her heavy backpack over my shoulder, it felt normal. We looked like every other boyfriend and girlfriend in that place and only we felt the ice flowing through our veins.

Spring

Chapter 16

The rains started in April and sandhill cranes dropped from the sky like crumpled paper bags. They took over entire fields as breeding grounds and filled the air with their strange dinosaur cries. Lambing season was over and the just-weaned lambs—fifty-eight had survived—filled one side of the barn with their high, incessant yelps and the ewes filled the other half with low, guttural groans that seeped out of the cracks in the barn siding into the yard where the wind waited to blow them away.

"I make about a thousand dollars a summer haying. And Dad'll get me on at the county this fall. He put in a word for me a long time ago."

I waited for Mary to nod or say something, but she didn't so I just kept going.

"And I called some contractors and told them I was looking for work. They're going to call me if they need an extra pair of hands. That'll pay good. Mason might need me early too. Calving season starts next month. But he'll probably call Charlie first, because of Kylie and all that."

She nodded a little at this but wouldn't look at me. The corner of her mouth was a tiny straight line, stitched up tight against whatever it was she was really thinking. We were in the hayloft of the Bonner barn, leaning against the musty hay, damp with the moisture of melting snow and thawing earth.

"And then Roman's lambs next year. They'll get top dollar. Like, two hundred fifty each, easy." This math I'd been salivating over for months. With ten ewes from Dad, he could easily sire twenty lambs, maybe more. "We can live in town at first, in a little apartment or something. After a while we can buy a place of our own. It'll work out. It'll be fine."

She stared down at the ring I'd given her. The black velvet box was balanced on her flat, open palm. It wasn't a ring I was proud of. I hadn't ever thought much about what kind of a ring I would get when I asked a girl to marry me, but I knew this wasn't it. The stone itself was no more than a chip, something the lady at the Kmart jewelry counter called a star. "You're sure now?" she'd said. "No returns or exchanges." So, before I even showed it to Mary, I said, "This is just for now. I'll get you something better soon. I promise." But at least in the dappled barn light the ring shone. It caught the long, dusty beams and sent them flying.

"Mary?"

She closed the ring box. "You've got it all figured out."

I took her free hand. "I'm just trying to make plans. School's done in a month. And then this fall, this September . . . This isn't just going to go away!"

She jerked her hand away. "You think I don't know that?" Her eyes were hard as cement, but at least she was looking at me.

"Then just talk to me. I'm trying to figure out what to do."

I reached out to her again. Gently this time. One finger at

a time, until her whole hand was in mine. And when she didn't resist, I pulled her closer, until she was in my arms and I held her, as lightly as possible, her hair barely touching my chin, afraid that if I held her any tighter, she would pull away and I never wanted her to do that again.

"Can't we just talk a little, Mary? Please. Just tell me this is right. Tell me this is what you want."

I could feel her shoulders moving with her breath, and slowly her fingers closed around the ring box. It seemed like forever before she spoke. But then at last, she did.

"Just like you said. A little place in town. It'll be fine. It'll work."

Each word worked its way into my chest, loosening the ice that had formed there in March and letting me take breaths I hadn't even known I'd been holding in since then.

"It will work," I said. "It will be good." And at that moment, I really thought it would.

Charlie and I sat at our table in the cafeteria.

"You want to head out to Dunbar after school?" he asked. "Suckers are running. You and me. No chicks. Like old times. A storm's on its way. They'll be biting."

"I got to give Mary a ride."

He leaned forward, serious. "Speaking of, I heard there's a little trouble in paradise."

"What do you mean?"

"You and Fancy. Kylie said there's something up with you guys."

The scooped-out feeling opened up in my chest. She'd been firm about keeping everything a secret till graduation. What had she told Kylie? What had Kylie told Charlie?

"Nothing's going on."

"Mary told her there was some stuff she couldn't talk about yet."

"What stuff?"

"Are you giving her the slip?"

"The slip?"

"You got to do it sooner or later. You can't be hanging on her like some dead weight while she's out in Cali."

I looked at him blankly. How did he know about California?

"What do you mean, Cali?"

"Are you shitting me, Lindt? She's got a bunch of acceptance letters from schools in California. And scholarships. A whole drawer of them."

"There's no way."

"Kylie's seen them. She told me. Art schools by the ocean. You knew this was coming, man. Just quit being a pussy and break it off. Quick and clean. That's the best way, if you ask me."

"That's some rich advice, coming from you."

"What's that supposed to mean?"

"Oh, you forgot? You're supposed to dump Kylie too! But that's right, the same rules don't apply to you. I've finally got something good, someone really special, and it's just eating you alive, isn't it, that I might actually be happy. So now you want me to break things off with Mary. Why? So I can be your sad little sidekick forever."

"You're losing it, man."

I rose out of my seat, leaning on my palms. "Your exact words were, 'I don't want to spend the rest of my life with Kylie, but she'll make senior year more fun!'"

Charlie's attention flicked to something behind me. His golden face turned white. He scrambled to his feet. There was Kylie, holding her lunch tray.

He put on his biggest, brightest smile. "Baby, what are you doing here?"

"My business class is visiting worksites today, so my lunch got moved up. I wanted to surprise you." Her voice was flat, robotic. Her lips barely moved. Her eyes slid to the side and down. "Surprise."

The thing about Kylie was she took up space. Not just her body and curls, but her voice was big, she was bossy. When she was in a room, she pulled everyone's attention to her, like she had her own gravitational force, her own set of physical laws. But now, she looked down at her tray and her shoulders drooped. She looked small.

"Finish what you were saying, Everett," she said. "Say it to my face."

"I wasn't saying anything," I said. "It was nothing." I didn't want her mad at me. If Mary had told her anything, she could tell it to the whole school; she could tell it to Mason and Mason could tell Mom and Dad.

"Is it true?" she asked Charlie. "What Everett said. Is it true?"

"No!" he said. "No."

No. Not so much in response to her question, but in response to the situation. No, he didn't want this to be happening. No, make it stop.

"I thought it was real," she said to herself. She looked like a bird that's flown fast into a pane of glass. She looked up at Charlie. "You said you loved me."

"I do! You know that! This is just a mix-up."

"My sisters warned me. They said you were a player."

"Come on, Ky. It's me. You know me."

He talked smooth and quiet, like someone soothing a wild animal. No sudden moves, no loud noises. But then I saw Mason flashing in Kylie's face. His hard blueberry eyes. His mouth drawn tight and thin. Like when he was about to ream us for the length of our lunch break, or the number of work hours we reported. She straightened up, like something inside her was growing.

"Listen up, everyone!"

The kids at the table next to us turned to watch. Then the kids at the tables next to them turned. It was like dominoes. Kids held their sandwiches mid-bite. Everyone in the hot-lunch line froze. Soon, the whole cafeteria was still. Every set of eyes was glued on Kylie. She turned to the room.

"Consider yourselves warned, people: This guy's a liar!"

She took two steps and smashed her lunch tray against Charlie's chest. Mashed potatoes and gravy slid down the front of his shirt. Tiny bits of chopped carrots and green beans stuck to the mess. Her slab of chicken landed on his boot and left a slimy smear behind. The plate and tray and utensils crashed to the floor. The room erupted in applause. Over the noise, I heard her lean into Charlie and say, "Don't you ever come near me again."

Then she turned to me. Mason incarnate.

"Is it true?" she asked. "For Mary too?"

I looked away.

"You and Charlie deserve each other." She lifted my tray from the table, the uneaten meal glistening and cold, and flipped it onto my shirt.

We walked back to our lockers in our undershirts. The lunch ladies had rinsed out our T-shirts and handed them back to us in knotted plastic shopping bags.

"I'm going to kill you, Lindt," Charlie said, slamming his locker, which was right next to mine since they were assigned alphabetically by class and there was no one between King and Lindt. "I'm going to fix things with Kylie and then I'm going to kill you."

"Let's see you try," I said, stretching out my hands, a wide-open target, dangling the soggy shopping bag from my finger.

"Is that an invitation?"

He came at me like some kind of bighorn sheep, gathering himself into a column, running full force. The impact sent me into the lockers.

We'd fought so often. Younger us, on the floor of his living room, him straddling me, pinning my arms over my head, dangling a string of spit over my face, slurping it up just as it was about to splat. It was play, right? Freshman us, him pushing me under the water in Dunbar and holding me just beneath the plane of air. *Your face, man!* Him and the other kids, hands on their knees, laughing, as I gasped. Older us, in the field with Mary, pulling off my shirt and pointing. *Lookit! Lookit!* He knew better than anyone how to hurt me. And now, now I had this one thing, this one special thing, and he couldn't even let me have that. I was done.

I pushed myself away from the lockers and started to pound him. There was no technique, no strategy, just my fists, his head, and hard. His mouth was a black circle of surprise. My hands were a blur. A lifetime of hurt found release. A lifetime of "It's all good, man." And I was aiming for one thing only. His face. Mashing his nose, his cheekbones. I wanted his eyes swollen shut. His fucking mouth swollen shut.

"Ev! Ev!" He curled his arms around his face to block me, but it didn't matter. There was no stopping me. There just wasn't. I yanked his arms apart and struck. I found his gut, and when he lowered his arms and doubled over, I went right back to his face. Sheep did not fight like this. Men did.

Everything disappeared and nothing hurt. Right hand, left hand, again and again. He slipped to the floor, crying out, "Stop it, stop it!"

But what I heard was *Lookit! Lookit!* and so I hit harder. He wasn't stronger than me. He never had been.

Beautiful Charlie didn't look so beautiful now. There was a

smear of blood under his nose. His skin was stricken and taut. The white blood cells and fluid were building. The horrible swelling I wanted would come. The bell rang. Lunch hour was over. The classroom door down the hall flew open. Soon the halls would be full.

I bent over him, and he flinched when my mouth got close to his untouched ear. I sniffed loudly. "You smell, Charlie." I sniffed again. "Like hog shit."

I tossed my shirt into the bottom of my locker. I would forget it there for the next two weeks and rediscover it, moldy and rank, when I cleaned out my locker the Friday before graduation. I wouldn't open the bag or try to wash it. I'd simply drop it in the trash. I would be a completely different person by then. Maybe I already was.

The storm came at the start of sixth hour. From the windows, we could see the clouds packed like sheep pressing their fleeces together, forming an impenetrable wall of wool.

Mr. Palinski whistled low. "Now, that's a doozy of a thunderhead." He opened his mouth to say more, wanting, I knew, to explain with words like "updraft" and "water vapor" what we were seeing, but instead, he listened with us in silence to the rolls of thunder coming out of the southeast. He raised himself on his toes and peered over our backs, tilting up his head to look through his glasses at the clouds as they climbed on top of each other and turned day into night.

The wind picked up and pushed against the delicate maples newly planted just a week ago in the strip of yard below. Their spare, red leaves whipped and spun away.

Charlie's seat was empty. I pushed up the window and pressed my head against the screen, scanning the parking lot. His truck was gone too. My hands ached, but the air was cool and damp against my skin, like unspooled threads of cloud tangled in my fingers. An enormous drop of rain splashed against my palm. Others speckled the sidewalk; soon they would cover every inch of it.

The bell rang and Mr. Palinski stayed at the window, gazing at the sky. "Careful going home, now, kids," he called to us absently.

I met up with Mary at her locker. She was wearing leggings and her dad's USCG sweatshirt, which she pulled at, lifting it away from her body. She dropped book after book into her backpack.

"You won't blow away with all of that."

"Some people actually study."

She closed her locker and started walking down the hall.

"Wait up." I hurried after her and took the backpack from her shoulder.

Outside, the wind plastered an empty McDonald's bag to the back window of my truck. The air brought the metal smell of storm to my nose.

I placed her backpack on the floor at her feet. She buckled her seat belt. She'd been busy doodling on her leggings, relining and darkening a vining flower that she'd drawn weeks ago. It ran the length of her thigh. She'd added thorns. Drops of blood. The words "Don't Touch." Which was exactly what I wanted to do.

I didn't start the truck right away. I watched the trees bending and the thunderhead roil. I watched the parking lot empty. My knuckles stung. I gripped the steering wheel and they looked like they would crack open. Tiny pricks of blood erupted across the ridge of my right hand. Mary didn't seem to notice.

"Kind of feels like we're the last people left on earth, doesn't it?" I said.

"More like we've been sucked up and dropped here. Are we leaving?"

The letters from the schools in California had been on my

mind since lunch. Maybe she had applied months ago and had simply kept them. Maybe Kylie was confused by what she'd seen. Even I'd gotten some mailers from schools. Glossy postcards with smiling faces: *Apply now! Visit today!* Maybe that's what Kylie had seen.

"Mary?"

"Yes?" Like I was a child she had to be patient with.

"That contractor I was telling you about? He called and said he could use my help in a couple of weeks. He's got some pole barns to put up and can use an extra set of hands. So, that'll be good."

"Yeah, that'll be good," she repeated.

"Mary?"

She turned to me. "Everett! Can we please leave?"

The storm clouds hovered over us, her long black hair was draped over her shoulder, her Jersey eyes looked so pretty. The question was balanced at the tip of my tongue. I held it there, unasked and unanswered. I wanted to hold this last moment of not knowing as long as possible. I wanted to freeze it or stretch it out. Make it last hours or days or years. I wanted to walk around in it, pay attention. But you could only hold things apart for so long. Eventually, they crashed together. It felt like something was dying.

I took her hand. "Charlie said you got into some schools?"

She watched the last vehicle in the parking lot pull away. She didn't seem surprised by the question. Maybe she'd been waiting for it. Maybe she'd shown the acceptance letters to Kylie just so that she'd tell Charlie, so that he'd tell me, so that I'd ask the very question I was asking now.

"I did."

"Like, recently?"

She shrugged. "A few weeks ago."

"Were you going to tell me?"

She lifted her chin. "Probably not."

"I don't get it."

"There's nothing to get."

"I mean, were you going to go?"

She looked out the windshield, splattered lightly with rain. The truck was parked facing north. Across the parking lot, we could see trees, a few houses. There were even more houses beyond our line of vision, Lincoln Elementary, the downtown area, and finally the St. Marys, flowing east and then south, constantly moving, even though we were standing still.

"Because we had a plan, Mary. Me and you and—"

"You had a plan."

"But you agreed. You said you wanted it too."

"I never said it was what I wanted. I never said any of this"—she laid her hands palm up, near her hips, gesturing to her belly—"was what I wanted! All my life I've done what other people want. My mom. My dad. Move here, move there. Stay here. This year was supposed to be the end of that. And then you came along. And it was nice! You were so fucking nice. You paid attention. And for someone like me, that's like candy. That's like crack. And you knew that!"

She pushed open the truck door and climbed out into the brewing storm. Her hair lifted like a cape.

"What are you doing?" I shouted.

"Walking!"

"You can't walk home."

"Watch me!"

She didn't just walk, she ran. She left her backpack and ran. I'm not going to lie; I thought about leaving her there. I wanted to tear out of there and just drive and drive and drive. Straight down Seymour. Straight down Three Mile. Straight down Riverside. Faster than was smart. So fast the truck would lift a little after each rise in the road, and the puddles would fan out like translucent wings readying for flight, and all I would feel was the jamming of my heart muscle against my ribs.

But I couldn't leave her. I got out of the truck and took off after her, not even knowing what I would do when I got to her. I caught the arm of her sweatshirt and pulled her toward me, but she kicked and screamed until we were both on the ground. Her elbows were in my gut and her hair was in my mouth. I'd wanted to hurt Charlie so bad, I'd wanted to crush him. With Mary, I just wanted to hold on. I held on to her tighter than I'd ever held anything.

"But I love you!"

"You don't love me!" she screamed. "You think you do. You want to love someone so hard, but it's not me."

That was when the sky cracked open. The type of sound that makes you look for an uprooted tree or a house split in half. The metal air curled up my nose just as lightning jumped from one cloud sheep to the next. They galloped across the sky, stretching out into thin dark streaks. The rain plastered Mary's hair in two long black ropes. The sleeves of the sweatshirt swallowed her, so that there were only cuffs where her hands should be. The wind pushed against the tiny half-moon of her belly.

"I do love you. I do." The real question came to me then. "Do you?"

She lifted the sweatshirt. Her belly was splotched with green and purple bruises. Some old, some new. Some very new.

"What did you do, Mary!"

She wouldn't answer. She tried to break free, but I wouldn't let go.

"You got to promise me you'll stop that, Mary. You got to promise me. Promise me!"

She didn't meet my eyes. She was wet and limp now. Her voice barely rose above the sound of the rain. "You'd think it could sense it. You'd think it would know."

"What?"

"Kick me. Your boots. I could never hit myself hard enough."

Oh God. I looked up at the sky. Rain poured into my eyes and mouth. The thought of my work boot stomping into her belly. I retched.

"There are things we can do, aren't there, Mary? There's time. We'll figure it out. Now that I know."

Her eyes snapped up at me. "You've always known!" She started struggling again but I held tight. I had her in a bear hug. I had hold of her right wrist. I was squeezing hard, so hard.

"You and Dad are the same," she said. "You only care what you want."

"No, that's not true. I love you, Mary."

"You love this idea of me. Me and your farmhouse. And your stupid sheep. You trapped me!"

"No," I said. "No. That's not true."

She looked me full in the face. Her eyes huge and dark. Her lashes clumped and smeared with rain. "Let me go."

I looked down at my fingers wrapped around her wrist, my arms—hell, my legs—wrapped around her body. Rain blanketed us. This was love? Slowly, I opened my hand. And then I opened my arms.

She pushed away from me and started to walk. She didn't run this time. She didn't look back. The sky cracked again and the rain, energized, fell harder. Water pooled on the pavement, and I sat in it, cold, miserable. Ten, fifteen minutes ago, I knew what lay ahead. I knew every step I was going to take. Now I didn't know a thing. All I could see was rain.

She'd left the truck door wide open, and the seat was soaked. Last summer, I'd made Jay ride backward on his knees because he and Chase had gotten in a water fight and his shorts were wet.

He'd stared out the back window, chin on the headrest like a forlorn pup, because I wouldn't let his soggy ass touch the upholstery. I didn't give two shits about the upholstery now. All I cared about was getting her home. I pulled up beside her and shouted through the open door.

"Get in!"

She kept walking. I rolled along beside her.

"You can't stay out in this," I said. "I'll take you home. I promise."

She studied my face. She was rubbing her wrist.

I parked and slid into the passenger seat. "Here, you drive."

She pulled out of the parking lot onto streets from another world. House windows were dark. Tree branches lay across the roads, there was not another vehicle to be seen, the odd afternoon darkness had not lifted, and the rain beat on the roof of the truck like jackhammers. The wipers couldn't go fast enough. They sheared water off the windshield in sheets. It was strange to be driven in my own truck. Her teeth chattered and I turned up the heat.

"I'm getting an abortion," she said.

I'd never heard anyone say "abortion" before. The word used up all the air in the cab, like how I felt as a kid saying "fuck" for the first time, ducking my head and looking around, waiting for doom.

"How—how do you even get one?"

Mary with her books. Mary sitting in the front of class. Mary using words like "portfolio." Of course she would know. "You can't, really. Not here." She hooked her fingers on the steering wheel, the way when I'd first met her she'd counted off the places she'd lived: "It's hundreds of dollars. There's a twenty-four-hour waiting period. The closest place is Saginaw, and—"

"Saginaw?"

That was three hours away.

She laughed dryly. "And you have to have your parents' permission. That's the icing on the cake."

She pulled into her driveway. The modular heaved in the wind. She put the truck in park, and I stared at the empty living-room window, imagining asking her dad for consent. I'd done exactly what he'd feared I would. And after the choice they'd made in the same situation seventeen years earlier, how could I ask my own mom and dad?

"There's one way though," Mary said. "New York."

"How is that an option?"

"Minors don't need consent. There's a center right in Buffalo."

"How far would that be?"

"Ten hours through Ohio," she said. It made Saginaw sound like a trip to town. "I can stay at Jen's."

Jen. The phone call. It hit me then. "You've been planning this. All along."

She looked away. Her jaw clenched and unclenched. "I'll get the money and I'll go. I'll find a way."

The money from the pole-barn work was weeks away. I thought about all the money I'd spent on that ring. All the money on gasoline and the starter. All the money on Roman and Fluff and feed. I'd done so many stupid things. So many stupid things.

I reached for her and she didn't push me away. I spread my hand over the firm rise of her belly, mindful of the bruises, the layers of tenderness beneath the wet fabric. All of this caused by me.

My voice was thick. "I'll get the money," I said. "I'll sell Roman."

Chapter 17

Mom's car was in the driveway, but not Dad's truck. He would still be clearing roads. The house was slick with rain and the yard glistened under my headlights. The tree swing whipped in the wind, but the lights in the house were on, so I knew we still had power. Lightning washed the sky white; seconds later, thunder bowled through the clouds. I dashed to the barn, straight to Roman. The lambs paced, unsettled by the thunder and lightning, but the ewes were calm, flicking their ears, eyeing me quietly.

Roman weighed as much as me now. There was no more of the puppylike ram lamb in him. He stood on wide-set, bulging rear legs. His chest was deep. He was silent and solid. His pen was cramped, and I thought how nice it would be to get him out in the field once it greened up enough, usually by the first week of June. He'd get the sun on him, he'd breathe the fresh air, he'd run. I could picture it.

But it would never happen. I was losing him. I'd lost Charlie. I was losing Mary.

I shook the gate on its hinges. I kicked it. I looked for something to hit. The stack of hay was closest. I pummeled it, over and over, until the dry stems split my knuckles at last. The blood mixed with the chaff, but it wasn't enough. I kept going until I couldn't raise my fist anymore.

My chest was tight, my breaths shallow and short. I lifted my shoulders, forcing my lungs open, sucking in the pungent, sour mix of wool and ammonia. I couldn't get what I needed from the air. I pressed my thumb under my sternum and tried to inhale. It hurt.

"I'll buy you back. This summer. Once I get more hay money. Whatever it costs me. I'll pay it."

The barn shuddered with a fresh barrage of storm. The lights flickered but stayed on. I backed out of the barn, holding my right hand in the crook of my left arm, and went into the house.

The lid on the Crock-Pot on the counter rattled. I knew I had to be hungry; I hadn't eaten since breakfast, but my stomach was numb. I felt funny. Like maybe I was going to throw up. Or that my hands weren't really attached. I looked down at them to make sure they were there.

Mom's eyes followed me as I hung up my Carhartt. It started dripping on the floor, slowly at first, and then faster as gravity pulled at the water.

"Ev, I've been worried sick."

"I know. I'm sorry. I had to give Mary a ride."

She grabbed a towel from the hall closet to put on the floor under my coat.

"You're soaked. Is everything OK?" She placed a warm hand on my cheek and stroked it with the edge of her thumb. I turned my face into her palm. I wanted her to read my mind, to know everything that was going on without me having to say it. Mostly, I wanted to hug her and breathe in her Downy, lanolin scent.

"Everything's fine." I showed her the best smile that I could.

Then I told my hands to hold the banister and I told my feet to climb one step after the other until I made it upstairs.

Jay was on his bed with his headphones on. He barely looked up as I peeled off my wet clothes and crawled into my bed. I was cold all the way through. I pulled the covers to my chin and closed my eyes and waited for the comforter to do its job.

"Dammit!" Jay said.

I opened my eyes. The room was darker. Silence blanketed the house. No refrigerator, no sump pump, just the wind and rain and thunder.

Jay's face was in my peripheral. "Power's out."

Then he went away, and I heard him run down the stairs. Katie murmured something to Mom. I smelled matches, the same smell as the sky when it cracked overhead. They were lighting candles. Katie always wanted candles when the power was out, even during the day.

Mom called up the stairs. "Ev, we're eating."

A few minutes later, she called up again. "Ev?"

I heard plates. I heard forks. Then, Jay was at my side again, looking down at me.

"You on your period or something?"

"Leave me alone."

He shook my shoulder. "Let's do chores before it gets too dark." I didn't budge. He pulled the comforter off. "I need help! Dad's not home."

I tucked my comforter around my shoulder and gripped it with my good hand.

He pushed on my shoulder. "Mom! Everett won't help!"

I shoved him back on his bed. He tried to come at me, but I grabbed him by the collar and walked him out of the room and into the hall. He stumbled back against Katie's door.

"You're fucking old enough to take care of the sheep!"

"You're nuts!"

I lunged at him, and he ran down the stairs. From the window, I watched him cross the driveway and go into the barn. The wind pushed the grass down in the yard and the rain pelted wet bullets at the house. I lay back down in the bed and pulled the comforter over my head. I stayed in the room all night.

Mom tapped at the door once. "Ev? Are you all right?"

"I just want to sleep." I lay on my side, facing the window with my back to the room, the door, the world.

Eventually, the rain stopped and Jay came back. The darkening sky was lonely and thick. There were no birds. The storm had sent them into hiding. The stars peeked out occasionally from behind the heavy curtain of green-and-purple clouds. Jay put on his pajamas. I felt him standing by my bed for a moment, breathing at my back, but he didn't speak, and I didn't move, and then he slipped into his bed.

Dad came home eventually. I heard his voice curling up the stairs like smoke, familiar, comforting, and I tried to close my mind's eye to the spinning thoughts in my head: the smell of the storm, the branches on the roads, the bruises on Mary's belly.

I lay in bed not sleeping. I saw myself as if from above: a young man lying with his back to the river and his face to the fields. His eyes were wide open, staring out his bedroom window where the slimmest crescent moon carved a spade of light out of the darkness. His brother lay in the bed opposite, slumbering peacefully in close proximity, but worlds and worlds apart.

I was standing in my boxers at the side of my bed before I fully woke up and figured out what was going on. The room was dark except for the thin bars of early dawn at the edges of my window blind. Dad was in our room screaming and I looked for the red numbers of the clock radio but it wasn't there. The power was still out.

Dad grabbed Jay by the arm and yanked him out of bed so hard I thought his spidery, pale arm would break.

"I'm moving!" Jay cried.

Dad turned to me. His lips were drawn back tight over his teeth. "Goddamn rams got out. Get your boots on. Both of you!"

Jay pulled on some socks and sweats and disappeared with Dad down the stairs. I found my undershirt and jeans from yesterday on the floor, still damp, and tugged them on. The door to Katie's room opened and she peered out, wild-haired, holding her rabbit, with her nightgown hitched up in her underwear.

"Why's everyone yelling?"

"The sheep." I was halfway down the stairs. "Just go back to bed."

The tongues of my work boots flapped clumsily as I followed Dad and Jay into the cold, wet dawn.

The wind was still up and there were slick, black tree limbs in the yard and swollen brown puddles in the drive, still reflecting moonlight. Dad's truck was idling by the house. The headlights carved grainy cones out of the murky morning light. Jay rubbed his arm as he ran.

There was no light in the barn, just the watered-down glow trickling in through the dust-and-fly-shit-covered windows. Out of habit, I reached out and flipped the light switch. My hand brushed a grand champion photo pinned to the wall and it fluttered to the ground. But there was no light, only the shadowy movement of the sheep catching slivers of morning light on their eyes and noses.

I felt a hand on my shoulder; it was Mom in her housecoat and barn boots, carrying a flashlight. She switched it on and swept the beam over the scene: ripped-open feed bags and torn bales of hay. The pens were trampled. The ewes were swirling, damn near running, in circles. The lambs moved around them loosely, hyped by the commotion and seeking half-forgotten teats. And something else too: Curly prowled among them, sniffing, pushing up behind the ewes. His nostrils flared and he moved through the creamy bodies like a dorsal fin. There were flecks of foam at the corners of his mouth. Where was Roman?

Dad slammed his hands against the gate. "Dammit!" The sheep dashed to the other side of the barn and bunched in the corner. Curly barely looked in our direction. He circled a ewe and nudged her, watched her with head high and lips curled, nudged her again, then mounted her.

Mom sucked in her breath. "Oh, Everett."

My eyes followed the flashlight beam. Roman lay prone in the yellow oval of light it cast. The lambs eddied around him, sidestepping his legs.

"What the hell?" I took Mom's flashlight and climbed the gate.

I could tell he was dead even before I lifted his chin with the toe of my boot. It dropped to the ground, heavy and loose. His poll was split and bloodied, and his neck was folded and bulging in the wrong places. Already his eyes looked like cloudy balls of ice.

I hooked my hands behind my head and stared down at his perfectly straight top and heavy legs, the fancy shag scalloping down his hocks. I doubled over. Then squatted because I could no longer stand.

"Is he dead?" Mom asked.

All I could do was nod. I couldn't speak. I couldn't breathe. I opened and closed my hand, aware suddenly that it was throbbing. Yesterday's details flooded back: Mary, Charlie, how I'd punched the hay, kicked the gate. Outside, the wind raged.

Caroline stepped out of the cluster of ewes, tall and ghostly in the hazy, damp air. She moved closer until I could hear her teeth grinding and could see her pink tongue flick over her nose. There were streaks of dirt and shit on her back. Curly had been there.

She scratched her forehead against my thigh and held it there, expecting me to rub her ears or cup her chin in my hand. I pushed her away but she stood there stupidly, waiting, sliding her jaw left to right. Her long bones. Low-set neck. The dopey cap of wool that hung in her eyes. I hated her.

"Fucking sheep!" I stuck my heel in her hip and kicked her away. She stumbled as she ran off, returning to the crowd of ewes in the corner, burying herself in the safety of their many bodies.

"Everett!" Mom said.

I turned around. Jay was halfway up the fence, ready to drop over and come look at Roman. "You stupid little shit!" In two strides, I was at the fence jerking him down. He locked his wiry legs between the metal rungs, but I pulled him off and shoved him into the ground. His boots came off with him.

"You let them out!" I growled, pinning him. "On purpose! Didn't you!" I could feel his puny collarbone shift and bend beneath my hands as I pushed into him.

"No, I didn't! I told you to help!" He was crying, which was what I wanted. Somebody should be crying, with Roman flat on the ground, legs stiff as fenceposts, and half the ewes with hoofmarks on their backs. He grabbed my wrists, trying to get me to let go, but I slammed him down again.

"You're going to pay me back for him! Every red cent!"

"Get off!"

Dad cuffed me on the back of the head. I hadn't even noticed him climbing into the pen.

"What the hell's the matter with you?"

Jay rolled away and clambered back over the fence. His socks were ruined and there was shit all over his back. Mom brushed him off. His face was red and wet, and I envied him for it, how he could show her that hot sadness. She touched his cheek, the way she'd touched mine last night, and he leaned greedily into the gauzy blue warmth of her housecoat, leaving smears of snot and dirt behind.

"He came out here by himself last night," I said. "And now look!"

"You should've helped!" Jay screamed, looking out from Mom's arms, his voice breaking into registers I could no longer reach.

"Enough!" Dad said. "We've got to get that son of a bitch out of there. He's done enough damage."

It took all four of us to separate Curly. Dad leaning on the halter rope, me leading his head, Mom twisting his dock, and Jay kneeing his ass. I held a new gate in place while Dad wired it tightly. We stood up the ewe and lamb pens and divided them again.

Dad looked down at Roman. It was too early for a chew, but I could see him working his lower lip out of habit. "His neck's broke," Dad said, squatting down next to him and running his hand over his body. "He didn't last too long against Curly, I bet." He stood and put a hand on my shoulder. "It's a gamble, son. Don't I know it. You put everything into these animals—your money, your hopes, your time. Everything. But they're just animals. And you might not want to hear this now, but you'll have more, all right? You'll get another ram. You'll have more ewes. You'll have more lambs than you can ever imagine." He grabbed Roman's front hooves and started dragging him. "Get his back legs. I'll help you get him in the loader."

We heaved him into the tractor bucket and his body rolled over on its back, legs pointing to the sky.

"I'm sorry, Ev," Mom said. "You had such big plans."

She was standing at the barn door with her arm draped around Jay's shoulders. The corners of her eyes were pinched with too little sleep and her housecoat was streaked with dark smudges, just like Caroline's back. The sun wasn't even a fingertip over the horizon and already there was too much in this day.

I drove the tractor out to the gully with Roman's body jostling in the half-raised bucket, like an offering to the roaring, storm-swept sky. The horizon buckled under the weight of the clouds. Sugar Island's dark-gray tree line was blurred and squashed, and I couldn't tell where the sky ended and our wide, flat field began. If I turned around, I was afraid the house and the barn would be gone. Each tire rotation brought me closer and closer to oblivion.

The track was pitted from the snow thaw, and Roman's legs knocked against the lip of the bucket at each dip, so I took my time, throttling down into the ruts and holes as the mud sucked at the tires.

Just as I reached the ridge, a needly, sideways rain picked up, pelting my back and plastering my T-shirt to my skin. I hunched over the steering wheel, hollow and cold, wishing I'd thought to grab my Carhartt before I left. I paused for a minute before tipping down into the gully. The car frame and washing machine, flaking and brown, had settled down into the earth a few more inches over the winter. The outlines of Fluff's grave were still visible.

I thought about the afternoon I brought Roman home. Katie had giggled because she expected something bigger. *Just wait till you see him and Fluff's lambs*, I had told her.

But he's still a baby, she had said, letting him nibble her outstretched fingers.

Next year, I'd said. *You just wait.*

I set Roman's body gently on top of Fluff's grave and I used the loader to slice open the earth and scoop out one for him. I slid him inside and covered him over.

"Together at last," I said, and cracked up a little. How would I get the money now? How could I tell Mary? Nothing made sense. I was shaking. I wrapped my arms around myself and felt the slick gooseflesh on my arms. My teeth knocked against each other. I was colder than I'd ever been.

Crows croaked like mad frogs as they watched me leave the gully. They clung to the flimsy tops of the chokecherries that ringed the field. The sideways rain battered the trees and bent them, threatening to tear off the hazy green dusting of spring's first buds.

Katie was standing in a puddle in the middle of the driveway when I got back, looking like she was standing on a shiny plate of clouds. Strings of wet yellow hair hung out of the hood of her purple raincoat and down her chest. The hem of her nightgown peeked out from under her raincoat just above her knees.

"School's canceled," she said.

"I figured."

She stepped out of the puddle, pulling up blooms of sand and dirt with the heels of her boots. The rain had let up and, without warning, the sun cracked open like an egg, dripping coral and gold over the heavy clouds in the east.

"Look at that!" she said, smiling up at the gold-leafed clouds.

I turned, still shivering, and stared with her while the clouds unfolded to make room for the morning sun, stretching clear across the sky, yolk-colored and new. It painted both of our faces in warm, rose-gold light. I rubbed my arms trying to work the fat beams into my skin.

"You hear about Roman?"

She nodded. "Did you put him by Fluff?"

"Yeah."

She crouched over an earthworm. "Why do they do that?" There were dozens of worms on the ground, pulling themselves over the gleaming gravel driveway. "They just get squished or dried up."

I bent next to her with my hands on my knees. “Mr. Palinski was just talking about this. I always thought it was so they wouldn’t drown in the rain, but he said when the ground is wet like this, they can move faster.”

“Where do they go?”

I shrugged. “Someplace new. Someplace better.”

We watched them bunch and stretch across the gravel, achingly slow. She picked one up that was already starting to stiffen up and launched it into the yard.

“That one moved real fast,” I said.

She bent her head back and laughed and her hood flopped back over her shoulders. Her little wet teeth shone in the morning sun.

“Is Mom inside still?”

“She’s getting ready for work.”

I left Katie in the driveway and went into the house. I could hear Mom in the downstairs bathroom. The door was open and the room was dim because of the power still being out. Already she had changed, freshened her hair, shoved the housecoat into the laundry basket. It was like the morning hadn’t happened. I watched while she lined her lashes. When I was little, I’d sat on the counter between her and Dad almost every morning while he shaved and she put on her makeup.

“Hey, baby,” she said to my reflection in the mirror. “Are you doing OK?”

“Been better.”

She stretched out her right eyelid and drew a perfect black line. “He was a beautiful ram,” she said. “You took excellent care of him. And Dad would probably never tell you, but he was just as eager to see how those lambs would turn out. He’s very proud of you.”

"Yeah, right."

"He is! And I am too. And all this means is that you try again, OK? That's what you do."

I nodded, and she stretched out her left eyelid.

"Dad wants you to go to Dr. Cavender's today and tell him what happened. Or call him if the power comes back on. Dad's worried about early breeding."

"I will." I pressed my thumbnail into the doorframe. "Mom?"

"Yeah, hon?" She looked at me again briefly through the mirror.

"Are you happy you married Dad?"

She set the pencil down and turned away from the mirror, looking at me directly. "What kind of a question is that?"

"I mean, did you ever have other plans? Did you ever want to live somewhere else or work somewhere else? Go away to college?"

"I did go to college."

And that was true. Class by class, semester by semester, she had finished a business degree at Lake State. There was a picture of us side by side on the couch: me, holding up my first report card; her, holding up a certificate for the dean's list.

"But, like, away for college. A big school or something. So you didn't have to take care of lambs or get shit on your shoes. Did you and Dad ever talk about not being together? Did you ever—"

She brushed a piece of hair behind my ear. "What's on your mind, baby? Is this about Mary? What she wants to do?"

Mary's pregnant! The words flashed in my mind. I saw them bold and in neon, blinking. With exclamation marks. I could almost hear myself saying them. Mom, of all people, would understand. She would hug me, she could help. But my mouth wouldn't make the words. Because she would also cry. She would be so sad. She would say that I of all people knew better.

I looked away, but she held my shoulders and made me look in her eyes.

"Everett, I have everything I ever wanted. I just had to go about it in a little different way, but if I'd have done things differently, I wouldn't have you. I wouldn't have your brother or sister or your dad. This house. My job at the credit union or my friends there. Everything works out, honey, and you make your happiness. You do your best with what you've got. And you just keep going, every day."

It was what I wanted to hear. That her life was exactly how she'd always wanted it to be. She would never change a thing. It was the story she wanted to believe; it was the story she wanted me to believe. Dad, in his way, was honest at least. He'd made a mistake and he didn't want me making the same one. I'd gone ahead and done it anyway. For once, I wanted her to admit that I'd knocked her life off track. If not for me, she would have left, she'd live in Detroit by Aunt Norrie, or even farther away.

"Just tell me the truth, Mom. Grandma and Grandpa Petersen don't have a thing to do with us. I know I messed things up. I know you wanted things different. Just say it."

The bathroom was so small. If I turned quickly, I would knock my elbows against the walls. I remembered kicking my heels against the cupboard door. How had I ever sat on this counter?

"Baby—"

"Stop calling me that!"

She crossed her arms. "You're hurting. This is not the time for this conversation."

"Just say it," I said. "I want to know."

Her eyes looked strange, one lined, the other not, like I could see two versions of her at once. One side, the armored face she showed others, the other bare, exposed. She glanced to the side, and for a second she looked just like the man who sold me the truck, pulling up a memory and playing it back in his mind, seeing who he had been when he was young. Mom grinned, something fast and fleeting, and then she took a deep breath.

"They never tried to know you or Jay or Katie. But it never had anything to do with you. You didn't mess up my life. You revealed it. You showed me who the people around me really were and how strong I was."

The house was eerily quiet, like the storm had sucked sound away as it passed. I listened for wind, birds, cars driving by, water rolling through pipes, but the only sound was the crisp brush of Mom's dress pants against the counter, the clack of her compacts and tubes as she rummaged inside her makeup bag.

She turned back to the mirror and started to line her eye. She blinked on her mascara. "I lived in town, you know. I was walking home after school. And your dad drove by, his arm hooked out the window. We weren't in the same crowd, but he drove by and waved, the way he does to this day, lifting two fingers, and all I could see were these glittering brown eyes in the side mirror, watching me until he turned the corner." That short, fading smile again. "We were inseparable. He was so sure of himself. So solid. And the Lindts were so different from my family. He had all these brothers and sisters. I don't know how they all fit in this house. There was so much food and noise and animals. Someone was always shouting, someone was always laughing, or angry, or crying. My house was like a crypt. 'We built the church,' Grandpa Petersen would say. So worried what people saw and said. When he found out you were on your way, he called me a whore. He said I should have kept my legs together. He said I wasn't his daughter. He wanted me to stay in the house until you were born and give you away. Grandma Petersen didn't say anything. She never would.

"I called your dad in the middle of the night. Grandma Lindt answered and she got your dad on the phone, no questions asked. I told him I wanted to leave. I told him to come get me right now.

I set the receiver down so slowly and gently that it hardly made a sound. I watched the snow through the kitchen window. It was falling in fat, beautiful flakes. Your dad came to the house with the headlights off, and I turned to look at the kitchen for the last time: There was my spot at the table where I'd eaten almost every day for the past seventeen years; there was the narrow space at the top of the fridge where I'd hid three issues of *Mademoiselle*; there was my backpack and Norrie's hanging on the wall. I closed the front door behind me and locked it, softly, slowly. I dropped the key into my purse but fished it out again and held it in the palm of my hand, staring at it. Snowflakes spiraled from the air and turned to water on my skin. They felt like kisses. I told myself God was blessing me. Each snowflake blessed me again and again. Your dad got out of the truck and stood by the passenger door. His boots were unlaced. He was wearing pajamas. There was snow in his hair. He said, 'You coming?' And I put the key in the mailbox and lowered the lid. I walked down the front steps and into his truck, and we drove away with no headlights, and it felt like we were the only people in the entire town, the entire earth, who were awake."

She leaned back from the mirror and studied her face. She pressed some powder on each side of her nose. "Grandma and Grandpa Lindt opened their arms to us. I never went home. I wonder about your grandma Petersen sometimes. What was going through her head that night and every night since. Nothing went on in that house without her knowing. She knew the levels of shampoo in the bottles in our bathroom. She knew the slap of the door, the creak of the floor. Maybe she lay in bed blinking up at the ceiling, holding her breath, feeling the weight of the night on her chest, lying still, so still, listening to the receiver click, the house key drop to the bottom of the mailbox, my feet crunch the snow on the front steps. Maybe she knew I was leaving. And maybe she let me go."

Chapter 18

Dr. Cavender was the only large-animal vet in the county. He was a tiny man and bald-headed. His head was shined as high as his boots. His office was in the main level of his house, an old farmstead halfway to Pickford. He'd built dog kennels off the back porch and there was a paved walkway to a leaning red barn in the back. The house and office were dark, but there was a truck in the driveway. I went around to the back and knocked on the door. Chair legs scraped the floor, the blurt of wood against wood, then the door opened.

"Young Lindt! What can I do you for?"

"Dad sent me to ask you about our sheep."

"Go around to the front and I'll open the office."

"Thanks."

Occasionally farmers would bring animals to him, but for the most part he traveled to the farms himself, assessed limping bulls, hogs that had wasted away, sheep with sore mouths and tapeworms. He treated what he could but never shied away from the inevitable cure—the bullet in the head. Always the most expeditious, economical treatment. Results guaranteed.

I was at Charlie's once when Dr. Cavender prescribed this treatment. He stood outside the pen and watched a hog breathe its rapid, shallow breaths. It lay motionless in the corner of the pen, damp straw around it. The other hogs were walking over it, nosing its hooves, dropping mouthfuls of feed on its back and behind its ears. Its snout was pressed into the shiny cement barn floor, scraped clean that morning, but already slick with urine.

"You better get it separated and then you've got two choices," Dr. Cavender had said. "You could fiddle around with a course of antibiotics. Could work. Could not. You could wait a day or two and see if it improves. That's what they would do downstate. Tell you to give it some cake mix watered down with milk, see if he'll take some. But pneumonia will spread fast. Shame to see them all go down."

Charlie kicked the gate. The hog flinched but lacked the energy to move. The rest of the hogs scurried to the far corner, watching with keen black eyes that followed the movement of our hands.

"Or?" said Mr. King.

"Or you could put a plug in this one's head and treat the rest."

Mr. King rubbed his chin, weighing a ledger sheet in his head. Sale price minus the cost of the hogs, minus the cost of feed, minus the cost of a vet call, minus the cost of medication. Minus one of the hogs. All of the minuses meant less profit.

"Charlie, run up to the house and get the gun," Mr. King had said.

It wasn't a surprise then that Dr. Cavender's response to our situation was flushing the ewes out and starting fresh in September. Those were his words: Flush 'em out.

The waiting room was empty and dark. There was no power, no patients. Even Donna, the office manager, was gone.

"So, Young Lindt, you've got a frisky ram." Dr. Cavender rubbed his hands together. "Got out and had a little fun, did he?"

"You could say that."

"Ain't the first farm with this problem. Usually, it's the damn Millers calling me each spring. Ain't got fences worth shit. How many head you got?"

"Thirty. I mean, twenty-nine."

"No way to tell which ones he got to, eh?"

"Some are marked up." I thought of Caroline. Her calm, white face emerging from the glowing dim of the barn. The streaks on her back. My boot mark. The streaks on Mom's house-coat. "But most you can't tell. He was out there with them almost twelve hours."

He whistled. "You could fiddle with pregnancy testing or let them go and try and sell any lambs this—let's see—October, but there's not much of a market for show lambs born in October, is there?"

"Not around here."

He nodded. "Well, it'd be easier if they could talk, wouldn't it? It'd make my job a whole hell of a lot easier. Better hit them all." He placed two vials of Lutalyse on the counter and told me the dosage. "You give them this in ten days or so. Two weeks is fine. Intramuscular. Keep an eye on them though. If any stop eating or won't keep their heads up, you call me."

I nodded.

"You need syringes and needles?"

"If you got them, yeah."

He dropped everything into a white paper bag and rolled it up. "Donna will send your folks a bill. Hell of a storm, wasn't it?"

"Trees are down everywhere. Dad got home late last night and was gone early this morning. No school." I took the bag from him and stepped to the door, then paused and turned back. "This medicine, Dr. Cavender, what does it do?"

"It resets the hormonal clock, so to speak."

"But what does it actually do?"

He eyed me for a moment then laughed. "You're gonna make me dust off my old vet books, ain't you, Young Lindt? What the hell? Nothing else to do today." He disappeared into a back room and returned a few minutes later with a thick blue veterinary manual. He flipped the pages and laid it on the counter, opened to a black-and-white illustration of the female sheep reproductive system.

"See that? Sheep ain't that different from humans, in some respects, anyway. The corpus luteum forms after the egg is released and sends out hormones telling the uterus to get ready for a lamb. Makes everything nice and comfy. The lining of the uterus gets thick and gives that fertilized egg a nice little home. The egg gets fertilized here, and then it travels down to the uterus. But this medication kills the corpus luteum. That's exactly what the name means. 'Luta' for luteum; 'lyse' for loosen. No corpus luteum, no hormones, no home."

As he spoke, he moved his finger from the ovary to the fallopian tube, to the uterus, and then right off the page.

I stared down at the book and swallowed. I checked behind me to make sure the waiting room was still empty. "What if—what if it already has a home?"

"Well, if it just happened last night, there won't be one."

"But what if there was."

He looked confused. "You mean if it's already moved in?"

"Yeah."

He rubbed his head. "And you wanted it to move out?"

I nodded slowly.

He thought for a moment. "Well, you'd dose them the same, maybe double it, but the effect would be different."

"What do you mean, different?"

"The uterus would contract. Violently. And—" He closed the book. "But that's not what you're dealing with here, son. If you get a ewe mid-gestation in some kind of distress, you call me then. You're putting them out to pasture soon?"

"Last week of May, usually."

"Well, there you are. You give them each a shot of this, you do the regular worming, you put them out, and everyone has a nice, fine summer. You'll be all set for fall breeding." He put a hand on my shoulder and led me to the door. "It's the right thing to do. Yessir, the right thing to do."

As I walked to the truck, the bottles of Lutalyse clinked against each other in the bag, and I took one out and held it in my open hand. It was a clear cylinder of glass, tapered at the top and capped with a flexible rubber stop. 100 ML. FOR USE IN ANIMALS ONLY. The medicine itself looked like water, a little thicker. There were a few bubbles inside, and they caught the sun and cast ripples on my palm. I shook the bottle and the liquid frothed into a loose foam that dissipated quickly.

A sudden wind carrying the putrid spring scent of the ditches pushed against the bill of my hat. *Everyone has a nice, fine summer.* I put the bottle back in the bag, rolled it up tight, and drove home.

Katie was watching TV, sitting with her knees in a W. Jay's music rolled down the stairs from our bedroom. It took me a minute to realize why this mattered. The power was back. All around was the sound of a house with power. The refrigerator hummed, the light fixture overhead buzzed, the voices of Katie's TV show rose and fell in waves, something in the cellar surged. I had one thought: Call Mary. Quickly, I dialed her number.

"Hello?"

Her voice was small and tinny, like a kid woken in the night.

I couldn't speak at first. My lungs were tight packed with sod; the heaviness was profound.

"Is that you, Everett?"

I pressed my hand into my chest. Then I opened my dirt-packed lungs and spoke.

"Roman's dead."

She sucked in her breath.

"But Mary, I got an idea."

Chapter 19

We drove to Rotary Island. The St. Marys was rushing and fast, flashing gray, full of melted snow and ice. The wind tangled and unwound the clouds over our heads. The ferry waited on the Sugar Island shore. Mary held her hands in her lap. I didn't know if I could touch her. I didn't try.

The sun was high overhead, and there were cars parked nearby. I kept looking to see if the drivers were looking at us. I craved darkness. But so far, we were still a girl and a boy watching the river, not yet become whatever it was that we would become. So far, we hadn't done one thing wrong.

"Do you have everything?" she asked.

I set the vials and the plastic-wrapped syringes and needles on the seat between us. There they were, white and undeniable between us on the velvet seat.

"Everything's brand-new," I said.

She picked up the Lutalyse and weighed the bottles in her hand. She inspected the needles and syringes. The plastic wrapping crackled. She was efficient, businesslike. Mom putting Russian tea-cake ingredients on the counter, setting the oven to 350 degrees. “What do we need to do?”

Her questions were flat, so matter-of-fact, so *eager*, it caught me off guard. I turned to her. “Do you get what we’re doing here? Do you get what’s going to happen?”

She’d never called me stupid. In all our months together. Not once. But she said it now. And not even with words. She looked at me like I was the smallest thing she’d ever seen.

“Are you seriously asking me that?”

I took the Lutalyse from her. I packed everything back into the paper bag. “This is crazy. Forget I even said anything about this.” The truck cab felt so small. I unrolled the window. Still, it wasn’t big enough. “This is for animals, Mary. Animals!”

She snatched the bag from me. Her eyes were angry black slits. She was inches from me, each word she said puffed against the skin of my face. “Do you think I’m going to let you just pack everything up and drive home? Drop me off and forget about this? Do you think I’m going back to your version of things, to hell with me?”

“I’ll sell the truck.”

“We’ll need it.”

“Then I’ll steal.” I could do something like that, bust the window at Rosedale Church. Take something shiny and gold. Plates or candlesticks. But once I got them, what then? I had no idea how to do anything. I was a fool. “Mason! He’ll loan me the money. I’ll tell him it’s for the truck. I’ll make something up.”

She laughed a dry laugh. She sounded tired. She sounded so old.

She held up the bag. “*This* is what we’re doing. This is what we have.”

I got out of the truck and stood on the rocks that had been hauled in to protect the riverbank. The chilled spring air pushed against my face. A seagull dipped low to the water but didn't land. I faced the river, listening to it strike the rocks, musical in its way. How long, I thought, until the river smooths these very rocks to sand? Ships the size of skyscrapers sailed here. Before them, canoes. And before them, the glacier, scraping the earth as it left, leaving water and clay behind. Nothing I said or felt meant anything to the river. The kicking rabbit of my heart meant nothing.

Then Mary stood beside me. I hadn't heard her get out of the truck. The gray-green water moved past our feet, carrying sunlight and pondweed, the bodies and eggs of water bugs and fish, scales, seeds, the sheen of gasoline and bright-yellow pine pollen, the shit of seagulls and geese, the oils of human bodies, dog hair and deer hair, the piss of elk as they dipped their giant bodies into the current and moved from island to island. Standing there on the shore in silence, I felt her press the Lutalyse into my palm, like it was some goddamned precious gift. Frankincense or myrrh.

"Show me," she said.

We got back in the truck, and I talked her through what to do. It was Jay all over again. Tip the bottle upside down, insert the needle, pull back the plunger to the amount Dr. Cavender had said, press out the air until a tiny clear drop of liquid beaded at the tip. Just like I'd done vaccinating the sheep a thousand times before. She rolled down her leggings and exposed her thigh, smooth and white in the afternoon light.

"You'll want to bunch up your thigh with your left hand and slide the needle into the muscle. The quicker the better. So you don't stop. So it's over."

She nodded and squeezed her thigh, held the needle to it, not yet touching. She took a deep breath.

"It'll hurt, Mary."

She bit her lip.

There's this sound that ewes make to calm their lambs after birth, a cross between grunting and cooing. It's the closest they get to singing, willing their stunted vocal cords to croon. While the lambs struggle to stand and blindly turn around, they follow that earthy lullaby. I never understood how they made that sound, how they could make themselves do what they weren't meant to do. But I understood it then. If you were desperate enough, you could make yourself do anything.

Mary pushed the needle into her thigh. "Shit, that hurts!" She turned her face in to her shoulder and held her breath. A pinhead of blood oozed. Three seconds. She'd done it perfectly.

"Are you OK?"

It took her a minute to answer. "I think so."

Her voice was tight. She moved slowly, sitting up, pulling up her leggings. She bent her leg, folding it to her chest and holding it, like she was getting ready for a run. Then she stretched it out, repeated this a few times. She rotated her foot.

"How long does it take?" she asked.

Again, the eagerness. "I have no idea." I felt panic pull at my lungs. There was no going back now. We were no longer just a boy and a girl watching the river. What were we now? Should we have brought towels? A change of clothes? I didn't even have a Band-Aid for that pinprick of blood. What exactly had been the plan?

"Then I guess we wait," she said. She lay back against the seat and closed her eyes and I tried to lie back too. We listened to the radio. The cars beside us left. New ones slid into the parking slots beside us. Eventually, they left too. We watched the ferry come and go, unload, reload, each round trip a half an hour.

"Maybe nothing will happen," I said. And suddenly this became my hope. One bottle of Lutalyse a little less full than the other. That's all. No harm in that. Two kids watching the river. We could be that again.

"Something better happen." She sat very still and closed her eyes, turned in toward herself, like she was listening to the sound of the blood in her veins. I studied her face. She lifted her chin, like she was basking in sunlight. Her forehead was smooth and relaxed. She looked like she might start humming. She hadn't looked this happy in months.

"Do you feel anything?"

She touched her leg. "There's a lump where the needle went in. It's hot," she murmured without opening her eyes.

"Massage it. We do that with the sheep."

She rubbed the spot with the heel of her hand.

"But you don't feel anything, like, inside?"

She shook her head.

The ferry left. It collected a load of vehicles from the island and brought them back. Her Keds tapped the floor. She folded her hands across her belly, laced and unlaced her fingers.

"It's taking too long," she said. "It's not working. What if it doesn't work?" She clutched at her sweatshirt. She was crying. I saw fear in her. Not that the medicine would work, but that it wouldn't. She wiped violently at her eyes with her sleeves. "Work!" she yelled to the ceiling. "Please work!"

Her hands turned to fists and she started beating herself, small sharp knuckles into the soft flesh of her own body. Those hands that I'd held as she walked the foundation stones, those hands that had touched my own body with such tenderness. Those fingertips stained the color of ash. I'd seen the bruises, but to witness this ripped the breath out of my lungs.

"Mary, Mary," I said to calm her and to get her attention. I held her hands and she collapsed into me. Her scalp was hot and damp. She felt like she was on fire, like something about to erupt. "He said maybe double it."

"What?"

Her eyes were swollen, red. Her sleeves were damp.

"Dr. Cavender. He said maybe to double it."

"Double it?"

"He wasn't being specific. It was a maybe. But that's what he said."

Already she had turned on her other side and started to push down her leggings.

She was shivering by the time I turned onto Three Mile. Tremors that seemed to start in her core and shake out through her hands. I turned on the heat, even though the day was mild, and pointed the blowers right at her. Her breath got rapid and shallow. I wedged my knee beneath the steering wheel and struggled out of my Carhartt.

"Put this on," I said.

The coat swallowed her, but it held my body heat, and it must've felt good because she seemed to settle for a minute and relax. I drove a few miles with a hand on her shoulder to keep her upright, but then she pushed me off and unbuckled.

"Pull over."

Every drop of blood was gone from her face.

I jerked the truck to the side of the road and scrambled out after her. She dropped beside the ditch and started puking. The cattails were puffed and old with last year's growth. There were shoots of phlox and tag alders. Everything wild and overgrown. The soil was damp and mosquitoes and no-see-ums clouded the air around us. I waved them away and gathered her hair from her face. Her skin was sticky. She hunched over and heaved. It took her forever to inhale. Too much breath out, not enough in. I cursed again not having towels, blankets, anything.

"I got you, Mary," I said. "I'm here." I was useless but I was there.

She stopped heaving and sat on the ground, and I patted

down the weeds around her. I sat beside her and felt the cold moisture seep into my jeans. She wiped her mouth with my Carhartt sleeve, a wet smear that darkened the fabric.

"We're going to the hospital," I said.

"No!" She bared her teeth at me. Her eyes were steel.

"I'll tell them this was my idea, Mary. I did everything. It was all me. This is all because of me." I took her hands again, begging. "Please."

She stood, using my shoulder to push off. Her knees and ass were wet. She was unsteady, a new lamb finding its legs. She got herself into the passenger seat. "You're taking me home," she said, and closed the door.

We made it to the modular without having to stop again. The road slipped away behind me, each mile just like the last, straight and flat, the ditches filled with pale, dead cattail stalks. Mailboxes were my only landmarks. There would be one painted like a Holstein at the farm just before Mason's. His would be shielded by an old pallet lined with reflectors. The modular's would be next. A simple black mailbox on a single post.

My eyes moved from the road ahead of me to Mary and back again until the Holstein mailbox came into view at last. Mason's house was next, and there was the modular, every window dark.

As I carried her inside, I thought about Christmas, how I'd spun her around in this very spot, swinging her in circles and watching the snow snag in her hair. The thin floor moaned under my steps as I moved down the hallway toward her room.

I laid her on her bed and pulled off the once-white Keds, graffitied with a school year's worth of flowers and waves, birds, my initials and hers. I set them on the floor by her closet. There was a blanket folded at the foot of the bed, pink with a satin trim. I draped it over her.

"You need anything?"

She shook her head and settled down into her pillow and closed her eyes.

Her face was pale, her eyes hollow. Her breathing was so strange. Long, slow inhalations, as though through a stalk of straw.

I sat on the floor by her bed while she rested. In the afternoon light, shadows gathered around her eyes and lips. I wished I could draw like her. I'd sketch the soft lines of her face: the way her bangs, split by a triangle of smooth forehead, fanned over her eyebrows; the way her mascara had pooled like oil at the corners of her eyes; the way her mouth, a little fuller on the bottom, parted slightly each time she breathed. The last thing I'd see before I died, I thought, was this face.

I picked up the sketchbook from her nightstand and flipped through the pages. Some were stiff and rippled with salt water. I turned the pages until the sketches ended and I reached an empty sheet. She'd wanted love notes and I'd never given her one. This, then, was something I could do for her.

I wrote:

Fear, is something that stops people from doing things. I would say Im one of those people. My fear is making a mistake. Its why I never wrote you and that was wrong, Its why I tried to be other people and not myself because I'm so fucking afraid of making a mistake. And being a mistake. In the field. I think I loved you right then and there. Your not afraid of anything. And when Im with you, I'm not afraid of anything either. But I am afraid now. I want you to find what you want. I love you, I do, no matter what you say

You're supposed to put periods at the ends of sentences. That's one thing Dumbfucks taught me. Ms. Weltzer told us that a hundred times. I could see her now, standing in front of class with her breezy scarf and big hair. When it's the end, she'd say, you put a period. Simple as that. But it wasn't that simple. I looked over the last line. It felt like the end of something, but it wasn't the end of me loving Mary. I put a comma instead and signed it, Everett.

Kids at school folded notes into elaborate shapes with interlocking tabs that were supposed to keep everyone but the intended recipient from opening them. I didn't know how to do any of that. I just pressed the words against each other and pinched the crease between my thumbnail and index finger, leaving a streak of dirt behind. I repeated this again and again until the entire sheet was smudged, and I couldn't fold anymore. I lifted the wire bail on the jar and dropped the note inside. It wavered behind the old blue glass like it was underwater. I wished I'd filled the damn thing up with love notes when I'd had the chance. Now all she'd ever have was just that one.

There was no sound in the house, not even a clock ticking, just the feathery ins and outs of Mary's breath. I walked over to the window and peered out. I could see the driveway from where I stood. I imagined Mary on school mornings waiting in this same spot for me to pull up the driveway, her fingertips on the windowsill, the outside air hard and cold, and her breath clouding the glass in temporary blooms.

Her bedroom window reflected the room like a mirror. In it, I saw the pages of pelicans taped to the colorless walls, dozens of them, over the headboard and framing the dresser, covering the back of the door. There was page after page of the long-billed birds soaring above the sea, flying with their necks tucked and the tips of their wings reaching like open hands, the horizon stretching wide and thin behind them. Some were taped in neat rows, others were placed randomly, as if she had put them up as she finished them, not caring where they landed. Her ceiling fan circulated the air and the sketches flapped against the walls.

I was surrounded by the fluttering wings, caught inside a flock midflight. All those birds with their wings open wide: the wind surrounding them and lifting them up, pushing them a little, so that all they had to do was lean, rotate a single feather, and the air would do the rest. Go anywhere. Do anything.

The clock radio on her dresser glowed, 4:17. I was suddenly tired. Bone-tired. My head and arms ached. I wanted to crawl under the blanket next to Mary and press up against the warmth of her body, close my eyes and not have to open them for another hundred years. But that wasn't my place. Not anymore.

She sat up with a hand to her abdomen. Her eyes were bright. "Help me to the bathroom."

She leaned on me as we walked down the hall. I helped lower her to the blue plush rug on the floor. I sat beside her, but she waved me away.

"Go," she snarled.

"There's no way I'm leaving."

"I don't want you here."

"I can't leave you. What if something happens?"

She stiffened and held her breath. She clutched the edge of the tub until the moment passed, then she started to breathe again. "I don't want you here," she repeated. The *t*'s were hard. Her voice was thick, deep. A half-growl. "Go!"

I stood, unsure what to do. I looked around the bathroom. I set out towels. I filled a Dixie cup with water. I dampened a washrag and handed it to her.

"But you'll call me? If anything happens? When it happens?"

She took the rag from me and pressed it to her face. "I'll call."

I backed out of the driveway and onto the still landscape of the empty road. The truck was the only thing that moved. Mason's cattle were in the fields on either side. Soon he would begin his daily patrols, scanning the greening pastures for the dark, wet shapes of fresh-born calves. It was the same year after year, like me cutting hay in July; willows flaming orange from the ditches in November; ice lacing the shores of the St. Marys in December; lambs coming in February. The cattle were always there in May, pulling fresh forage into their mouths, milling together to rest for the night, the moonlight spilling over their backs. Next spring and the spring after that, it would be the same.

The cab was lonely, and the road stretched south forever. I turned left at Rosedale Church. What would God do to me, I thought, if Mary died? The St. Marys didn't care, but God did. I conjured the pastor's wife in my mind. She offered no sliver of scripture to give me hope like she did when I was a sad little kid with a dead lamb. I was going to hell. Jail first and then hell. And I'd deserve every second of it.

But she wouldn't die, would she? Her dad would come home, his day on the river over. He'd hang up his Coast Guard uniform and wonder where she was. He'd hear her. He'd see her. If anything happened. He'd take her to the hospital, and she'd be fine. He'd call the police and they'd take me away. I'd go willingly. Willingly. And she'd be fine.

I jammed the gas pedal against the floor and the truck took its time responding, but when it did, the force of it pressed me against the back of the seat and for an instant I was frozen, shooting forward as the fenceposts slid by in a gray-blue blur. The truck topped out at 85 miles per hour. As it crested the Nine Mile ridge, it wanted to leave the earth. I felt it bunch like a cat on its haunches, readying itself to leap. I lifted my foot from the pedal and the momentum launched me into the air. My body left the seat before the seat belt snagged me from the air and pulled me back. I hit the gas again. I whooped.

Charlie was there with me then. I felt him. It was summer again. Our fishing rods rattled in the bed of the truck and his red-and-white cooler took up the seat between us. We had the windows down, and he perched on the door, slapping the roof. I stretched out my hand, feeling a warm sleeve of sunlight on my bare arm.

Make money, catch fish, pop Kylie's cherry.

Get grand champion, I'd said.

I laughed at those two stupid rednecks with their goals. I missed them. I could drive to Charlie's now—it was only four miles behind me. Tell him I'd messed up, make things right again. Maybe he, who'd needed my forgiveness so many times before, could give it to me now. But nothing I said would change what I'd done. There was no going back. I turned on the radio, blaring it. The sun was hours from setting, and if I could have, I would have just kept driving forever.

Chapter 20

She didn't call. I sat in the living room watching TV with Katie, just feet from the phone, jumping at every call, wanting it to be her but feeling so relieved when it wasn't.

I pushed my dinner around the plate.

Mom laid a hand against my forehead. "Still not yourself?"

I ducked away.

"What did Dr. Cavender say about the ewes?" Dad asked.

I had to think for a minute: The female sheep reproductive system. Dr. Cavender's hand moving from ovary to fallopian tube to uterus and then sweeping off the page. *Might need to double it.*

"He gave me some Lutalyse."

"Where is it?"

"In my truck."

Katie watched me with her owly blue eyes.

"You seem funny," she said.

Mom tried to feel my forehead again.

"Stop it, Mom. Jesus!" I stood. The microwave blinked 6:45.

Mr. Williams would be home by now. I couldn't stand it anymore. "Can I use the phone in your room?"

There were two phones in the house: the one on the wall in the kitchen; the other in Mom and Dad's bedroom. I closed the door behind me and sat on their bed. It was quiet and dim in there. The voices in the kitchen were muted and buzzy but I could make out a few words. I heard my name. I heard "Roman" and "worried" and "Mary."

"Hello."

Mr. Williams's icy voice didn't terrify me anymore. I was happy, so happy to hear it.

"Is Mary there?"

"She's busy."

"What do you mean?"

"Do I have to spell it out? Indisposed. Been in the head all night."

"Is she OK? I mean, is she all right?" I would go there. I would drive right there and tell him everything. We would take Mary to the hospital and everything would be OK.

He was silent as though listening for something and, hearing it, said, "Seems fine."

"Seems fine?"

"You need your ears checked? Good night."

"Wait! Can you have her call me? Mr. Williams? Sir?" I gripped the phone, waiting, but the line was already dead.

I went back out to the living room and sat on the couch. I watched TV. Not really watching, just seeing. Meaningless flashes of light and color as every thought in my mind exploded: She seemed fine. Her dad was there. She would call me. A sitcom. A crime show. A million commercials. The eleven o'clock news. I thought I heard sirens. Long cries stretching down Riverside Drive, getting closer, louder. He had called them then. They were coming.

"Everett! You hear me?"

Dad was looking at me, waiting for an answer to a question I hadn't heard. Mom was gone to bed. Jay and Katie long asleep.

"You've been sitting there like a zombie all night. Your mother said good night and you didn't even move."

I rubbed my face. "I don't know. I was just—I was thinking."

He eyed me for a moment. "I said the road commission's hiring summer workers in the next week or so. You get on now and it could turn into something permanent this fall. I told Smitty you'd call."

I nodded.

"You all right?"

"Yeah," I said. "Call Smitty."

It was the night that wouldn't end. Of all the things I would be ashamed of that night, the worst was that, somehow, I slept. I dreamed the ewes were out. I ran into the lawn, trying to get them in the barn. The grass was cold and wet on my bare feet. I got a group heading in the right direction, then they blew apart like dandelion seeds. One of them was Fluff. There she was in the flesh. I yelled for Katie to come out of the house and see. "You'll never believe it!" I shouted. I left the rest of the ewes and followed Fluff. I would get her. I'd bring her back. Katie would be so happy. Fluff trotted down the driveway and into the road. Not fast, but I couldn't catch up. A car was coming, the headlights got bigger. I yelled for Fluff, I ran, hard, but couldn't reach her. "Don't look!" I yelled to Katie. "Don't look!" The car blared its horn and Fluff turned around and said, "I'm not a sheep!"

I kicked off my covers and tugged on my blind. It rolled up a few inches and I peered out onto the front lawn. No sheep. The moon was high and bright overhead. Katie's swing hung motionless in the night air. The clock radio said it was almost three AM.

Jay lay on his belly, soundless and still except for the almost imperceptible rise and fall of his comforter. His arm dangled off the side of the bed. I shook him. I squeezed a fistful of the skin on his back.

"Jay!"

"Ow!" He reached around and rubbed his back. "What's the matter with you?"

"I don't know."

He lay back down. "Go downstairs then!"

I pushed open Katie's door. She was asleep on her back, arms at her side, mouth slack. I picked up her rabbit from the floor and tucked him under the blanket. I played with her fingers. She was wearing a cheap tin ring I'd gotten her out of a quarter machine. When the plastic bubble had rolled out into her waiting palm, she looked at me with shining, happy eyes. "I was hoping I'd get the ring," she'd said.

I knocked lightly on Mom and Dad's door. "Mom?" No answer. I stepped inside. The polished light of the moon painted a window-shaped square across the foot of the bed. Mom's forehead was pressed against Dad's shoulder, one of her hands rested on his side. They breathed in unison; the room was peaceful.

"Mom?" If she wakes up, I will tell her everything. I waited, but she didn't stir. And I wasn't even sure I'd said her name out loud.

Outside, without my Carhartt, the air was damp and chill, like a thousand tongues licking the back of my neck. When I opened the barn door, ninety-one pairs of eyes turned to me, and I almost choked on my delight. Most were standing around slumbering, dimly chewing. Always chewing. Some lay with their shiny legs folded under them. I climbed into the pen and

Caroline came forward. I knelt before her and pressed my face into the sour nape of her fleece. I stroked the spot where I'd kicked her.

"I'm sorry, girl," I said. "I'm sorry for what I did to you."

Light swept through the window and Caroline withdrew to the safety of the other ewes. I opened the barn door and watched a truck roll to a stop in the driveway. The headlights lit up the yard. Mr. Williams's truck. This was it then. He was here. The driver's door swung open.

The hoodie, the shoes. It was Mary. She got out and walked toward me. She held my Carhartt in her arms.

"You didn't call me! You didn't call!"

I ran to her and fell on my knees, relieved she was there, standing before me. Alive.

"Why didn't you call?" I held her hips. I ran my hands up and down her legs. I bit the fly of her jeans. The top two buttons were open. They were metallic and sharp against my tongue and teeth. She knelt down and leaned heavily against me, a runner who has finished a great race. She was pliable, tired. I breathed her in, a new sticky smell, the smell of night air and clay and sinews undone.

She put the Carhartt in my hands.

"Don't look," she said.

But I did. I unwound the sleeves and turned so the moonlight and headlights illuminated the taffeta lining of my coat. I saw things I'd seen before. Things from the lambing floor. The makings of something. A claybaby. Half-formed. Unfinished. I folded the jacket back up, thinking it shouldn't feel so light, so empty.

"I don't know what to do now," she said.

I pulled her to her feet, thankful for action, for the end of the waiting. I knew exactly what to do.

We crossed the moon-bleached field on the four-wheeler. I squeezed the throttle with my right hand and supported Mary with my left. A shovel was wedged between us.

She sagged against me as we rolled over brittle clumps of orchard grass not yet woken by the last few days of tepid sunshine. But the roots are alive, I thought. The crowns were already pulling nutrients from the soil. In a month, the entire field would run with shin-high blades of green, the insects would be back, and the ewes would lower their faces to the earth again.

The night air was soggy. Mary's hair spilled over her shoulders, smelling of sweat, shining like water. The spring peepers were so loud I heard them over the four-wheeler engine. At the lip of the gully, I stopped.

Mary raised her head. "Here?"

"Just on the other side. Can you walk?"

"I don't think I can make it that far."

I stepped on the barbed wire so she could walk over the fence, clutching the Carhartt bundle tight against her chest, then I carried her and the shovel down the gully, over broken tree limbs and the blanched stems of last year's pasture grass. It wrapped round my ankles and pulled at my pant legs, but I didn't stop, I didn't stumble, I didn't set her down. The creek was full and fast, joining other milky rivulets, widening and deepening as they flowed east and met the St. Marys. There was no stepping over it, so I walked through, and the water filled my boots, icy snowmelt water. The claybabies would be easy to find now, I thought. Up the other side, I turned and saw the house and barn, the fields stretching north and south, the foundation stones, and Croft's Place. Beyond that was the river, Sugar Island, and Canada itself. My whole world was here. This was the center of everything.

I set aside the sod first, then scooped out shovelfuls of crumbly brown dirt that turned to clay the deeper I went. Three to four feet would keep the coyotes away. Mary watched me thrust the shovel in and out of the dirt. Her face was pale and drawn, and she sat so still that it seemed any movement would use up too much energy. I felt others watching me too; generations of Lindts silently gathering, recognizing my movements, my skin, the slope of my shoulders; witnessing me open the land, putting something inside. How many of them had stood in this very spot, shovel in hand? What else had they planted in these fields?

"It's ready."

She held out the Carhartt bundle to me, and I placed it in the earth.

"This too." She reached into her kangaroo pouch and took out the Kmart ring box. I nestled it in next to the Carhartt. I pushed in the soil and used my hands to fit the puzzle pieces of sod back together. Something broke inside me then, like a river pushing down an old brick dam. Tears came. I pushed the heels of my palms into my eye sockets, but there was no stopping them. There had been so much doing. Now came the feeling. I turned away from her, but out there alone in the night there was no hiding anything from each other. It was the end of things. It was the end of everything.

I turned over the shovel and tamped down the sod. "It's done now," I said. "It's all done."

I sat beside her and looked up at the night sky. It was pure and heavy above, comforting in its size because it made me feel small. I looked down at my blackened hands.

"When I was a kid, like eleven or so, I was biking home from Charlie's and I went past a bull in a field. It was always there. It had this chain hanging from its nose that it would step on if it tried charging. And, I don't know why, I wanted to see if I could touch him. So, I said, 'Hey, boss, boss,' and he got closer and closer. He came right up to the fence. And I scooped up some gravel from the side of the road and pelted him with it, as hard as I could. Just over and over. And he started thrashing around and tossing his head. I thought he'd tear the chain right out and I took off on my bike as fast as I could. I fell and scraped my hands up. When I got home, Dad found me in the kitchen, running my hands under the faucet. He pulled my hands from the water and turned them over, firm but gentle. They were still bleeding. I told him I was just biking by, and the bull went nuts. And he said, 'Let me tell you something that bull's fool owners don't know. It doesn't cost a dime more to keep a good animal than a sorry one. All the sorry one's going to do is pass the ugliness on.' I couldn't meet his eyes, because the tenderness of his touch was rare, and I was afraid I'd end up telling him how I made the bull come close, how I'd thrown the rocks. Because if I told him that, he'd know it wasn't the bull that was ugly—it was me."

She turned to me. "Do you want to know why I liked you? Why I really liked you?" The moonlight stretched our shadows wide and long before us. A breeze lifted the baby hairs that framed her face.

"Why?" I asked.

"Everywhere I've lived, I'm from somewhere else. The new kid. The stranger. Standing out, noticed but not really seen. But you—you can name this plant." She pulled up a purple curl of vetch. "Those trees. You know exactly where that water is running. You know the path the glacier took. You know this place and it knows you. You are known here. And not just by the people. But the animals. The sheep recognize you. Every single one of them. They see you. And I wanted to know what that was like. I wanted to feel it, even if it was just for a little while. What it was like to be known. For my footsteps to matter. To leave something behind."

The grass was night-wet. I threaded my fingers through it. The diluted dirt streaked my hands. I wiped them dry on my jeans.

"Mary," I said. "Can I hold you?"

She nodded and I lay down beside her for what I knew was the last time. I held her so that all the lines of our bodies touched. The chorus of spring peepers poured down like rain.

"Mom and Dad got married and had me young. And they're happy, you know? They work really hard but they're happy. I wanted us to be like that too. I wanted that more than anything."

She was quiet for so long I thought she had fallen asleep. I sat up a little to see her face. She was blinking up at the stars, dry-eyed.

"It felt good to be wanted."

I drove slowly back to the house, not wanting to get there, because there was nothing left but for her to leave. I eased the four-wheeler over the ruts in the field, gently, gently. I memorized everything. The shade of her hoodie. A purplish red. Even more purple in the dark. One drawstring knotted, the other side free. The darkness changed the color of her shoes. They were bright white again. Almost glowing, as though she had just climbed out of Mason's dually and first placed her foot on the field. I felt her sharpness against my chest, the hardness of her skull under my chin. Shorn of my Carhartt and her dad's sweatshirt, she felt so light she might float away.

We reached the yard. There was no stopping that. I watched for a lamp in the house to flip on, Mom's shadow at the door. But the windows stayed dark, the barn was almost invisible. The security light cut a dim tent of light around the utility pole. I turned off the four-wheeler and for a moment, there was silence. Then our footsteps on the gravel, the stones shifting under our weight. Sensing us, the sheep called from the barn. Lone voices at first, then many together. Restless, eager for pasture.

Soon, I thought. *Summer's coming. You'll be out soon.*

"I could sleep forever," Mary said.

And I felt that way too. I would sleep. I would wake. Tomorrow was the day for selecting show lambs. Three for Jay, three for Katie. They would train them all summer, and I would help, but there would be no more showing for me. That was finished now. Every summer of my childhood had ended with me in the show ring leading a lamb. From now on, I would be outside it looking in.

Mary opened the door to her dad's truck, and I helped her inside. She was tiny in the truck. She looked so young. I knocked on the glass and she rolled down the window.

"You sure you don't need me to drive?"

"I'll be fine."

She turned the key and shifted the truck into drive, but my hands were curled around the door. The truck rumbled under my fingertips, craving movement. I couldn't bear the moment speeding away. The details were changing too quickly. The first hum of dawn glowed over the St. Marys River. The day's first robin gurgled. Everything was covered in the strange indigo light of the coming day.

She touched my hand, the last time she would touch me. It was quick, like touching feathers, and the heat of the engine moved the air around us. We were caught up in a brief column of wind. Every event that night had unrolled to this very leaving. I stepped back and she lifted her foot off the brake. The truck lurched forward. The moon, still hanging like a thumbprint in the sky, glinted off the hood of the truck.

Remember this, I thought. *Remember this.*

Author's Note

I'd like to acknowledge the land on which *A Good Animal* is set. For thousands of years, it has been the home of the Three Fires Tribes known as Anishinaabe: the Ojibwe, Ottawa, and Potawatomi. I'm grateful to live, work, and write on this land.

Acknowledgments

A Good Animal would not exist without Ryan Maurer. I wish for every writer to have the immovable support and fierce love that I had while writing this book. I didn't know what I was getting into when I started writing, and it's a good thing. I would've given up. I almost did, many times. But I had Ryan, and he never wavered. Not. Once. And here we are on the other side, a book in the world.

My daughter, Hannah, was one of my earliest readers. Her tears told me the story was true. Brent, my son and biggest cheerleader, wrote me the casserole song and watched over my shoulder with a huge grin as I hit Send.

For the haying lessons, the personal writing retreats at the hunting camp, and a childhood filled with 4-H and all the good animals, I thank my parents, Susan and Spencer Shunk. My sister Deanna Shunk, for claybaby hunting and getting me in and out of the sheep business—the shots and shearing and breeding and birthing—all of it. It's all in here. I'm indebted. And to my other sisters, Karrie Gilbert and Marcey Thorne, thank you for a lifetime of support.

My agents, Carrie Howland and Zoe Howard, took a chance on me and my weird little sheep book. Their editorial notes were a continuation of my writing education.

From the very first conversation I had with her, I knew my extraordinary editor, Claire Cheek, "got" this book. Her thoughtful questions deepened the story and, most importantly, helped me know Mary.

I thank these talented, meticulous, and magical individuals at St. Martin's Press for transforming a sprawling Word doc into a beautiful book and placing it in readers' hands: Austin Adams, Jen Edwards, Young Jin Lim, Lauren Riebs, Kiara Ronaghan, Lisa Senz, Anne Marie Tallberg, Layla Yuro, and Jess Zimmerman.

Christina Clancy was an early champion of the book. I hope someday to encourage another new writer as much as she has encouraged me.

Michael Hertz, MD, MPH, mentored me through Michigan's reproductive freedom for all ballot initiative and lent his medical expertise to this book. I'm honored to call him my friend.

Fellow Inkling and Yooper sounding board, Jan Kellis, helped me call myself a writer. She knew Everett and Mary first and best.

My Writing Buddies are smarter than me and make everything I write stronger: Judith Ugelow Blak, Ruby Carlson, Vivian Clausing, Kim Elliott, Hannah Heller, Mj Joung, Sam Mireles, Glenna Penner, Rebecca Marks Rudy, Pam Weiss, Rachel Wineberg, and Marion Wyce. I'm grateful to Stanford's Continuing Studies Novel Writing Certificate program for bringing us together, and am grateful especially to instructors Sarah Stone, Nami Mun, and Jack Livings for their guidance during the program and after.

Much appreciation to Kirsten and Aaron Daru for their support of my work through the Daru Writing Fellowship at the

Tahoe Writers Retreat. The company of my Writing Buddies, the dedicated writing time, and the beautiful setting filled with Steller's jays and giant pine cones were instrumental to the development of this book.

Further thanks to the Glen Arbor Arts Center in Glen Arbor, Michigan. My time as a Suzanne Wilson Artist-in-Residence was a period of quiet reflection and self-actualization in one of the most stunning places on earth.

Last, I thank the sheep: Polka Dot, Jumperoo, Frank, Stella, Frances, and Vincent. And my little calf, Corey. He is in my heart always. I will never stop writing about him.

About the Author

Libbey Brown

Sara Maurer lives with her family in Michigan's Upper Peninsula. She earned her bachelor's degree from Albion College and master's from Eastern Michigan University. She honed her creative writing craft while completing Stanford's Continuing Studies Novel Writing Certificate program. Her short fiction can be found in *Dunes Review*, *Hominum Journal*, and *The Twin Bill*. *A Good Animal* is her first novel.